"An intensely sexual love story." —*Kirkus Reviews*

"Addictive, delectable reading." —*USA Today*

"Wicked good storytelling."
—Jaci Burton, *New York Times* bestselling author

"Holy hell HAWT." —*Under the Covers Book Blog*

"Suspenseful. . . hella sexy and hot. [The hero and heroine's] erotic relationship is good enough to make one's toes curl." — *RT Book Reviews*

"One of the sexiest, most erotic love stories that I have read in a long time." —*Affaire de Coeur*

"A sleek, sexy thrill ride."
—Jo Davis, national bestselling author

"One of the best erotic romances I've ever read."
—*All About Romance*

"Nearly singed my eyebrows." —*Dear Author*

"Fabulous, sizzling hot."
—Julie James, *New York Times* bestselling author

EXORCISING SEAN'S GHOST

BETH KERY

ONE

BELLE PAUSED IN THE HALLWAY, her hand frozen on the key in the lock. She glanced over her shoulder at the sound of the door across the hall opening. Excitement bubbled in her belly when she saw Sean Ryan leaning casually in the doorway of his condominium.

"You know, they say it's unhealthy for people to work the kind of hours you do."

She shivered. Her next door neighbor's voice always had that effect on her, like if she turned her body in just the right way, that low, gruff tone could scratch her just where she needed it the most.

"Well you would know since you must put in an average of eighteen hours a day at the office," Belle teased back.

Initially she had been a little nervous when she'd shared an elevator with her next door neighbor or passed him in the hallway outside of their condominiums. He looked almost ten years older than her, for one. Plus his sheer size and his vibrant masculine energy intimidated her as much as it drew her. But one look in his eyes and she'd been a goner. Intelligence and humor shone in them, but so did a sexuality so potent, it immediately melted through even Belle's considerable reserve.

She knew his gaze could also become as incising as a surgeon's scalpel. She supposed that expression was much more familiar to Sean's colleagues down at the U.S. Attorney's office, never mind the people who were unfortunate enough to be prosecuted by him.

Presently, her eyes lowered—seemingly of their own accord —over Sean's thighs.

"What's the occasion? I've never seen you wearing jeans," she said. Every time they'd run into each other in the hallway, the elevator or the foyer of their condominium building in the past Sean had been wearing a suit, usually with his tie in various stages of disrepair—either not yet tied and just looped around his neck in the predawn a.m. or loosened and limp in the hours close to midnight when he was finally coming home.

"It's a special occasion. I'm making dinner for you. I've been waiting for over an hour for you to come home," he said with a mock put-upon expression.

For a moment she wondered if she'd heard him correctly. Sean Ryan, the handsome, renowned, powerful U.S. Attorney for the northern district of Illinois, was asking *her* to dinner? She said the first thing that came to mind.

"You're kidding, right?"

"About the fact that I'm making you dinner? No. At least, I'm hoping you don't think one of my meals is a joke." His eyes narrowed on her. "You haven't been talking to any of my friends about my cooking, have you?"

Sean smiled when she laughed. Her laugh was like the rest of Belle March. Golden. Although he was admittedly on edge about her response to his invitation, he couldn't help but let his eyes rove over her with slow, deliberate appreciation. She was wearing her hair down today. He'd already decided was the only way Belle should be allowed to wear it. Binding such glory ought to be a crime. Lustrous golden curls hung several inches below her shoulders. Almost from the first second he'd laid eyes on Belle, he'd wondered if her hair would be as soft as it looked if he rubbed a curl between his thumb and forefinger.

In less guarded moments—usually while desperately trying to sleep at night—Sean had much more illicit fantasies about sinking all of his fingers into it greedily, pulling her head back to expose her throat, fisting those curls while he drove into her softness.

He loved her skin. He found himself getting an erection at the most inopportune times during his workday when he daydreamed about finally exposing her breasts to his gaze. Then maybe he'd know the secret of whether Belle March tanned lightly to achieve her golden, apricot-colored skin shade, or if God had blessed her with that gorgeous color uniformly.

In his position as a U.S. Attorney and as a special prosecutor in high profile cases—cases that often involved prosecuting terrorists, organized crime figures and powerful government officials—Sean thought it was wise to remain unattached to any organization or individual. The fact that it was wise for him to remain uncommitted both politically and personally had never bothered him much. His sexual needs were important to him. But he'd always managed to adequately meet them without making obvious headlines or becoming overly involved.

His take it or leave it attitude had come to a grinding halt just a few weeks ago. He recalled the moment perfectly.

He'd been racing into his condo lobby, hurrying to take a

quick shower and still make a business dinner in time to be only nominally versus unpardonably late. Just as he approached the elevator, the door began to close.

"Hold it." He'd stuck his hand aggressively into the two-inch gap in the doors and forced them back open. He'd only paused when he fully took in the woman in the elevator who was staring at him in slight alarm. Sean stilled in the midst of loosening his tie and clawing at the top button of his shirt. For a few breathless seconds, they'd just stared at each other. He'd been trapped by a pair of wide, soft, golden-brown eyes. When the woman blinked once and glanced down over him, Sean's gaze had followed hers.

He'd grinned sheepishly, realizing that in his haste he had unconsciously begun stripping even before he got to his condo.

"Sorry. I didn't mean to startle you. I'm running a little late and…" He'd waved his hand vaguely as his voice faded. He had come to the startled realization that he was tongue-tied. It was a whole new experience for him. He'd always thrived on the nimbleness of his brain and tongue.

But this woman was…golden. Everywhere. She reminded him of honey and freshly ripened peaches. Her legs were long and her calves and ankles were beautifully shaped beneath the tailored skirt she wore. He'd hoped his eyes didn't widen when they skimmed across her chest. Her white silk blouse and open suit jacket were all in perfect taste, but her clothing couldn't completely hide the fact that this slender, elegant female must fill out a C-cup generously.

"It's okay," she had assured him. He'd sensed her shyness, but he would have had to be dead not to also notice that her eyes didn't hold sexual interest, no matter how nascent. And just as if she'd known that he'd just jerked to attention in his briefs, she gave a little smile that managed to be utterly innocent and completely wise at once, a smile of mystery…a Mona Lisa smile.

And that, Sean supposed, was when he began his battle with himself about whether or not he should ask Belle March if he could see her. She wasn't like the experienced women that he'd seen in the past, who may not have loved his solitary by necessity lifestyle, but who had understood and accepted it, nevertheless. Belle wasn't the kind of woman who he could sleep with one night, and then forget about until the next urge for female companionship struck him.

The phone call he'd received from his boss twenty-six hours ago should have only reinforced the necessity of staying away from Belle March.

But the grimness of that new reality had somehow increased his already intense focus on her. Sean just couldn't seem to silence her unique siren call. He'd left work tonight at a record-breaking early hour, knowing that he was finally going to succumb to his need. The laws of nature always had their way in the end, didn't they?

Or at least that was what Sean's rationale had been.

Belle glanced down over her work clothes in rising dismay. She'd been at the office since seven that morning. Somehow her fantasies about spending an evening with Sean Ryan had never involved her wearing a wrinkled skirt and a blouse with a coffee stain on it.

"Do I have time to change before the dinner that you're making is ready?"

"I'll give you fifteen minutes. That'll give me time to rewash the dishes."

"Rewash the dishes?" Belle asked slowly.

"I better. It's not like my dishes ever actually get *used* or anything. Come to think of it, I might have to unpack them still…"

Belle took her opportunity as he puzzled out the location of his dinnerware and turned toward her door. She was having dinner with Sean Ryan, the man she'd been obsessively preoccupied with since the moment she'd first shared an elevator with him. And she only had a precious few moments to prepare herself.

"Okay. I'll see you in a few minutes then." She was fumbling clumsily around with her keys when she heard Sean's rich husky voice call her name from behind her.

"Belle?"

"Yes?" she asked distractedly over her shoulder.

"I guess that means the answer is 'yes'? You do want to have dinner with me?"

Her fumbling stilled and she glanced back at him. He was leaning in his doorframe watching her with an expression of satisfaction. Belle realized that she'd never seen him wearing short sleeves in the past. His upper arms were solid with delineated muscle. His forearms looked appealingly strong and masculine beneath a light dusting of dark hair.

"Oh. I…yes," she finally got out breathlessly.

"Good. If you're not over here in fourteen minutes and thirty seconds I'm coming over there to get you. Ready or not."

She was struck dumb for an instant by the desire that flashed into his striking eyes as he murmured the sentence with a playful seductiveness that still managed to sound like a sensual threat.

"Do you *swear* that you made that meal?" Belle asked Sean

almost an hour later as she placed her utensils in her completely empty plate.

Sean paused in the action of raising a forkful of tender chicken toward his mouth. He was considerably behind Belle in eating for several reasons. In the first place, he couldn't help but admire her as she tucked into the meal he'd prepared. He'd learned to appreciate the fruits of honest labor from both of his parents, and he liked seeing someone enjoy his effort. Plus, he appreciated the fact that she obviously wasn't one of those women who ate a spoonful of peas for dinner, and then complained about looking fat.

The second reason he was behind her in eating involved the fact that he suspected that Belle was an excellent psychologist, because she was very easy to talk to. He felt a little mortified when he realized that he'd just spilled his guts to her about everything from getting a football scholarship to Yale, but still needing to work as a valet at the Ritz Boston Common to afford college, to growing up in a working-class Irish neighborhood, to his close relationship with his parents, who had passed away within a year of each other several years back.

"I swear I cooked it. What makes you accuse me of dishonesty so casually?"

She smiled when she saw the mock injury on his handsome face. "Oh, let's see. What could possibly make me suspect that you aren't the type to make a delicious home-cooked meal? Could it be that you had to wash your dinner dishes before we ate off them? Or maybe it's just because I read in the newspaper recently that you and your staff are practically solely responsible for keeping Lucio's restaurant in business."

Sean looked surprised. "They said that? We give our fair share of business to that Greek place on— You read an article about me?" he asked abruptly.

"Yes. It's not that surprising. You can't blame me for being curious can you? You have a fascinating job, and you are my next door neighbor," Belle said quietly. She was glad that her voice sounded even and that if she had blushed, the damage had been minimal.

Sean popped the chicken into his mouth and studied her for a moment while he chewed. "I'm not complaining. You have my full permission to be as curious about me as you want, in any way that you want."

This time she couldn't have prevented the color from staining her cheeks for anything. To cover her discomfort she picked up her glass of Chardonnay and took a sip. It was her burden, this proclivity to blush. She hated it as much as someone else might hate a scar or an unsightly burn.

Her uncontrollable blushes reminded her all too painfully of her childhood stutter. Both tendencies fought their way to dominate center stage when Belle least wanted to be noticed. For a good part of her childhood, she'd suffered from a speech impediment that had perhaps only emphasized her natural tendency for reserve. By the time she reached adolescence, her years of hard work with a speech therapist had paid off. Only during times of extreme stress did her stutter return.

But the deficit had left a mark on her. By the time she began to develop sexually, she was behind her peers in the skills needed to navigate the complicated world of teenage boys and dating. To make matters more complicated, her bearing and manner didn't convey shyness and uncertainty but instead a cool aloofness that didn't match her inner perception of herself. She only knew that something about her seemed to put men off, intimidate them. And the few who had been strong and confident enough to try and get to know Belle better had never awakened her passion. Not fully.

Until Sean came along.

She inhaled slowly to chase away her embarrassment before she continued. "There *was* other evidence that I should have taken into account before I accused you of not actually cooking this. Such as the fact that your mother and father owned a restaurant and that your father was the cook, although your mother ruled the kitchen at home."

"You were actually listening to all of that stuff I just said?" Sean asked incredulously.

"Why wouldn't I? Learning about your background was interesting. Now I think I'm beginning to understand why the media seems infatuated—if a little wary and confused—by you, and why anybody who's even dreaming about turning crooked must be shaking in their wingtips, and hopefully thinking twice about ever committing the crime. You really are what the media suspects and criminals fear: a genuinely honest and driven prosecutor. I think the people of this area are lucky to have you, Sean."

He paused for a moment, taken aback by her simple honesty. Impulsively he leaned over and took her hand in his. Her hand was small, beautiful and elegantly shaped, just like the rest of her. "Belle, how old are you?"

Her lips parted in surprise, not only at the unexpected question, but at his sudden intensity. A lock of dark hair had fallen forward attractively on his forehead. The impact of his blue eyes was even more startling up close.

"Why?" she asked dazedly.

"Because I've never seen a grown woman, especially such a beautiful one, who blushes as often and as intensely as you do. I've certainly never tried to seduce anyone like that." When Sean saw the expression on her face and felt her instinctively try to pull away from his hand—probably to shield her embarrassment—he held her tighter and laughed.

"I like it. When you blush."

She stilled. She studied him anxiously to see if he was teasing her but she saw no humor in his eyes, only the steady warmth of rising desire. "You do?"

He nodded slowly. For a few seconds they soaked in the sight of the other in silence. Belle didn't move when Sean lifted his hand and touched her cheek, feather light. When his thumb reached her full lower lip, he pressed into the flesh with more avidity.

"Belle?"

"Yes?"

He leaned closer toward her over the corner of the table. Their faces were only inches apart.

"I just said a few seconds ago that I wanted to seduce you, and you're still here with me. Should I consider that a good sign?"

"I-I don't know," she said uncertainly. But part of her knew, the part that instinctively swayed forward when she felt Sean's warm, fragrant breath misting her face. "You mean... right now?" she wondered.

He smiled tenderly and palmed her jaw.

"Yes." When he noticed the way her golden eyes widened at his answer he added gruffly, "Don't worry, Belle. I'm going to take it slow with you. You're a woman to be savored. There are things you should understand about me first, before you decide if this is what you want," Sean added dutifully, despite his rising arousal. Then he inhaled Belle's subtle floral scent and all traces of humor and caution faded. For a second he forgot about her innocence and the need to keep a safe distance. "Maybe just a kiss?" he murmured as if to himself. "They say it's best to get it over with...makes both parties less tense to just . . . "

He dipped his head and kissed her. The feeling of her soft warm lips, her singular taste and the sexy sound she made with her surprised indrawn breath blended together, creating a sweet, intoxicating haze. When he felt her caressing him back with rising eagerness, his desire unfurled. He sent his fingers deep into her soft curls and palmed the back of her head. She tasted more delicious than he'd ever imagined a woman could. He plucked at her lower lip, insisting that she open for him so that he could taste more of her.

They made a shared sound of gratified arousal when her lips parted, and he sank into the hollow of her mouth. His other hand came up to her jaw and held her firmly for his kiss. His tongue thrust boldly, rhythmically. When he finally raised his head and looked down at her, there wasn't a hint of apology in his blazing blue eyes for the fact that he'd just fucked her mouth thoroughly with his tongue. Belle couldn't think of any other way to describe what he'd just done to her…

"That didn't exactly work the way I thought it would," Sean admitted distractedly as he watched his thumb caress her moist, plump lower lip. She obediently opened for him. His cock jerked.

"It didn't?" she wondered with bemusement. "I thought it went…pretty well."

"It was supposed to lessen the tension between us, not make me want to take you on top of this table right this second Belle," he growled with amusement next to her lips. Even though he was planning on separating himself from her, he couldn't resist the lure of her sweetness. He dipped into her again with a slow, sexual rhythm that soon had him sweating, and Belle squirming restlessly in her chair.

He forced himself to tear his mouth from her. He cursed softly. "I'm going to have to watch myself around you. You taste like sin and heaven mixed together."

"You don't have to, Sean. Watch yourself, I mean."

He examined her closely, absorbing the trust in her large, beautiful eyes. It humbled him a little. It also forced him to face harsh reality. "That's very generous. But it's not really that simple. There are some things you should understand before you make your decision. The type of work I do…there are risks."

"What kind of risks?" she asked, puzzled. She startled slightly in protest when he straightened in his chair and moved away from her. Anxiety rose in her when she saw him sweep back his dark hair with restless fingers and sigh heavily.

"You said that you've read some newspaper articles about me. Did you ever read anything about me being in any relationships with anyone?"

"No," Belle said cautiously after a moment. "They always say how close you are to your staff, how loyal they are to you. But they never said anything about any personal relationships. You…you're not trying to tell me that you're secretly involved with someone else, are you?" she asked with a sudden flash of dread.

"No, that's not what I'm trying to tell you, Belle," he said patiently.

"You're not married…or involved?"

Sean just shook his head. "Not involved in the way you're talking about. I've never cared so deeply about someone that I would feel compelled to draw them into the possible messiness of my life."

Belle glanced around Sean's condominium. Her eyes lingered on a picture of a grinning, dark-haired girl on top of a pony—the goddaughter he'd told her about during dinner, no doubt. It was the only personal item she saw in the room. Messy? If she had to guess from the appearance of his place, she'd surmise that Sean Ryan's life wasn't so much messy as it was sterile. His condominium looked like it had been furnished and decorated to be a vacation home or a time-share unit, a place where people moved in and out in transience. It was comfortable enough, luxurious even. But it wasn't a home.

"You mean that your first priority is always your job?"

Sean opened his mouth to deny it but shut it quickly. "Maybe that's part of what I was trying to say. I'm not sure to be honest with you. But what I was mostly getting at is that becoming involved with me could be dangerous, Belle."

She stared at him doubtfully. "Dangerous?"

Sean gave a lopsided grin. "Sounds a little grandiose and melodramatic, doesn't it? That's what part of me keeps thinking too. But I've had to have FBI and FPS protection at various times during my career, most recently when I was the special counsel in the case against Ahmed Aten."

She stilled. "Ahmed Aten? The man who was responsible for the explosion on the United States Army base in Germany? You were the prosecutor on his case? But he was a known—"

"Terrorist?" Sean nodded as he studied her reaction carefully. "I serve on the U.S. Attorney's office subcommittee on terrorism. I've prosecuted a number of cases involving either direct or indirect terrorist activities and gotten guilty verdicts in all of them. Almost twenty men are doing time because of me, men who are deeply involved in worldwide terrorist organizations. That's more indictments for acts of terrorism against the United States and its citizens than any other U.S. Attorney has ever won. It's not a big surprise that I've made the 'wish you were dead' lists of any number of men who live by codes of fear, vengeance and violence. I'd expect nothing less from them."

"You don't seem very concerned about it."

He shrugged. Belle wondered if she hadn't first fallen in love with him at that moment. He naturally downplayed it but she recognized his courage for what it was. She instinctively knew that Sean didn't believe he was untouchable. His attitude wasn't the carefree insouciance of a youth who believed he would live forever despite the foolhardy, risky actions he took. Sean knew the inherent dangers. But he did the job and he did it exceptionally well, because he believed what he did was right.

"I could also meet my maker after getting plowed over by an exhausted shopper while crossing Michigan Avenue after work one day. We're all going to die sometime. I'd rather not cringe in my condo and wait for it."

"Sean, are you trying to warn me to stay away from you?"

Hesitation showed clearly on his handsome face. "Maybe. A little. I don't do things halfway in my work, Belle."

She shook her head. "I don't know what to say. It was good of you to bring it up." Her eyes met his uncertainly. "But I don't think I want to be. Warned off, I mean."

A grim smile tilted his mouth. Maybe Belle was naïve and inexperienced, but there was more to her statement than just bravado. "I wasn't just talking about danger to me, Belle. I was trying to tell you that the reason I don't become close to people personally is that they could become endangered too. People who are close to me could conceivably be at risk. I can't take you out publicly, date you in the way that a woman like you deserves. Especially now."

"Why especially now?"

Sean surprised himself by hardly hesitating before he answered her. The news hadn't broken yet to the press. "Ever since U.S. special forces caught Tariq Sahid two nights ago in Afghanistan."

Belle's eyes widened incredulously when she recognized the name of the man who was likely one of the most wanted terrorists in the world.

"They did?"

Sean nodded grimly. "Allen Shively has informed me that I'm the top candidate to be the special prosecutor on the case against him."

Belle recognized the name of the Attorney General for the United States. "That's good news isn't it? For your career?"

"It's the opportunity of a lifetime. And I think I can do it, Belle, nail him good and hard. If someone had asked me awhile back if I was happy about it, I would have laughed at the ridiculousness of the necessity to ask the question."

"What happened to change your mind?"

"I saw you standing on that elevator two weeks ago."

"Oh," was all she said after a tense silence.

"Yeah, you made me a little speechless too," Sean said with a smile. He watched, fully enraptured, as color bloomed again in her cheeks. "But now you can guess where I'm coming from. The timing is incredibly bad."

"I'm not afraid, Sean. My father is a circuit court judge. Like you, he's sent his fair share of criminals to prison and even received the occasional threat, both against him and his family. And like you, he's never let it stop him from doing his job."

Sean studied her closely. So she *wasn't* as inexperienced in these matters as he'd assumed. "Your father is Richard March? Of the thirteenth circuit?"

Belle nodded. "He seems to have a lot of respect for you," she said softly.

"From what I've heard of your father, I would say the same of him."

"I'm not afraid, Sean," she repeated. She reached over the corner of the table and caressed the dense muscle of his shoulder. She liked the way her touch caused Sean to go utterly still. His eyes gleamed and his nostrils flared slightly, as though he were capturing her scent. Despite his obvious reaction to her touch, he frowned.

"But maybe you should be."

He couldn't believe he'd just said "maybe". The overpowering lust that he had for Belle was making him stupid. Would he really risk endangering her just to get his rocks off? He sighed in disgust and stood. "Listen, I just wanted to have dinner with you and get to know you better. There's no reason for us to worry about this now. Not if it's just dinner."

Sean could tell from doubtful expression on Belle's face that he hadn't completely convinced her, even if she was going to go along for the time being. She stood and began to clear the table. He reached out and grabbed her hand.

"Leave it," he ordered quietly. "I'll get it later. What I want is for you to come over here into the living room and tell me every detail of your life, just like I did to you during dinner. I'm nowhere near as good a listener as you are, but just do it as a favor to me so that I don't feel so guilty for being a conversation monopolist," he joked as he refilled her wine glass and handed it to her. He kept her hand in his grip and led her to the couch, where he plopped down next to her. When he noticed the flush on Belle's cheeks he touched the right one softly. His amusement shifted to awe.

"Why don't you start off by telling me how such a beautiful, sophisticated, smart woman could reach the ancient age of twenty-six and still blush when a man just touches your hand."

Belle glanced away. "I don't. I mean, not usually." Her eyes looked almost apologetic when they met his. "Not with other men."

Every rationalization for why he shouldn't make love to her faded into oblivion at her honesty.

She made a soft, trapped cry of alarm in her throat when she saw the way Sean transformed at her statement. One second he had been warm and tender. But in the next a primal, hot look suffused his eyes. The next thing she knew he was devouring her. Belle moaned at the impact his kiss had on her body.

"You shouldn't say things like that if you don't want to end up in bed, Belle," he murmured grimly against her neck as his open, hot mouth sucked at her greedily. He knew that he was likely marking her tender skin but he couldn't seem to stop himself. His lust overpowered rationality. He filled his palm with her breast, overflowing it.

He cursed. His cock instantly transformed into a leaden pillar. He'd been wrong in speculating that Belle was secreting C-cups under all of her sedate clothing. The firm, delicious breast that he currently massaged in his hand must fill a D.

"But I *do* want to, Sean."

He couldn't stop himself from gently squeezing her breast and running his thumb and forefinger over her nipple, finding the way they peaked beneath him so responsively incredibly exciting. But he did manage to raise his head and examine her. Her eyes were glossy and dazed with desire. Her lips were dark pink, moist and slightly swollen from the way he'd just kissed her so aggressively. Was it possible that she was as hot for him as he was for her? Sean knew that he wouldn't be able to stop himself from discovering the answer to that question, despite the fact that his gut told him that she was too innocent for what he had in mind.

"You sound pretty confident about that. You've done it before? Gone to bed with men that you knew as well and as long as you knew me?"

A trace of uncertainty went through her. She wondered if Sean saw doubt on her face because his fingers stilled their tormenting activities on her breast. She made a low sound of protest.

"Belle?" Sean prompted quietly.

"No," she finally admitted.

He had to focus on the mechanisms necessary to let go of her breast. "And you're trying to tell me that you wouldn't mind it? Knowing that I can't see you publicly, openly? You'd settle for that, fucking me at night, in secret?" His bluntness was intentional. Belle needed to know what she was dealing with, and he wasn't just talking about the circumstances of his job.

Yes. Belle stifled the automatic response that flew to her lips. His casual use of such illicit language turned her on more than she liked to admit. "It wouldn't be forever, would it? Us having to keep things secret?"

"No, but…" Sean paused, his mind racing, his body straining for the release that at this point he knew he was only going to find inside this woman. Her obvious innocence clawed at his consciousness though. "Aside from all of that stuff with my job, what about your experience? You've been with men before, right? Been involved, had affairs."

When he saw her hesitation he cursed soundly.

"I have been with a man before, Sean," she insisted hotly when she saw his reaction. "I'm not as naïve as you seem to think. I've just never…"

"What?" Sean asked when she stopped abruptly. "You've never what?"

Her chin came up. She wasn't going to cower in front of him like she was ashamed. There was nothing wrong with her, other than that her history and circumstances hadn't provided her with a desirable outlet for her sexual energies.

"I've never had intercourse with a man."

He stood up abruptly and crossed the room. He studied the city lights outside the window like he'd never seen them before.

Jesus, she'd just told him she was a virgin. It was an unprecedented experience for him. As if all the available evidence that he should walk away now hadn't *already* been damning enough.

"Sean . . . "

"It's okay," he said when he heard her voice behind him. "I was just thinking. We'll wait," he said with sudden decisiveness. "You're probably not on birth control, right?" She shook her head. "And I should go for a doctor's appointment, have tests, and make sure everything is okay before I put you at risk. I practice safe sex, but I won't take the chance of harming you," Sean explained patiently when he saw her amazed expression.

Her spine straightened with irritation at his authoritarian pronouncement. She could very easily imagine him barking off orders in just such a manner to his staff. "Just like that? You get to decide for both of us?"

One dark eyebrow rose in surprise at her unexpected reaction. "You want to file a complaint about it?" he asked darkly.

Her shoulders went back, thrusting her breasts forward. She experienced a small sense of triumph when Sean's suddenly brisk, businesslike attitude was broken as his eyes lowered to her chest. "There are other ways we could make love until then."

Blood drained from his brain to his cock at her calm challenge. Reason was once again replaced by lust.

"Oh and I suppose you're an expert at all of those ways," Sean replied sarcastically. For some reason her insistence that they purge their lust right here and now infuriated him as much as it excited him. It must have had something to do with the fact that he had an instinct to protect Belle March as much as he needed in a very primitive way to screw her until he fell over from exhaustion. Something in him demanded that he make her completely his.

He closed his eyes tightly, but the image of doing just that was still waiting behind his closed eyelids, tormenting him. He took a deep, steadying breath. "We'll wait. It's true that there are safer ways than others, but I don't know if I'll be able to stop myself once we start--"

"You'll stop yourself, Sean. I trust you."

He opened his eyes slowly and focused on her. She was sitting on the edge of his couch. She'd changed into a pair of low-riding, faded jeans and a light blue cotton shirt. Although her jeans hugged her round ass and hips with enticing snugness, her top was loose and only skimmed her breasts. It bothered Sean, the way she hid the bounty of her breasts, just as much as it irritated him when she bound the glory of her hair.

"You're serious about this, Belle?"

Her eyes widened slightly when she saw the sharp gleam in Sean's eyes that belied the stony expression on his face. He began to move toward her with the slow, intense focus of a predator.

"Of course," she managed.

"Prove it, then. Take off your shirt and bra."

She swallowed to bring moisture to her suddenly dry mouth. It was true that she wanted him, but her breasts were not a promising place for him to start. She'd always been self-conscious about them. She envied the streamlined beauty of small-breasted women.

"Belle? You said you were serious," he prompted. He watched as she grabbed the bottom of her shirt and lifted her arms.

"Stop. Don't move."

Belle halted abruptly at the lashlike quality of his voice, her elbows tangled in the shirt above her head.

"I said don't move," Sean said softly when Belle started to lower her arms.

Her eyes were huge as Sean came to stand in front of where she sat on the couch. She made a sound of protest when Sean took her hands and moved them behind her neck with her shirt still binding her elbows.

"Sean, what—"

"You said you trusted me, Belle. Have you changed your mind so quickly?" he challenged with distracted amusement. His eyes were busy appreciating the sight of her breasts encased in a snug nylon bra. When he'd put her hands behind her neck, it had made her spine curve and forced her breasts to thrust forward. He reached down and massaged her breasts with both hands.

He groaned roughly.

"Your're so beautiful. I'm glad that you don't show them off for other men, but I don't want you to hide them from me." He reached over and released the front clasp of her bra with a deft flick of his wrist. His actions brought him nearer to her. Belle found her face less than inch away from his crotch. The outline of his stiffening cock was clearly delineated against the fabric of his jeans. For a second she couldn't seem to unglue her eyes from that impressive sight. But then she realized that Sean hadn't moved after he'd pushed the cups of her bra off her breasts. Belle's eyes flew up to meet his. She could tell by the steamy look in his eyes that he knew what she'd been studying so hungrily.

Sean smiled and glanced back at her bared breasts. He knew her secret now. Belle's skin was that gorgeous color uniformly. Her nipples were a delectable peachy coral shade. He began to finesse her with his hands, alternating between massaging the flesh with his palms and teasing the responsive tips with his fingers. A sexy little moan leaked past her lips.

"You looked surprised when I said you have beautiful breasts. Why?"

"Because I don't exactly share your opinion," Belle admitted, lost in the erotic sensation of his hands on her breasts and the depths of his heated gaze.

"I can't expect that you'd share my feelings for them," Sean said wryly. "I think it's only fair to tell you something though. I've lost count of the number of times I've jerked off thinking about fucking your breasts."

She blinked in amazement.

He grinned when he took in her reaction. "It's one of those 'other' ways of making love, honey. It's safe enough to silence my concerns. Don't tell me that you're going to chicken out on me now."

"No…of course not. I was just a little surprised, that's all." She made a sound of protest when Sean's hands slid off her breasts and he backed away a step.

"You're going to find out soon enough just how crazy I am about your breasts." He reached forward and palmed the back of her head tenderly. "I'm crazy about all of you, Belle. Hold on a second. Don't move," Sean cautioned when he saw her shift her shoulders as though she would rid herself of the binding shirt. "I like you that way."

When he returned he was carrying a bottle of lotion that he'd retrieved from his bathroom. He kneeled down in front of where she sat on the couch, his eyes never leaving hers as he pumped some of the lotion into his palms and warmed it by massaging his hands together.

As Belle watched his preparations and took in his hot gaze, her breasts seemed to thrust forward even farther of their own accord. Her nipples pebbled, hungry for his touch. When he finally took her flesh into his palms, a low, shaky moan escaped her lips.

"You may not like your breasts much, but they certainly like to be touched. You're so responsive," Sean murmured appreciatively. Her skin was already like silk but it was pure pleasure to slide over her dense firmness so smoothly with the help of the lubricant. He fondled her thoroughly, but he was careful to avoid the pointed tips. He watched with fascinated arousal as her nipples distended and puckered even without direct stimulation.

Belle strained forward in his palms, desperate to have him touch the crests, but he easily maneuvered around her. She groaned.

"What, honey?" Sean prompted, knowing full well the source of her frustration.

Belle's shyness was forgotten, submerged by the liberation of her desire.

"Why aren't you touching the centers?"

"Because. Your nipples are reserved for my mouth and I don't like the taste of lotion."

She moaned and thrust forward, instinctively trying to graze her hungry flesh across his stroking palms. Sean laughed softly as he moved his hands to avoid her nipples. "Play fair, Belle. All you have to do is ask. Tell me what you'd like."

"For you to suck on my nipples," she admitted huskily.

He reached around and pulled the shirt binding her elbows and wrists off her. "Hold them up for my mouth then."

He almost came in his jeans at the sight of her skimming her hands beneath her shapely, slick breasts and offering herself to him. He took a moment to get control of his sharp lust before he leaned forward and tongued first one nipple and then the other. She made a trapped sound of arousal.

"Sweet," he murmured before he fastened on her right breast, hard.

She gave a startled scream. His initial licks on her had been slow and languorous, contrasting largely with the way he currently sucked and tongued her with hot-mouthed greed. She realized how close she was to coming. Her hips moved restlessly, instinctively seeking out the means to release the sudden almost cruel bite of pleasure that clutched her at her sex.

"Oh God, Sean, I think I'm going to—"

She gasped when he reached down and touched her unerringly through her jeans, never breaking the suction on her nipple. Belle surged up and rocked against him, mindless of what she was doing. The tight knot of tension burst. She cried out raggedly and shook in orgasm.

His eyes opened as he continued to stimulate her, taking in the sight of her face as she climaxed. The spasms that coursed through her body caused her breasts to tremble and shake. He sucked harder. Belle awarded him with renewed tremors of orgasm and a sharp cry. He reluctantly released her nipple, feeling his cock jerk in response to the popping noise it made when it sprang free of his mouth.

"Lie down on the couch, Belle," he ordered tensely.

She lay back and watched him as he stood and attacked his clothing. His t-shirt went first, revealing a flat, muscular abdomen and narrow waist that tapered upward beautifully to muscular shoulders. She could see his small, dark brown nipples through chest hair that wasn't excessive but was still entirely masculine. An enticing, narrow path of hair swirled around his bellybutton only to disappear beneath a pair of white briefs. Sean stretched the elastic band wide and sprang his cock. He shoved the briefs and jeans down his long thighs, kicking the clothing off his ankles impatiently.

Her eyes widened when he straddled her. He paused when he fully took in the look on her face. Christ, he could understand why she was so freaked out. His cock looked a little ominous. It was dark where it lay against the paleness of her belly, the veins prominent. He couldn't remember ever feeling this hard, this ponderous, this stretched with pure need. His hips surged forward on her soft skin of their own accord, unmindful of her look of fascinated alarm. The smooth head of his cock nuzzled the bottom curve of a firm breast. Sean leaned down over her, bracing his hands on the armrest behind Belle's head.

"Does it turn you off, Belle? That I want to do this?" he asked with quiet intensity. Every muscle in his body was tense with arousal. He felt like he could snap like a rubberband. He would stop if she wanted him to, but it was going to cost him more than he liked to admit.

"It's not turning me off, Sean. Just the opposite," she assured him. Her thigh muscles clenched tightly over the stinging pulse of arousal at her sex when Sean smiled.

"Good. I thought you were looking at me like I was a total pervert for a second."

She laughed softly. His cock jerked in response to the golden sound. They glanced at each other and shared a look of aroused amusement. He palmed one breast.

"Squeeze them together," he requested tensely. "Make a nice, tight little place for my cock, honey."

Belle moaned at his words. Her thighs were squeezing her sex so furiously that she wondered if it was possible to have an orgasm just from hearing Sean talk dirty to her. She did what he said, pushing her breasts together tightly. His cock nudged forward eagerly but Sean hesitated. When Belle glanced up uncertainly, he shook his head in awe.

"*Look* at you. Push your nipples together for me."

He dipped down, quick as a snake, and tongued the two nipples that she made meet with her fingers. She cried out.

Desire shot like an arrow straight to her sex. She moaned at the stabbing pressure.

"You're my fantasies come to life, Belle," he murmured as he leaned forward again, took his stiff sex in his hand and slid it into the crevice of her breasts. "Sweet Jesus," he muttered as he surged forward. He set a quick pace, watching every stroke of his cock as it disappeared between her flesh only to poke forward again, almost touching Belle's chin.

"Is this turning you on, honey?" Sean asked after a minute as he plunged harder, feeling his balls slap against her breasts. The sight of her breasts' upward bounce when he thrust into them would be scalded into his memory forever.

She stared up at him in stunned arousal. His muscles were straining and defined in aroused tension. A slight glaze of perspiration gilded his dark, smooth skin. He looked like some pagan fertility god.

"You have no idea how much," she said.

"So tell me," Sean insisted through clenched teeth as he pumped more strenuously.

Belle panted. She glanced down at the sight of his dark cock surging between her much paler breasts. "My underwear is soaking wet and I wish my hands weren't otherwise occupied because I think that I would explode at the smallest touch."

Despite the sexual intensity of the moment, Sean's eyes widened in surprise at the honesty of her response. "Christ," he muttered between tense lips. "Just give me a minute, honey, and I'll make sure you come as many times as nature will allow."

Her smile was the essence of womanly mystery. She tilted her chin down to see him better. "I can reach you with my mouth," she murmured.

Despite himself, Sean faltered in his thrusting. Damn. Had she really just said that or was lust making him hallucinate? And had Belle really said she was a virgin? The realization of what he was doing to her with her full consent made him scold himself for having preconceived notions about her desires. "You don't have to, honey. The lotion…"

She leaned forward, flushed lips parted. "I don't care. I want to taste you."

Sean surged forward so hard that her breasts sprang up several inches. The heaven of Belle's warm, suctioning mouth waited for the head of his sock at the end of the stroke. He shouted out at the sensation, pressing his hips forward to prolong her caress. Christ, she didn't take him in her mouth like she was inexperienced, not by any stretch of the imagination. He felt his balls pinch with a vice-like pressure. He was about to come, and God it was going be *so* good. He stroked once more, then twice, both times jiggling her breasts forcefully, both times sinking into the wet, clinging warmth of her mouth. He wanted to explode into that sweetness, but he forced himself not to push his incredible luck.

She started when he suddenly raised himself with one foot on the floor and reached down to her jeans. He ripped open the button fly violently. He shoved his hand inside her panties. She cried out shakily. He slid two long fingers along her clit and began rubbing her firmly. His whole arm jerked back and forth, biceps bulging, in an insistent demand. He glanced up at her face when she called out his name sharply.

"You weren't kidding," he muttered, nostrils flaring. "You *are* soaking wet. I'm going to come on your beautiful breasts. Come with me," he ordered starkly.

It wasn't a request. His eyes on her were slits of cool fire.

He took his erection into the hand that wasn't stroking her and pumped.

She screamed, her eyes wide, igniting under the impact of his talented fingers and the intensely erotic vision of him. She forced her eyes open, not wanting to miss the sight of his cock stretching impossibly longer before he came. White, ropey streams jetted onto her breasts. His uninhibited, ragged shout of pleasure turned her orgasm up a notch.

The seconds ticked by. She slowly released the pressure on her breasts as Sean's ragged breathing began to calm.

She glanced up only to see that he was watching her steadily.

"What are you thinking, Belle?"

She read his expression. "I'm not regretting it, Sean. If you must know, I was thinking about how incredible it was. I was also thinking that I doubt there's another man alive who could have talked me into doing it. I know there isn't one who could have made me love it so much."

Her heart squeezed in her chest at the potent flash of his grin.

TWO

The Following Year

BELLE'S GRIEF-INSPIRED dreams could be cruel at times, evoking feelings of fresh panic and emptiness. Tonight they made her want to howl with a powerful desire that was destined to go unfulfilled.

She loved to treat Sean to both slow, sweet, teasing sucks and fast, furious, face-fucks that culminated in him gasping for air, shouting out his hilarious, arousing combination of nonsensical curses and divine imprecations, eventually coming in her mouth in record time. She knew which kind he'd want tonight.

His tension level about the Tariq Sahid trial had been escalating steadily for the past few weeks, although Sean rarely spoke of it. Belle could just sense it in the rigid lines of his jaw and the tension that coiled in his muscles. The press had been hounding him since someone on his staff had leaked that he'd received multiple death threats following the announcement that he would be the special prosecutor in the Tariq Sahid case, threats that the Federal Bureau of Protective Services and the Federal Bureau of Investigation were taking very seriously.

Not that Sean was talking about that much either. None of it changed the fact that he had a job to do.

Belle wanted to bring him a measure of relief, a catharsis for his stress. So she didn't waste any time tonight, sucking him deep and strong and setting a brisk tempo. The pants to his suit were still around his ankles. They'd barely been inside his condominium for twenty seconds before she was kneeling in front of him.

Sean growled deep in his throat and fisted her lush blonde curls when she began to tease a testicle with her hand at the same time as she sucked him to the back of her throat.

"I'd like to light up that asshole who taught you how to do this, but I guess I should thank him from the bottom of my heart too." He gave a guttural groan and held her head steady. Belle let him fuck her mouth, concentrating on stilling her gag reflex. His hips pumped into her steadily at first but with increasing irregularity as he grew nearer orgasm. "Ah, honey, you're so sweet. Hum me a little tune."

Afterwards he held her tightly, laughing softly into her hair. "I think I'm earning a first class ticket straight to hell."

"Why?" she murmured. Her sex throbbed dully for him. Sucking Sean always turned her on more than she cared to admit. But he would make her come many times before the night was over. His blowjob had just been the equivalent of a very dry martini after coming home from work, something to take the edge off after a hard day. They'd begin again in the bedroom soon enough in earnest.

"For fucking the mouth of a virgin with the face of an angel," Sean muttered wryly, stroking her cheek. "When I come back from my trip out east I'll be able to make love to you, right?"

Belle looked up into his penetrating blue eyes and nodded. She would be on birth control for the prescribed period of time by then. "You could now, Sean. We don't have to wait. You could use a condom." She could tell by his smoky stare that the idea appealed to him. But although Sean was lustier than Bacchus himself, she'd learned firsthand over the past weeks of being with him that he was also highly disciplined once he'd made a decision.

"Quit tempting me," he warned huskily. "A man is only with the woman of his dreams for the first time once in a lifetime. I want it to be perfect. I want to feel every sensation of being inside of you."

"But…"

"No buts about it. When I come back from my trip, I'm going to make you mine. Completely. Constantly," he added with a sense of wry inevitabily. "He reached up and filled his hand with her breast. He growled low in satisfaction. "Not that I haven't staked my claim on most of you already. Let's go to the bedroom, Belle…"

Belle awoke with a groan at the sound of Ellie's bark.

"Bad timing, girl," she whispered irritably at her dog. Her sex felt tight and heavy from her hyper-realistic dream about Sean. How long would these dreams continue? It had been fifteen months, three weeks and four days since Sean had been killed. Yet there seemed to be no end in sight to Belle's suffering. His powerful ghost still haunted every sleeping and waking moment.

But her dog was apparently having an urgent biological imperative of her own. Belle staggered out of bed and threw on a t-shirt and jeans, having no other choice than to deal with the practicalities of the present.

The first flush of dawn gilded Lincoln Park with a soft, hazy gold. As Belle walked farther and farther away from

North Avenue, she was encapsulated in an island of peaceful nature in the midst of an urban sea of steel and concrete. She loved this time of the day, when promise hung most thick in the air. The still dawn stood in stark contrast to her restless, grief-filled nights.

Her usually sedate Irish setter seemed especially energetic this summer morning as she tugged at her leash. Even though she wasn't supposed to—there were strict leash laws in Lincoln Park—Belle removed Ellie's leash and let her run. There wasn't a soul in sight and Ellie never wandered far.

The Irish setter disappeared behind a copse of tall ever-greens. Belle immediately spotted her dog when she entered the clearing, but Ellie wasn't alone. She nosed a gigantic black and tan dog that looked to be at least thirty-five or forty pounds heavier than her. But Ellie seemed far from intimidated. If their fascinated circling and nuzzling of each other was any indication, this was an entirely friendly meeting.

Belle glanced around the area, wondering about the owner of the black and tan dog. At first she thought the clearing was empty. She held up her hand to shield the sun streaming into her eyes from the east, brightened by the reflection off Lake Michigan. Her gaze caught on a figure standing in the shadows of the evergreens.

She blinked twice, squinting, and lowered her hand. It was a tall man wearing faded jeans and an untucked t-shirt. Belle had the distinct impression that he'd been watching her steadily since she'd entered the clearing. That realization and his shadowed, vaguely sinister appearance made her first few steps toward him slow and reluctant.

Once she was within fifteen feet of him, she chastised herself for being paranoid. He was a completely ordinary-looking man. Well…not exactly ordinary. Quite extraordinary really. But nowhere near as ominous as she'd imagined a few seconds ago. It was the shadows of the trees that clung around his already dark features that had provided that dangerous quality. Or maybe it was the two-inch scar that ran from his temple over his right cheekbone that contributed to his enigmatic appearance.

"Good morning," he greeted quietly when she finally got within speaking distance.

"Hello. They really seem to have hit it off, huh?" She waved at their dogs.

The man nodded once, but he didn't remove his stare from her. Belle noticed that despite the shadows, his eyes were a clear cerulean blue. A prickly sensation feathered over her forearms. He didn't speak as he studied her intently. Shockingly, she felt her already partially aroused body quicken further beneath his stare. She hadn't bothered to put on a bra for her and Ellie's early morning walk. The material of her t-shirt abraded her erect nipples, causing an achy, prickly sensation.

"I didn't know that Copenhagen's tail actually could wag that wide until now," he said.

She took in his grin and the flash of even white teeth in his dark face. Her mouth fell open. *Talk about potent.* She glanced away abruptly, unsettled by her thought.

"Copenhagen? Is he a Great Dane than?" she mused.

"Partly. Allegedly. The only thing I know for sure is that he's a one hundred percent pain in the butt. He's got some Great Dane in him, along with some shepherd and bloodhound."

When he stopped speaking Belle's gaze was drawn back to him like metal to a lodestone. His arms were crossed casually over his chest, his jean-clad thighs were slightly spread and his knees were bent just a tad as he watched the cavorting animals.

It was an entirely male pose, confident and lazy at once. The sight of hard thighs and the thickness between them compelled her eyes to linger. Whoever this man was, he didn't need to flaunt his masculinity. It spoke for itself, loud and clear.

"But that's not why I named him Copenhagen," he added gruffly after a moment.

Belle dragged her eyes away from his crotch guiltily, only to notice that his gorgeous light eyes were fastened on her breasts. Was her aroused state obvious to him?

"No? Why then?" she asked, glad to have something to focus on other than the fact that she found this man vastly appealing. It struck her that although they were carrying on this mundane conversation, beneath the surface, a very different communication was taking place, a subtle but potent nonverbal sexual exchange.

What was *wrong* with her? She didn't typically respond to men in this way. The exception had been Sean, of course. She'd practically liquefied the first time Sean had speared her with his blue eyes.

Her eyes widened as the realization dawned.

Oh. So that was the reason for her furiously frothing libido. This man reminded her of Sean. Both men were tall, lean and muscular. Like this man, Sean had had hair so dark brown that it looked black in the shadows. And the striking light eyes that created such a breathtaking contrast against dark hair and skin…those were similar too.

But also different, Belle admitted to herself. This man's eyes were colder and sharper than Sean's had ever been.

"I named him after Wellington's horse," he said.

His deadpan answer made laughter tilt her lips despite her former thoughts about his coldness. "Any particular reason for that?"

He shrugged broad shoulders. His eyes gleamed with warmth as he took in her amusement. "He's as big as a horse. I grew up a city kid. I didn't know that many horses' names, but I read a book about Wellington and Napoleon when I was twelve years old. So I knew the name of at least one horse."

She opened her mouth to question him, but her attention was diverted when her usually sedate, calm dog suddenly pranced and leaped forward with a playful bark. Copenhagen loped after her energetically. Belle looked over in surprise at the man beside her and they shared a smile.

"I think your dog is seducing mine," he said quietly. "What's her name?"

"Ellie." She'd thought of defending her pet's honor, but instead she just shook her head in amazement. "She really is acting like a big flirt, isn't she? I've never seen her act this way. Has Copenhagen been…neutered?"

When he didn't immediately reply she glanced over at him. His expression looked vaguely guilty. "Uh no. I kept meaning to get around to it but…"

Belle couldn't help but smirk.

"What?" he prompted with a slow grin.

She shrugged, hoping to look nonchalant, and kicked the toe of her shoe idly in the grass.

"Professional cliché. I'm a psychologist, so…"

"Oh I get it. You're going to make some annoying remark about me projecting my castration fears onto my dog. Is that it?"

She laughed, pleasantly surprised by the astuteness of his comment. "Well I did say it was a cliché. I hate to be predictable so I won't say another word. Or you can interpret me, since I've never had Ellie spayed."

His eyebrows rose in a sardonic expression. "Guess we

better keep a close eye on them or nature is going to take its natural course."

For a few seconds his heated gaze held her in a sensual spell. Her mouth fell open in deepening sexual awareness. Her tongue swept anxiously over her lower lip. His eyelids narrowed as he stared at her mouth. She blinked once, disoriented when she realized he'd spoken again.

"What about you?"

"Excuse me?" she asked, dazed. Surely he wasn't asking her if her reproductive organs were intact or not.

"Your name. I'm Jack. Jack Caldwell."

"Oh. I'm Belle March." The early summer morning was cool but Jack Caldwell's hand was warm when he fully encompassed hers in a handshake. It struck her after a moment that he hadn't let go. She forced herself to reclaim her hand. He re-crossed his arms and rocked back on his heels casually.

"Do you and Ellie walk out here often?"

"Yes. It's our regular haunt."

"But not at night."

Belle gave him a puzzled look. His tone had been almost stern. "Sometimes, but usually not this far into the park. I try to stay closer to North Avenue."

Jack frowned at her answer. "You shouldn't come into the park alone. It's dangerous."

Belle choked back laughter. Not only his words, but his sudden hard expression took her completely off guard. The thought struck her that it was the type of thing that a person said to another when they were in a relationship, not when they were complete strangers like she and Jack were. Sean used to preach to her about where she took Ellie out at night.

"Why would you say something like that?" Belle asked with amusement tinged with wariness. "This neighborhood isn't dangerous. I've lived here for almost two years now and never seen any crime."

"The worst kind of crime is usually invisible. I wouldn't expect that you would see it," he answered impassively.

"Are you a cop or something?" Belle couldn't shake the idea that she knew him. How else could it possibly make sense that a complete stranger would sound so natural admonishing her for her personal habits? Not to mention that her body was responding to him as though it knew him in the most primitive way.

He grinned mirthlessly, adding to his piratical air. "Much worse, actually. A lawyer." Belle stilled when he pinned her with icy blue eyes and shrugged negligently. "That is, unless you have a thing for lawyers. They say some women do, despite the complete unnaturalness of it."

A whirlwind of unexpected emotions rose up through her gut and stifled her lungs, preventing her from inhaling.

"What's wrong?" Jack's expression of grim amusement vanished only to be replaced by tense alertness when he saw her stricken expression.

"Come on, Ellie," she managed in a strangled voice. When the Irish setter ignored her she managed to get out a second request in a louder voice.

"Belle?"

She didn't turn at the sound of his voice, but busied herself with fastening Ellie's leash on her collar. "Yes?"

"I asked you a question. What's wrong?"

She straightened too briskly, making half of her precariously balanced hair came loose from the fastener that secured it on her head. She muttered irritably and reached for the hair clip to release the rest of it. A curly tendril caught. She pulled at it too hard, making tears spring up in her eyes.

"Nothing is wrong. I just need to get going, that's all," she muttered as she yanked at the clip in increasing agitation.

"Calm down."

Belle blinked and stilled. Jack Caldwell had just issued an order, no matter how softly it had been murmured.

He leaned down over her. She held her breath. Her entire awareness focused on his fingers gently removing the errant tress from the teeth of the clip. For a split second his gaze left his task and met hers. Knowing full well that she watched him, he glanced down at her heaving breasts.

"Nice t-shirt. Did you go to Yale?"

Belle's breath froze but she managed to shake her head. "Northwestern. A…friend went to Yale." Her nipples pulled tight as he continued to caress them with his stare. Belle had always been self-conscious about her breasts, feeling like they were too large for the rest of her body. It was rare for her to be in public without a bra on, but she hadn't really figured on running into anyone—let alone a man like Jack Caldwell. But he didn't seem to mind her size. If anything, his expressive gaze was downright wanting. He dropped one of his hands from her hair. Belle tensed.

Dear God, he wasn't going to—

He *was*.

She moaned shakily in disbelief and paralyzing arousal when he ever so gently pinched a pebbled nipple between a thumb and forefinger. His eyes slowly rose to meet her gaze. He carefully studied her dazed, mesmerized expression as he rolled her nipple between his fingers. She inhaled raggedly at the exquisite sensation, breathing in the scent of Jack Caldwell.

"What the hell?" Jack muttered half in alarm, half in amazement when Belle stumbled as she abruptly pulled away from him. It took him a second to fully absorb the expression on her face. His hand immediately went out to her shoulder to steady her.

"Christ, you're shaking," he added in disbelief when he felt her tremor through the thin material of her t-shirt. "Belle? I know how that must have seemed to you but you're not *afraid* of me, are you?"

"Y-you-you smell l-l-like…" She immediately stopped when she realized she was stuttering. Her gaze scoured his face, unconsciously undertaking a desperate search.

His eyes became crescents of cool flame when he narrowed his eyelids to study her.

"*What*?"

She swallowed with effort. "Nothing. I'm s-s…" Her eyes shut in frustrated concentration as she tried to overcome the shameful reoccurrence of a childhood stutter. "Sorry. Come on, Ellie."

She had to tug on Ellie with uncustomary harshness to get her to part from her new friend. Belle never turned around to see if Copenhagen—or Jack, for that matter—followed until she safely entered her condominium lobby. Once there a backward furtive glance told her that she and Ellie had made the return trip through the park utterly alone.

————

Belle kicked off her shoes when she entered her condominium and sank shakily into a living room chair. For several minutes she sat there and stared blankly into space. Ellie's nose on her hand and a low, mournful whine brought her back to reality. She petted her dog's dark auburn coat.

"You have reason to be worried, Ellie. I think I'm finally cracking up."

Her analytic clinical skills clicked into gear. Why would

she be having such an extreme delayed grief reaction to Sean's death? Why hadn't her unusual response occurred earlier, instead of more than a year after the fact? It didn't make sense. She had gone through a difficult bereavement following Sean's unexpected, violent murder in a car bombing. It had only made it worse that she couldn't grieve openly. She suffered in secret, and still did.

"Promise me that if anything ever happens to me you won't reveal our relationship to anyone. Do you understand, Belle? No one. And swear that you won't go anywhere near the funeral services.

Promise *me, Belle."*

She had finally promised so that Sean would stop badgering her about such a frightening topic.

A few moments later, she found herself staring blankly into her refrigerator while tears rolled down her face. She slammed the door shut and grabbed a paper towel to dry her face.

Of course, the reason for her near psychotic-like behavior in the park earlier—letting a stranger grope her, believing that Jack Caldwell's scent was identical to Sean's—made complete sense, clinically-speaking, if she was willing to accept the obvious facts. Maybe she was ready to move on with her life, experience herself as a sexually viable woman again. What did it matter that she hadn't come to that realization with Clay Rothschild, the man she was currently dating? She admitted to herself that she was very attracted to Jack Caldwell, despite the fact he was a complete stranger. Was it any surprise that her unconscious mind was only allowing her to make that admission within the context of acknowledging his similarities to Sean?

She stood in the kitchen, her head bowed, her defenses lowered by pain. As memories of Sean flooded her awareness she acknowledged one thing as fact. No matter how his loss still caused her daily suffering and perhaps always would, Belle would have chosen to love Sean all over again in a second even knowing how brief their time had been together.

Even knowing that hell waited for her in the end.

She clenched her eyes shut, groping in her lonely darkness for images of Sean, saddened by the way time was making the cherished memories so blurred and ghostly.

THREE

SEAN'S FACE leapt unbidden into Belle's mind's eye yet again the next evening as Clay kissed her goodnight at the entrance to her condominium.

"Are you sure you don't want me to come up?" Clay asked in a low husky voice next to her lips.

She was glad that he hadn't noticed the way she stiffened when he kissed her. She'd been casually dating Clay Rothschild now for two months. He was an associate at Holloway & Croft, one of the most prestigious law firms in the country. According to her good friend Sheila Livingston, who had introduced them, Clay was an up-and-coming star in the firm.

Belle couldn't help but think of Jack Caldwell's sardonic blue eyes. *Unless you have a thing for lawyers. They say some women do, despite the complete unnaturalness of it.*

Belle shook her head briskly to rid herself of the uncomfortable memory. "Not tonight, Clay. It's been a long day."

He hid his frown by kissing her temple. He asked himself daily why he continued to see Belle March when she almost ritualistically denied him access to her bed. But the fact of the matter was, despite her damnable coldness she was pretty near the perfect woman for him. She was beautiful and smart. Clay loved her face and body, although he truthfully could have done without the big tits, even though Belle's were firm and shapely. Clay preferred small-breasted women with responsive, sensitive nipples. Women with big breasts reminded him of cows.

But he couldn't expect complete perfection could he? Belle had the type of background and breeding that complemented Clay's image of what he wanted to be. Her father could provide him with innumerable desirable political and personal connections that would boost his career.

There was also the fact that her refusal to sleep with him only fueled his attraction to her. Clay wasn't used to being denied anything he wanted. He wanted Belle, and her elusiveness only made him more determined to have her.

"Remember that I'll be picking you up early tomorrow night," he said. "A bunch of people from the firm are getting together over at the bar at The Peninsula before we go to dinner."

Clay leaned down over her and held her gaze. His sun-streaked dark blond hair fell forward rakishly. The thought struck Belle that most women would have given up a few years of their life to have a man as gorgeous as Clay Rothschild look at them the way he was looking at her right now. But all she wanted to do was step away. She had to refocus her attention to even absorb what Clay was saying.

"It'll be an absolute necessity to have a few drinks before I have to kiss up to this new partner. Everybody acts like the guy is the second coming, but he seems to have decided that he hated me from the moment he saw me," Clay complained.

"I'm sure it's your imagination," she replied, smoothing his lapel distractedly. "He's probably just got a lot on his mind, moving to a new city, taking on a new job. Maybe he'll lighten up at his welcome dinner. It doesn't seem likely that anyone would dislike you instantly."

Clay dipped his head. She froze. "Are you saying that you like me, Belle?"

"Of course I do. Why else would I go out with you?"

"Sometimes I wonder about that myself," he admitted.

Guilt flickered into her awareness. She'd been wasting his time. Her experience with the stranger in the park the other day had taught her one thing—she wasn't completely numbed-off sexually like she'd assumed she was since Sean's death. Her lack of desire when it came to Clay had nothing to do with Sean's loss and *everything* to do with the fact that she just wasn't attracted to Clay.

"Maybe you're right," she admitted.

Clay stopped her abruptly with a brisk kiss on her mouth. "It's okay. I'm sorry for pushing you. But you must know how attractive I think you are, how sexy. It's not a crime that I want to go to bed with you is it?" When he saw the protest on her lips he stilled it glibly. "I know. I know. It's not a crime that you should want to wait, either." He kissed her again, this time more lengthily. When he raised his head his grin was warm and charming.

"I'll see you tomorrow at six thirty, okay?"

Her smile hid her hesitancy as she nodded.

Her doubts about continuing her relationship with Clay had only increased by the following evening.

She quickly inspected her appearance in the bathroom mirror before she went to answer the phone. It was probably the doorman telling her that Clay had arrived. Despite her uninspired, automatonlike efforts at preparing herself for the evening, Belle had to admit that the end result was pretty good. The tawny-colored, sleeveless, belted sheath dress that she wore with matching leather heels accentuated her coloring. In deference to the warm summer evening she'd put her hair up, but a few loose tendrils softened the style. When Belle saw Clay's appreciative look as she opened the front door to greet him, her anxiety rose a notch.

She didn't want to be inspiring glances like that from Clay when she was planning on breaking up with him later that evening.

The large bar at the Peninsula Hotel had a clublike atmosphere with several conversation areas consisting of leather chairs and deep, decadently comfortable couches. When they arrived Clay expressed his surprise at the number of people who were already there. Belle knew by then that Clay was a social creature by nature.

"Clay looks like he's in exceptional form tonight," Angela Winthrop, another attorney whom Belle had met several times before, commented with a wry grin. Belle followed Angela's glance at Clay. They'd only been there for fifteen minutes but he was already half finished with the second of the stiff martinis that he favored. He was standing a few feet away joking loudly with several of his friends and co-workers.

"To be honest with you, I'm not sure that he is." As a psychologist she knew that the frenetic, almost manic mood that Clay exhibited likely was more a sign of emotional turmoil then genuine happiness. "I think he's worried about that new partner. He's going to be working for him a lot, and for some odd reason, Clay is convinced that the new guy hates him. It's got him on edge."

Angela took a sip of her drink and shook her head. "He's not imagining things. We've all noticed it. The new guy really does seem to have singled him out. Clay can't do anything to please him." Angela's brown eyes widened when something caught her attention at the entryway to the bar. She leaned over and whispered, "Speak of the devil."

Belle began to take a casual sip of her wine as she nonchalantly followed Angela's gaze. She lowered her wineglass without ever taking a drink.

"*That's* the new partner?" she asked hollowly.

"Yeah, I know. Gorgeous, isn't he?" Angela whispered conspiratorially close to Belle's ear. "You'd think that scar would make him ugly, but it just seems to highlight the perfection of everything else. Not that he's exactly a pretty boy to begin with. Rough-hewn, if you know what I mean. I'm willing to bet he's got a cock bigger than Zeus' in those pants. And that scar… He's really got that sexy pirate thing going on, don't you think? Belle? Belle? *Stop*," Angela hissed, barely restraining her laughter. "You're staring. Jeez, he's staring right back," Angela murmured in fascinated amusement.

Belle tried to drag her gaze away, but only succeeded in turning her head. Her eyes stayed locked in the trap of Jack Caldwell's stare.

Her heartbeat escalated to an alarming rate as she finally succeeded in ripping her stare from his and turning around. She took a long, very unladylike draw on her wine. After a moment, she noticed that Clay and his group had also noticed Jack Caldwell's entrance into the bar. His friends watched their new boss with covert interest, while Clay cursed quietly under his breath.

"Shit. What's *he* doing here?" Belle heard Clay mutter to one of his friends.

"Shut up, Clay. It's his welcome dinner tonight, isn't it? Christ, he's coming over here," his friend John McNair whispered in surprise.

Belle felt like she couldn't breathe. The ten or twelve young people who sat around her all seemed aware of the man who approached even though they tactfully avoided staring at him and continued their conversations. After a few seconds, however, even their forced conversations ceased as they looked over with surprised speculation to the spot just behind and to the right of Belle. Clay's mouth fell open in confused disbelief.

"Belle?"

She stood slowly and turned to face Jack Caldwell. He stood less than two feet away from her. Even with her heels on he seemed to tower over her.

"Hello." Her voice sounded calm enough. Thankfully her back was to Clay and his friends, so they couldn't see how flushed her face had become. But Jack noticed it, Belle was sure. She doubted those blue eyes missed much of anything.

"We met the other day in the park," he said.

"I haven't forgotten." Her blush deepened at her statement. As if she was likely to forget Jack Caldwell or the fact that she'd let him play with her nipple after knowing him for five minutes.

"How is Copenhagen?" she asked abruptly, trying to rid herself of the embarrassing, arousing memory.

His grin was as potent as she recalled.

"Eating me out of house and home. Although I have to admit he has been moping around a lot ever since he met Ellie."

Belle laughed. "You know, come to think of it, Ellie has been a little moody too."

"You left so quickly. It disoriented Copenhagen and me. Were you okay?"

Her laughter stilled at the intensity of his quietly asked question. He'd leaned forward when he spoke. She doubted that any of the people behind them had heard what he said. His eyes were like searchlights on her, demanding an honest answer. Her lips opened to give it.

"I guess there's no need for me to make introductions."

Belle blinked and glanced over at Clay, who was suddenly standing by her side. She didn't even notice that Clay put his arm around her waist in a casual gesture of possession until she saw Jack Caldwell's eyes lower. When he met her gaze again briefly, his expression was impassive, but his eyes were like ice.

"Brilliant assumption, Rothschild."

Jack turned and walked away.

"Damn," Clay whispered bitterly. He grabbed Belle's arm and forced her to sit down. "Why didn't you tell me that you knew him?" he demanded in a whisper as he came down next to her.

"You're hurting me. Let go of my arm, Clay," Belle insisted in a no less irritated voice.

He complied, but his focus on her didn't lessen. "Belle?"

"I don't really *know* him." When she noticed his look of disbelief, she added, "I mean I do. But I just met him briefly a few days ago. It's not a big deal."

"You could have fooled me. He arrowed over here like you were his only friend in a room full of strangers. Are you sure he's not a crony of your father's or something?"

"Of course not. Or at least not that I know of. I told you, I just met him briefly a few days ago. It was in Lincoln Park. Our dogs had a thing for each other."

Belle took a sip of her wine and followed it with a deep breath. She needed to slow down her racing pulse. Jack Caldwell was gone now. Surely she wouldn't have to speak with him again for the rest of the night.

The vague emptiness in her chest made her remind herself forcefully that *not* seeing him again was a *good* thing. She could objectively understand her attraction to him when she'd thought his presence in her life was just a random, bizarre, one-time incident. It was more difficult to analyze the strength

of her response as Jack became more of a real, fleshed-out individual who just *happened* to be leaning on the bar across the
room from her, chatting amiably with a pretty, dark-haired
woman.

It became all that more difficult to rationalize her reaction
to him when they went to the Shanghai Terrace later, and Jack
Caldwell sat down in the empty chair next to her. Belle stared
at his back incredulously, but then had the presence of mind
to look away when she realized that his attention was
completely focused on the woman to the other side of him. It
was the same dark-haired woman he'd been talking to earlier at
the bar.

Clay leaned forward and checked out the seating arrangements. He smirked. "Looks like Jack Caldwell is straight after
all. We all thought he was gay. Well, all of us but Angela.
Caldwell brought that creepy assistant O'Sullivan with him
from his old law firm. We figured they were butt buddies,"
Clay said quietly as he made a subtle gesture with his eyes
down the table. Belle noticed a brown-haired man who was
sitting diagonally across from them—O'Sullivan, apparently.
The man returned Belle's casual glance with an implacable,
steady stare.

"What law firm did you say that Jack Caldwell was with
before?" she wondered, barely moving her lips.

"Ellsworth and Burke out of Boston," Clay muttered
distractedly. "He comes from blood almost as blue as yours.
At least on his mother's side. His father is a U.S. Senator,
but Caldwell's roots on that side are working-class all
the way."

Clay didn't seem to notice Belle's irritated glance. She
couldn't understand his obsession with class. But Clay seemed
absorbed as he stared at his new boss's back intently.

"Maybe he's just making things look like they're on the up-

and-up for the other partners. Joyce Hollister would be the obvious choice to stake his claim as a hetero."

Belle's hand shook slightly when she took a sip of water. "Cut it out, Clay. If he's gay, it wouldn't be any of your business. He's not though. Gay, I mean."

Clay's green eyes flickered in surprise at Belle's sharp tone, and then transferred over to where Jack Caldwell was leaning close to Joyce Hollister in focused conversation.

"Yeah, I guess you're right. Most of the guys in the firm have a serious lech for Joyce." When Clay noticed the change in Belle's offended expression, he caressed her upper arm with smug reassurance. "The guys who aren't already dating the most beautiful woman in the city, that is. That leaves me out."

She had to force herself not to lean over and give the supposed source of such universal male lechery a more serious inspection. She managed not to do it during the entire time one of the senior partners stood and welcomed Jack Caldwell, and while Jack gave a witty, humorous speech in response. Belle even made it through the first course without studying the subject of Jack's undivided attention. Clay seemed to be reassured by the fact that Jack was ignoring his date, and began to attend more fully to his friend's conversations.

She was toying with her Kung Pao chicken when she noticed Jack stand up. She glanced up instinctively and met his stare. He held it as he sat back down slowly. Belle realized that he'd stood while Joyce Hollister excused herself momentarily. Her darting, curious glance made her heart sink. Joyce *was* very pretty and she had the type of sleek, boyish figure that Belle coveted.

"You look bored, Belle," Jack observed dryly.

"Do I?" she asked with surprise. How was it possible to be bored seated next to him?

He nodded. "Surely this can't be too exciting for you. A

room full of lawyers." His blue eyes sliced past her to the back of Clay's head. "I see that you *are* one of those unfortunate women who find lawyers attractive."

Belle didn't know how to respond so she merely glanced down at her food.

"I sat down next to you for dinner on purpose."

"Oh?" she asked with forced casualness after a moment. "I was wondering how I rated being seated next to the guest of honor."

"I wanted to ask you for some advice."

Belle glanced over at him, surprised. "What kind of advice?"

Jack shrugged and leaned subtly closer to her. Belle found herself staring into a pair of blue eyes that were unsettlingly in their impact. His suit was dark, just like his hair and skin. It was cut well, accentuating the breadth of his shoulders. Belle inhaled the clean, spicy smell of his cologne. Beneath it she caught the rich scent of his skin. Had she been wrong in thinking it was like Sean's? She unconsciously breathed him in more deeply, suddenly not caring if there was a similarity or not.

"Professional advice. You said you were a psychologist?"

Despite herself, Belle laughed. "You can't be serious. It wouldn't be ethical for me to sit here and counsel you over dim sum and Kung Pao chicken."

"Okay. Forget about being a psychologist. I just want your opinion on something. As a friend?" Jack asked smoothly before he took a sip of water.

She hesitated. Of *course* they weren't friends. They hardly knew each other. "I'll listen if you want me to," she eventually murmured.

He smiled. Her gaze flicked downward hungrily to catch

sight of his white, even teeth. When she glanced back into his eyes, his gaze was warm.

"That's all I ask. Here's the thing. I have a good friend. He lost his wife in a tragic accident a little over a year ago. He hasn't been able to get over her death."

"How terrible for him."

"Yeah. It hit him really hard. I've been really worried about him. The thing that I wanted to know is, how long do you think it takes most people to grieve the loss of a loved one?"

For a few seconds she just stared at him, speechless. His steady gaze unnerved her. "Jack, that's not a question I can answer without knowing the circumstances. It's different for everyone."

"Yeah. I figured you'd say something like that. That wasn't really the question I had anyway."

"Jack," she halted him. "You're not talking about a friend, are you? You're talking about yourself. You're the one who lost someone."

His eyes narrowed warily. "Why would you say that?"

"Intuition," she replied softly.

Their gazes clung. In some corner of her consciousness, she became aware that Joyce had returned and was noisily dragging her chair to the table, probably trying to get Jack's attention so that he would re-seat her.

But Jack didn't budge.

"It really is a friend," he said.

"Okay," Belle replied evenly, willing to go along until she got a grip on this conversation. On Jack Caldwell in general.

"Here's the thing." He leaned toward her even further. Belle could clearly see the black line that delineated the outer rim of his iris, the way the blue was darker toward the pupil and lightened to a mesmerizing cerulean as it moved outward.

"My friend recently met a woman whom he finds extremely attractive."

Her brow crinkled slightly at that statement. "Okay," she said uncertainly.

Jack seemed to notice her confusion. "See, he hasn't been with another woman since his wife died. He just couldn't bring himself to do it. Didn't have the desire."

Understanding dawned. "Oh, I see. And now he's met this woman, and he's attracted to her and he's feeling…?"

He gave a small smile. "Dazed and confused about it. The thing of it is, this woman whom he finds himself so attracted to?" He paused and waited for Belle's nod of acknowledgment. "She reminds him a lot of his wife. Do you think that's unhealthy?"

Belle forced herself to look away, to focus on some other object in the room so that she could get her bearings. A dreamlike quality assailed her consciousness. What were the *chances*? How likely was it that Jack Caldwell was confessing something that almost exactly paralleled *her* personal experience of meeting him?

"I think it's probably natural, Jack." Her voice sounded distant and unfamiliar to her own ears. "Your friend is likely ready to end his grieving process, to feel alive again. His awakened sexuality is just a natural expression of that."

"Belle?" Jack's voice was hard and insistent, breaking through her haze of unreality.

"Yes?"

"What about the fact that the person my friend finds attractive reminds him of his wife? Doesn't that seem a little sick?"

The subtle insecurity in his tone of voice managed to completely break her feeling of being in The Twilight Zone. Recognizing the vulnerability in such a strong man unexpectedly activated her protective instincts. "Of course not, there's nothing sick about it," she assured him passionately. "The woman probably isn't as similar as he imagines. He's likely just ascribing those familiar characteristics to her in order to increase his comfort level with being with her and to decrease his guilt. It's an unnecessary but *perfectly* understandable defense mechanism."

Jack's right eyebrow rose a fraction of an inch as he studied her. "I knew you would be a good psychologist. So do you think it would be okay for my friend to pursue this attraction he feels for this woman?" he asked nonchalantly as he took a bite of his dinner.

Belle's mouth fell open. Where had his vulnerability gone? His attitude was almost blasé. Unintentionally, she stared across Jack to the woman who sat next to him, who was trying not to seem obvious about listening in on their conversation.

"I don't know," she finally muttered irritably. "That will have to be his decision."

"Whose decision?" Clay asked.

Jack didn't roll his eyes at the interruption, but the hard frown he gave Clay gave the equivalent effect.

"Uh…a friend of Jack's," Belle supplied after a flustered moment.

"How long have you two been seeing each other?" Belle glanced over in surprise at the urbane smoothness of Jack's question. Clay must have been encouraged by his tone of voice, because he jumped in to answer.

"A few months."

Belle tried to unclench her teeth when she felt Clay's hand on her shoulder. She saw Jack's sharp gaze flicker downward, taking in the caress. She resisted a strong urge to shake Clay off her.

"It seems like longer, though," Clay continued. "Personally, I'm looking forward to it being a lot longer. She's not the kind of woman you want to let go once you've had her."

The narrowing of Jack's eyes appeared to be his only initial response. Then he picked up his highball glass and finished off the remainder of the amber liquid with one swallow.

"Sweet. I'll just give you two lovebirds a little privacy then," he murmured with only a trace of sarcasm before he turned his attention back to Joyce.

————

"I wouldn't if I were you, Jack," Tom O'Sullivan warned in a misleadingly calm tone.

Jack paused in his action of opening the car door and scowled at Tom. "You aren't employed to be the moral voice of my consciousness."

"It's a no-brainer. You're reacting emotionally because of what you saw at dinner."

Jack hit the dashboard with a resounding smack. Tom's answering careless shrug made Jack want to substitute his friend's skull for the dashboard.

"I'm just saying that if you go in there you're going to regret it," Tom repeated.

"Like I wouldn't regret not stopping that asshole, weasel, sycophantic—*fuck it.* I'm going in there. I'm not sitting around all night and imagining the look on his punk face when he's coming inside of her. People have been known to go crazy from stress like that. Get off your ass and help me get through the lame security at the front desk or rot in here all night for all I care."

Tom sighed and unbuckled his seat belt reluctantly. "Jesus, Jack. All *night*?"

Jack didn't deign to answer. His expression was furious as

he flung open the car door. "Are you coming or not?" he growled before he slammed the door so hard the car rocked.

Tom rolled his eyes and calmly got out of the car. He'd been carefully watching Jack, Belle March and Clay Roth-schild all night. Jack's normally acute powers of observation must be dulled by repressed lust and jealously. Otherwise he would immediately have known that Belle March was about as interested in screwing Clay Rothschild as she was in having intimate relations with the ancient doorman who currently snoozed behind the front desk of her condominium.

"You're going to regret it, Jack. You know I'm right," he said in a quiet, sing-song tone of voice that he knew Jack would find annoying. Tom casually lifted the old man's limp hand and waved the security card that was grasped in it over a magnetic plate. The glass doors buzzed open obligingly.

"Shut up," Jack said so softly, but so chillingly, before he passed through the security doors that Tom did just that. Tom wasn't stupid. He'd seen some tape of Jack back when he was playing college ball. He'd been one hell of a defensive back, not as bulky as some, but lightning quick, focused and smart. He could read the line like he read a jury. And when he hit, it was with a concentrated smack of power that was guaranteed to abruptly end the play. So Tom couldn't help but pity Clay Rothschild at that moment.

Jack could be a real bear when the rare mood struck him.

———

Belle's forehead was still pressed to the front door of her condominium. It was taking her a moment to recover from the ugly scene that had just been enacted with Clay seconds ago. The image of his outraged, alcohol-reddened face popped up in front of her tightly closed eyes.

"This is bullshit Belle. You led me to believe that you were finally going to have sex, and you're dumping me instead?"

She started when someone thumped aggressively on the other side of the door. She opened her mouth to tell Clay to go away, but the memory of the shocked, disoriented look on his handsome features right before he'd walked out a minute ago made her reconsider. Her guilt got the best of her. She swung the door open.

"What? All comers are takers tonight, Belle?"

"*Excuse* me?" Belle muttered in dawning disbelief. Her amazement only increased as Jack Caldwell stalked past her and glanced around her open living and dining area before turning around. Ellie ran toward Jack and gave a friendly bark followed by some furious tail wagging. She frowned at her dog's uncharacteristic enthusiasm. Jack petted the dog distractedly, despite his obviously turbulent state. She blinked twice, sure she must be dreaming.

"You just open up wide for anyone who comes along? Don't you think that's a little dangerous?"

"What are you *doing* here, Jack? How dare you barge in here and start preaching to me?" Belle said, rising indignation melting away her shock. She may as well not have spoken though, for all the effect it had on the tall, furious man who stood in front of her.

"Where is he? Back in the bedroom?" he asked in an eerily cold voice.

"What are you talking about? *Jack?*" she shouted as she began to follow him as he strode down the hallway. She paused by the telephone in the living room, but then passed it without picking it up. Jack Caldwell may have a screw loose, but she wasn't afraid of him.

She thought twice about that assessment, however, when she took him in, walking back toward her a few seconds later.

His size, the dark coloring of his skin, hair and suit and the strength of the repressed emotion that seemed to roll off him in waves, made her feel like she was caught in the eye of a powerful approaching storm. He'd already checked the bedroom and den. He peered into her empty bathroom before he continued down the hallway. Belle found herself backing away from him warily as he stalked toward her. She backed all the way into her kitchen.

"Where is he?"

"Who?" Belle asked shakily. Her refrigerator door halted her backward progress. Jack kept coming until he loomed down over her.

"That sniveling brat that you call a boyfriend," he answered with a calmness that belied the fire flashing in his blue eyes.

"Clay?"

His lip curled up derisively. "Yeah, *Clay*. Where'd he go?"

The back of Belle's head came to rest on the refrigerator door as she craned her neck to look up at him. "That's none of your damned business, and you know it," she replied disdainfully. "Now will you kindly get out of my way and get out of my—"

"I'm not going anywhere."

A disbelieving puff of air dislodged from her throat at the calm finality of his tone. "*Yes.* You are, Jack. Should I even bother to ask how you knew that Clay came up here? What, are you *spying* on me?"

Her eyes searched his intently when he didn't answer her immediately. She became aware of the sound of her rapid heartbeat in her ears. He studied where her neck and shoulder came together as though he were considering taking a bite out of her there.

She shivered.

"*Jack?*"

His eyes moved hotly over her face before they met her gaze. "I'm not spying on you. I was coming here to see you and I saw you leading Clay up here. The expression on his face was as basic to read as the ABCs. The little bastard thought he was going to get laid. Do you deny it?"

Her eyes widened in disbelief when she realized the source of his anger. And it was true. Apparently Clay *had* come up here tonight thinking that they were finally going to have sex. Still, that didn't excuse Jack's behavior.

"I'm still not getting what business it is of yours if I admit or deny that a dozen men came up to my home tonight to get laid."

"Then your powers of perception are a hell of a lot lamer than I had imagined, Belle," he said acidly before he leaned down and covered her mouth with his.

The sound of protest that rose in her throat was obliterated as utterly as a thin piece of tissue paper would have been when it came into contact with an inferno. She felt submersed, totally inundated by the taste, the scent and the sensation of Jack Caldwell. When she realized that she was yielding to him, she tried to resist. Her mouth broke away from his and she gasped for air.

He didn't seem to mind her temporary refusal of her mouth. His hands came up to cradle her head possessively. His firm, warm lips kissed her cheeks, her nose and her eyelids. Belle sagged against the refrigerator. She didn't stop him when he buried his fingers in the knot of hair on the back of her head and released the clasp.

"You should never wear your hair up."

She moaned when she felt his breath and then his lips caress her outer ear teasingly. His fingers entwined in her hair with blatant possession, loosening it and molding it to maximize the pleasure of his seeking hands.

"Jack?" Belle whispered desperately when he placed his hot, insistent mouth over the opening of her ear and kissed, then licked, then created suction. Her thighs clamped together to still the sharp ache at their apex. To her amazement, he seemed aware of her need because he dipped his knees and abruptly pressed his lower body into her, stroking her sex with his cock. She whimpered in harsh, awakened need.

"What, Belle?" Jack asked distractedly as he transferred his attention to her neck. He rocked his erection against her and groaned in satisfaction. "God you taste good. Everywhere."

The tiny sound she made in her throat was that of an animal that knew it had been mortally cornered by a predator. "No," she whispered weakly. But blood pooled between her thighs, the pressure mounting from the friction of his rigid, pressing cock.

God, she wanted him at that moment—more than she could recall ever wanting anything.

"Jack?"

"I heard what you said. I'm not deaf," he said against the side of her neck. His hands lowered to shape the curve of her hips and the indentation of her waist. His palms slid up sensually over the soft fabric of her dress until her full breasts were plumped up for the inspection of his heavy-lidded gaze. "I'm just listening to your body instead of your mouth. Your breasts are saying yes," he said huskily before he bent his dark head and tongued an already erect nipple directly through the fabric of her dress and sheer bra.

Belle gasped. Her nipples pulled tighter, beading up almost painfully against his warm, moist tongue. He nuzzled one breast while he fondled the weight of the other. She sighed raggedly at the feel of her flesh in his massaging palm.

Instinctively, her hands sought him. His hair felt thick and vital against her eager fingers. Her fingertips rubbed sensually against his scalp, unconsciously pressing his hungry mouth to her breast, granting him complete access to her.

He finally straightened and stared down at her with fiery eyes. He held her gaze as he moved his hands to the zipper of her dress.

"We hardly know each other, Jack. It's not right," she whispered desperately.

"True and false. We may not know each other. But I've got a feeling you're not going to find it any more *right* this side of heaven," he replied grimly.

FOUR

THE DOUBT that mixed with the desire on Belle's face irrationally irritated Jack. He toyed with her zipper at the middle of her slightly arched back.

"You look beautiful tonight," he said quietly.

"Thank you," she whispered, tilting her mouth up toward him. He bent down and kissed her with a controlled, finessing mouth.

"When I take off your dress, what will I find underneath it?"

Her neck strained back as far as it could so she could catch every nuance, every texture of his kiss. When his question soaked into her consciousness she made a small sound of distress, but she didn't stop feverishly returning his kiss.

"What? I don't know…what kind…of a question…is that?" she managed absentmindedly.

Jack shifted his body and stared down at her. "I thought about it for a good part of the evening. Now I want you to *say* it, Belle. Tell me what you're wearing under your dress."

He watched her steadily. Her cheeks were flushed with arousal. Her eyes looked like warm liquid amber. Jack saw the moment she realized what he was asking of her, that he was forcing her to give herself to him instead of just allowing herself to be taken.

She licked her lower lip anxiously. He'd moved slightly away. Her body ached for the return of the pressure of his hardness, the pleasure wrought by his talented mouth.

"I...just a bra and underwear," she finally admitted in a thready whisper.

"You're wearing some kind of stockings," Jack stated matter-of-factly. When he noticed how her eyes skittered away uncomfortably he spread his large hand at the side of her neck and jaw, tilting her face, forcing her gaze to meet his.

"Thigh highs," she admitted softly.

"Excuse me?" Jack ducked his head, trying to catch her words.

"Jack, don't do this." She was mortified at the aroused reaction her body was having to their verbal exchange. She was hyperfocused on the sensation of the fingers of his left hand idly playing with the zipper of her dress at her back. His stare on her was merciless, demanding. "Thigh highs," she finally sputtered in a louder voice. "You know...they just come up to your thighs so they call them—"

"Very nice," Jack murmured. He slid her zipper down to her lower back, pausing to palm the upper curve of her ass. He felt her still beneath him when he slid one long finger entirely down the crevice between her ass cheeks, pausing to skim lightly over her tiny, sensitive asshole with his fingertip. Jack saw her eyes widen with surprise and anxiety, but he kept his finger on her for several seconds anyway, holding her gaze, gently caressing her. He saw her cheeks flush bright pink. His fingers played with the band of her panties after his slow, leisurely tour back up her crack.

"These panties are silk. What color are they?" he wondered casually.

She bit her lip to still the gasp of pleasure that she experienced at his extremely intimate caress. *Why am I letting him do this to me?* She'd never even *considered* allowing anyone to make free with her like this. No one but Sean, that is. But not even Sean had ever dared to touch her in the way that Jack just had.

"They're just...nude, flesh-colored, I think," she finally said almost apologetically. It would have been better if she'd worn something a little sexier, racier. She thought her concerns were reinforced when she saw Jack scowl. He reached up and slid her dress off her shoulders. With a brisk nudge at her hips it fell obligingly down around her ankles. Belle gave a small cry of alarm when she felt his hands on her butt and hips, lifting her. Her breath came out with a puff of surprise when he plopped her ass down on the cool granite of her kitchen countertop. His eyes flared as they roved over her. He trailed two fingers along the lacy edge of the stocking, and then penetrated the top, caressing her bare thigh with a long finger—up and down, up and down—in an intensely sexual, suggestive slide. All the while, his stare was fixed on what he was doing.

She felt her clitoris pinch tight in anxious pleasure.

"That's what I thought. No factory would ever be able to match the color of your flesh," he said hoarsely. His hands spanned her sides and plumped her breasts upward for his appreciative gaze. His dark head lowered. Belle almost choked with desire at the sudden sensation of his mouth on her breasts. Her head fell back against the cabinet with a thud.

"Christ, you're beautiful. Your skin is the color of apricots and you taste even sweeter," Jack praised unevenly as he nipped and licked at her breasts. His marauding mouth lowered over her belly. He found her bellybutton and pierced it with his tongue. His hands cradled her hips possessively. "Say you'll take me here, Belle." He kissed her lower belly as his arms caught beneath her thighs, rolling her back on the counter. "Say you'll take me here."

"Jack," she cried out, the thin fabric of her panties the only thing separating her sex from his hungry, hot mouth.. Her nerve endings quivered in pleasure. When she noticed that his brilliant blue eyes were watching her steadily, insisting on an answer, she responded mindlessly.

"Yes. *God*, yes."

He straightened slightly. Their gazes locked as he slid her panties down her thighs and over her ankles and shoes. When he finally glanced down over her, he groaned. He leaned forward and pressed the rigid column of his cock against her pussy, rocking against her.

"Look at you. Like heaven and sin mixed together."

Her eyes sprang wide. Perhaps he noticed the stiffening of her body, because he suddenly went very still. The room seemed to swim around her. The only thing that stayed steady was a pair of blue eyes that pinned her steadily to reality . . .

. . . No matter how impossible that reality might be.

"Sean?"

Her incredulous whisper hung in the air in the tense silence that followed. Even though she'd uttered only the one syllable, it seemed to echo repeatedly in her stunned aware-nesses. Belle held her breath until her lungs began to ache, but still the man whose arms enclosed her didn't answer.

Jack watched the single tear that fell down Belle's cheek and he felt a heavy, leaden coldness press down on his chest.

"Who the hell is *Sean*?"

When she didn't immediately answer he demanded more harshly, "Why are you calling me Sean, Belle?"

She just shook her head. Another tear rolled down her

cheek. Her childhood disability had just been reactivated. Her brain had forgotten how to communicate with her tongue.

A muscle twitched in his cheek when she refused to answer him. "Oh I get it. I'm not up here filling in for Clay Rothschild but for this Sean guy, right? Is that it?"

Her shaking head and silent tears were his only response.

His eyes were cool flames as they studied her. "Did *he* ever do this? Ever strip you bare and make you come on the kitchen counter? Did he, Belle? *Tell* me." He queried relentlessly. He cursed viciously as he watched her lips open as though she would speak, but only tears seemed to have been granted access to leave her body. Her gaze on him broadcast a myriad of strong emotions, but Jack could only decipher amazement and wariness. He recognized the need for ruthless emergency measures. His jaw hardened and he deliberately spread her thighs.

"Because that's exactly what I'm going to do. And I have so little pride that you can shout out to the high heavens another man's name when I do it, and I won't give a damn as long as I get to taste you," he breathed out ominously.

That managed to cease the flow of her tears. Belle clenched her eyes shut in painful anticipation when he tilted her back, bent down over her sex, and proceeded to drink from her like she was the very chalice of life. He began stabbing at her clit with a stiffened, ruthless tongue then teasing her, gliding and rubbing sinuously, before he switched back to roughly agitating the nerve-packed flesh. He fastened on her and applied a steady, eye-crossing suction before he tongued her again. She was lost. Emotion and sensation barraged her in a distilled, potent rush. Her fingers sank into his thick hair desperately, begging for release without words.

Jack must not have been in the mood to make her suffer for long. He answered her by forcing one knee back into her chest while he tilted his head. The suction he applied to her clit was like a smart bomb, precise and shockingly effective. She screamed.

The name she chanted repeatedly as violent spasms rocked her and her head bumped rythmically against her kitchen counter was *not* Sean Ryan's.

"Damn."

That single, emphatically muttered word was the first thing she heard when she surfaced dazedly from deep realms of pleasure.

He stood, replacing his mouth with his hand, firmly pressing her slick clit with his thumb while two fingers sank into her snug channel. "Come on, Belle. Give me more." He thrust into her, groaning when he felt her muscular walls clasp and pull at his fingers, drawing him further inward. She cried out sharply. He held her head, cushioning it from the cabinet as another shudder of pleasure rocked her.

"Jack?" she eventually murmured. She sagged limply on the counter. Her thighs were up around his waist. Her fingers were still buried in his hair.

"That's right, honey. *Jack*. Remember the name, because I want to hear it coming from your lips a lot more." Perhaps to emphasize the point, he corkscrewed his fingers as he left her pussy, making her post-climactic, sensitized nerves shiver into life again. She shuddered and whimpered. He lifted her to him and whispered harshly in her ear, "Wrap your legs tight around me."

She was only vaguely aware that Ellie trailed them eagerly down the hallway, or of Jack's wry comment—"Sorry, Ellie, you're not invited"—before he closed her bedroom door with a bang. He lowered her down on the bed. Her duvet cover and pillowcases felt cool and soft against her heated, prickly skin. She watched through heavily lidded eyes as he rapidly undressed, glad for the dim light of her bedside lamp. Appreciation and renewed arousal seeped into her awreness as she took in the vison of his hard, lean body.

"You're beautiful," she said softly when he stood before her, naked.

Jack laughed roughly as he lowered himself over her. "No. I'm old and beat-up and scarred." He growled with masculine gratification when he pressed their naked skin together. "You're the beautiful one, Belle." He kissed her. She glided her hand down his muscular back and felt him shaking. She pulled away from his kiss.

"Jack? Are you okay?" she whispered. How could such a big, powerful man be trembling beneath her fingertips? It awed her.

He nipped hungrily at her parted lips. "I *hurt* for you. Take me, honey. I can't wait a second longer."

She complied, in complete agreement with his need. She watched as he spread her thighs, and then introduced the tapered, engorged head of his cock to her entrance with his hand.

Air hissed over his lips at the feeling of her narrow entrance. Christ, she was so warm. So damn wet. So *small*. He saw red for a moment. Lust blinding him, he flexed his hips. He remained in the same place. He struggled wildly to find restraint amidst a clawing, primitive need to mate.

"You're so blessed sweet, honey. But you're resisting me. Take me. You promised, Belle," he grated out darkly. He barely acknowledged her sound of dismay, so focused was he on the feel of her adjusting to him. He thrust determinedly when he divined the slight give in her soft, harboring body. He shouted out in triumph as he firmly pressed into heaven.

His eyes widened. He braced his upper body off her and stared down at her. For a tense moment, the sound of their mutual panting breath filled his ears while she squeezed his cock maddeningly.

"You're a virgin?" he managed.

"I don't think so, technically," she panted as she looked up at him with anxious eyes. Sweat glistened on her brow. "Not anymore."

Emotion slammed into him. He clenched his eyelids shut, fighting it.

"*Shit*. Ah Belle, I'm sorry. I thought…you and that kid. It's been driving me half crazy to think…" He swallowed convulsively. He was buried in her to the hilt. Her muscular walls clutched him in a thoroughly pitiless grip of hedonistic pleasure. Agony and bliss pummeled him from every direction.

"It's okay," she soothed. "It doesn't matter. This is what I want. *Jack*."

His head came up at the sound of her saying his name. She shifted her pelvis down and up again, stroking him. They both groaned. "This is *exactly* what I want," she insisted.

He couldn't have stopped himself then if a bomb went off in her living room. He began to thrust, trying to spare her the full length of his cock, the force of his hips. His eyes rolled back in his head at the heady pleasure of stroking her, even in that measured manner.

"Is it okay?" he hissed after a minute. His facial muscles were pulled tight with restraint. She fit him like a second skin that had been removed and then shrunken about two sizes before it was squeezed back on him. He used all of his control not to ride her hard. "Am I hurting you?"

"No. No, it's *so* good."

In truth it was so much more than *good*, Belle realized. It hurt a little, true, but the slight pain only spiked her pleasure. She relished the feeling of him filling her. His steady, firm strokes were causing her to swell and pulse and blossom again with desire. He stretched her, the smooth, steely head of his cock rubbing some magical spot deep inside, a place she hadn't known existed until he touched it. She loved watching his handsome face, seeing it pull tight with ecstasy that she knew to be a reflection of her own. Her fingers went up to stroke his back, hips and tensing, muscular ass, at first gently and later more desperately, encouraging him, silently begging him to fill her all the way.

Jack felt her fingernails sink into his ass with a grip that he knew would leave him marked. He responded naturally, thrusting higher, harder, deeper. He groaned gutturally. The headboard of her bed began to thump rhythmically against the wall as he brought the head of his cock almost fully out of her and sank back into the heaven of her.

When a measure of rationality hit him, when he realized that he'd been pounding her good and hard, he glanced down into her face with concern. He paused when he saw how tight her face was, thinking he'd hurt her.

Then she began to tremble all around him, milking his cock, her tight channel pulling him deeper and deeper. Heat rushed around him.

"Sweet Jesus," he managed in awe before he bent and ate her tiny, sexy cries of climax. He fucked her with wild abandonment then, forgetful of caution. It was her smooth muscles rippling in orgasm that did it, clasping him greedily further into her depths, teasing him into heights of orgiastic bliss.

He plunged deeply one last time.

He shouted out sharply in that suspended second before orgasm, thrusting aggressively, claiming another half inch, instinctively needing to explode at Belle's final limit. His cock jerked viciously inside of her...swelling...straining...

He closed his eyes. He roared as orgasm slammed into him.

Afterward Jack removed her shoes and stockings, caressing her thighs, calves and heels tenderly as he did it. He did the same for the bra that she still wore. Neither of them spoke when he lay down again next to her and gathered her into his arms.

After several minutes he whispered, "Are you all right, Belle? I was rough with you."

She nodded, liking the feel of his crisp chest hair against the softness of her cheek. "Better than all right," she murmured, sounding content.

Jack gloried in her response until Tom O'Sullivan's words rose to haunt him. *You're going to regret it, Jack. You know I'm right.* His mind went back to the moment that he'd breached her with all the finesse of a battering ram. He stifled a groan of regret.

When he moved restlessly and began to sit up, she stirred against him. Her skin felt like smooth silk. His cock jerked and throbbed, eager to be back inside her already.

"Where are you going?" Belle asked.

"Bathroom," he muttered.

When he'd returned to the bedroom a minute later hoping that his crisis of guilt and arousal had passed, Belle was sitting up against the pillows. He didn't know if he was glad or irritated that she'd covered her body in a sheet. Personally, he wanted to spend the rest of the night pleasuring her, trying to make up for his previous blatant insensitivity. But he could completely understand how she might not be in the mood for that after he'd pushed his way in here tonight, insulted her, robbed her of her virginity...fucked her like he was a horny teenager with a seasoned whore.

"Are you ready to tell me now?" Belle asked, breaking into his mental self-recriminations.

"What do you mean?" he wondered cautiously as he sat down at the edge of the bed.

"You know what I'm talking about," she began in a low, tremulous voice that escalated in volume as she spoke. "I'm asking if you're ready to tell me why you keep insisting that your name is Jack Caldwell. And how could you have *possibly* rationalized letting me think you were dead, Sean?"

FIVE

FURY SEEMED to have taken the place of blood in Belle's body. As she spoke, it seemed to pound through her veins until she thought she would explode with it. Even her hair felt like it was bristling with electric rage.

"*Say* something, damn you. I may have just made love to you, but I swear, Sean Ryan, I'm over that. I'm ready to kill you right now unless you say something really good to stop me."

She waited, but the only response to her accusations was a steely stare.

"Sean?" Belle asked angrily. "Why aren't you saying anything?"

This time, she was acknowledged with a small shrug.

"Give me a second, will you? What the hell am I supposed to say? I'm not accustomed to speaking to women who are stark raving mad. I'm still soaking in the fact that you didn't just call out a different man's name while we were fooling around, but that you actually think that I *am* that person." Jack shook his head slightly, as though trying to get a clear focus on unfolding events, and failing miserably. He blinked and looked over at her incredulously after a moment.

"Sean *Ryan*? Is *that* what you said?"

"Why are you *lying*?" Belle asked with amazement and dawning hurt. She'd suspected it from the very beginning. True, she'd convinced herself afterward that she was wrong, rationalized her strong response away until she thought it had disappeared. But earlier, in the kitchen, his words—*like heaven and sin mixed together*. Surely two different men wouldn't say that while they were with her.

Or would they? The logical part of her brain pushed itself forward through the morass of her emotional chaos. Her experience with men wasn't extensive. Maybe it *was* the kind of thing that men said to make a woman willing. Maybe it was a line, like *you're so beautiful you make me hurt* or *I've never felt this way about another woman*.

No. *Sean* hadn't meant it like a line.

Sean hadn't. But *Jack* probably had.

Oh, shit.

Her hands shook when she covered her face with them. Panic rose in her chest, a familiar and hated feeling that she knew all too well from her dreams since Sean's death. *Of course* they were two different men. So what if they looked a little alike? The similarities that she'd glommed onto were minimal at best. She'd heard Clay refer to Jack's past, his family, his job. Jack was an acquaintance at best, an almost stranger at worst.

And she'd just fucked him in her desperation to believe that Sean was alive.

When she felt his hands on her forearms, heard him say her name, she twisted at the waist away from him. She lowered her hands but refused to look at him. She focused all her energy on preventing the mortifying telltale sign of her body's trembling.

"Will you just go?" she managed.

"I'm *not* going, Belle. Not when you're like this."

"I'll be all right." He didn't move. Desperation rose in her. "I'll beg you if you want me to, but please…just leave Jack. I made a mistake. Maybe you're right. Maybe I *am* crazy. Just forget that it ever happened."

"As if that's likely," he scoffed disbelievingly.

"If it's not possible then I'll deal with it."

"How?" he demanded aggressively. "Are you going to get a lobotomy or something? Because short of that I don't see how it's possible for you to forget it or deal with it, *especially* if you don't plan on talking about what the hell is going on with you. For Christ's sake, Belle--"

He halted his tirade abruptly when she made eye contact with him. She looked like she'd just been put through one hell of an emotional ringer and was currently being forced through an even tighter one. He took a deep, uneven breath.

"I'm sorry for shouting. That's the last thing you need when you're upset."

"The thing that I'm upset about is that you *won't leave*," she cried out. "Can't you see it will make me feel less uncomfortable if I didn't have to…to *look* at you anymore?"

She panted shallowly as she watched him. Regret lanced through her awareness when she saw the hurt incredulity on his face, the way his mouth went white at the corners. It only amplified when he stood, not breaking her stare until he bent to retrieve his clothing. She shut her eyes tightly. In her current state of emotional turmoil, the sight of his rugged masculine beauty made her want to burst into tears.

"You may be stubborn, Belle, but I'm more stubborn," she heard him say.

"Please, Jack…"

"Enough. I'm going. But you haven't heard the last of this."

————

"*Belle*? What are you doing here?"

She closed her eyes, trying to tamp down her irritation at the sound of the voice behind her. She forced herself to turn and face him.

"Hello, Clay. Angela, John. Hi, Phil," Belle added when a fourth man joined their impromptu circle in the lobby of a high-rise on Clark Street. Clay and his friends had pounced on her so unexpectedly that she didn't have time to formulate a good lie. "I had a doctor's appointment in this building. And you? What are you all doing here?"

"There's a great Japanese restaurant here. Are you sick or something?" Clay asked solicitously as he stroked her arm. When he noticed her look of surprised discomfort at his touch, he added, "Go ahead, guys. I'll catch up with you at the office."

She smiled wanly as she said goodbye to the others. She felt exhausted after her session with the psychologist who had been referred to her by one of her partners in the group practice. The meeting had left her spent. She didn't have the necessary defenses in place to lie when Clay asked her again why she was seeing a doctor.

"I'm not sick. I had an appointment with a psychologist."

Clay barked with laughter. "What for? *You're* the psychologist, for God's sake."

She rolled her eyes. "Right. Next you'll be insisting is that a lawyer never needs a lawyer." She turned her back on him and headed for the exit onto LaSalle Street. They hadn't spoken for three nights, not since she broke up with him—not since the night she'd gone to bed with Jack Caldwell. Her stride broke at the intrusive, vivid memory.

"I'm sorry, Belle. Really. That was insensitive of me," Clay said breathlessly as he caught up to her. He'd assumed she'd slowed down for him, Belle realized. He took her arm and moved her to the side of pedestrian traffic that flowed through the lobby during lunch hour. His green eyes became liquid with apologetic anxiety as he stroked her shoulder. Belle couldn't help but think that his expression was rehearsed to create automatic forgiveness. "I've been in hell since the other night. Why haven't you returned my phone calls?"

"I'm sorry. I've been preoccupied."

Clay dipped his head and murmured intimately, "Were you seeing a psychologist about us? About our relationship?"

She frowned at his self-centered assumption. "Why I was seeing psychologist is my own business. And we don't have a *relationship*, Clay. Not anymore," she reminded him.

His comment about the psychologist had refocused her mind on her worry. She'd couched her confession to the psychologist earlier in anonymous terms. But because of her serious case of out-of-control lust the other night, she hadn't been as circumspect with Jack Caldwell. She'd unintentionally broken a promise she'd made to Sean over a year ago, and spoken Sean's name to a near stranger. She needed to rectify that error as best she could. Belle couldn't imagine that it would matter at this point, but a promise was a promise. She couldn't believe she was going to purposefully try and see Jack again but…

"You're being too hasty about all this," Clay said. "We need to talk more."

She sighed. "Maybe you're right," she said after a pause. "I think I'll walk back to Holloway & Croft with you."

"What do you mean you want to talk to *Jack Caldwell?*" Clay asked ten minutes later as they stepped off the elevators at Holloway & Croft. He was still sullen at the fact Belle had reinforced the idea that they were *definitely* no longer an item on the walk over to his office. An ugly look had settled on his usually handsome features. He gripped the flesh of Belle's upper arm so hard that she cried out in pain.

"I was wondering what was going on between you two the other night." His eyes flashed. "Are you letting that son of a bitch fuck you, Belle?" When she just stared at him in disdainful disgust, he shook her, unmindful that they were standing in the corridor of a sedate law office.

"Answer me," he hissed.

She bristled. *This* was certainly an eye-opening experience.

"Go *fuck* yourself, Clay? And let go of my arm while you're at it. You're going to need your hand."

"You frigid little—"

Clay stopped abruptly. His facial muscles pulled tight with surprise and pain, bewildering Belle.

"The lady asked you to let go of her arm. You let go of hers and I'll think about giving you yours back," a cold, quiet voice said behind Clay.

Her eyes widened in amazement when Clay released her arm. His body was unnaturally thrust backward and to the side through the grip of the man that was behind him. Clay cursed when the man pushed him down the hallway, away from Belle, before he released him.

"You're not going to get away with that," Clay sputtered, still cautious enough to keep the volume of his voice low in the office corridor.

"You mean I'm not going to get away with helping a woman when you were assaulting her on Holloway & Croft premises?" the man she recognized as Tom O'Sullivan asked pointedly.

Belle choked back a nervous laugh. She silenced it when Clay's outraged gaze slid over to her and sizzled. Tom O'Sullivan's cold stare seemed to make him think twice, however. She thought she caught both the words "frigid" and "fag" in Clay's muttered tirade when he finally turned and walked down the corridor.

"Bad day for him, I guess, being bettered by a man he believes is gay," Tom commented with a careless shrug. His green eyes sharpened on Belle. "Are you here to see Jack?"

When she nodded reluctantly, Tom moved aside and swept out his hand in an "after you" gesture. Her eyebrows rose in appreciative amazement when Tom led her into the anteroom of Jack's large, luxurious corner office a moment later.

"He's still at lunch but if you can wait a few minutes he shouldn't be long."

"Thank you for that…earlier," she said. She was admittedly confused by Tom O'Sullivan's relationship with Jack, but she automatically liked the quiet, steady-eyed man. She put out her hand. "I'm Belle March."

"Tom O'Sullivan. I work for Jack," he said as they shook hands. Belle wanted to ask him what exactly he did for Jack. He didn't really seem like the administrative assistant type, but she didn't want to apply stereotypes. Tom didn't give her any opportunity to ask questions, however. He opened a paneled wood door and led her into Jack's private corner office.

A few minutes later Jack stuck his head into Tom's office. "I'm back. Thanks for the tip about the restaurant. I think Bob Scalini came when he tasted the fettuccini Alfredo. No doubt there's been some earth-shattering news in the thrilling world of mergers and acquisitions while I was gone?" he mumbled with a weary expression.

"Nope. As boring as ever. Dave Keski called and oh, yeah —Belle March is waiting for you in your office."

Jack's bored expression instantly altered. "Belle? Is *here*? Fuck!"

"What?" Tom asked, alrmed at Jack's intensity as he hastened out of his office.

"*The picture*," Jack hissed ominously over his shoulder.

"Oh shit. The *picture,*" Tom mouthed.

Jack paused to calm himself outside his office door, but then he heard the sound of shattering glass. Biting back a vicious curse, he threw open the heavy door.

Belle gravitated over to the grouping of picture frames in Jack's mahogany built-in bookcases. The photos that one chose to display were always telling. She studied a photo of a handsome couple in their late fifties on a sailboat, dressed with an elegant disregard that screamed money and privelege. Jack's parents, she guessed, vaguely recalling Clay's comments about them. Her thoughts were reaffirmed when she picked up a picture of the same couple with a different Jack—a more relaxed, grinning, scarless Jack—and a lovely, exotic-looking brunette. Was this the wife of the supposed "friend" that Jack had referred to at his welcome dinner? She set down the picture abruptly, but her betraying eyes kept wandering back to the beautiful woman tucked in Jack's arm.

The next photo made her grin widely. It was Copenhagen, posing with as much regal bearing as possible when drool leaked from his slouchy jowls. She lifted the fourth photo.

For a moment she just studied it with a puzzled, bemused expression. A low roar started up in her ears.

It was a picture of two young men, both wearing Yale football uniforms. It must have been a post-game picture. It had been a win, judging by the young men's exultant expressions. Their hair was damp with sweat. Their blue eyes sparkled with life and the promise of bright, seemingly endless futures. Shivers poured through her.

When the photo fell from her frozen fingertips, Belle hardly registered the sound of tinkling glass. All she could think of was how it was impossible that Sean—*her* Sean—could have his hand pressed with such playful familiarity against Jack Caldwell's neck, as if he were in the midst of ribbing him on about something when the camera flashed.

As if they were the best friends in the world.

She couldn't have asked for more solid, damning proof that they were two separate men. For some reason that five-by-seven photo staring up at her from the floor had the same effect as if she'd been at Sean's funeral, seen his casket, the funeral procession, the freshly dug earth of his grave...

They were all images that had been denied her.

Just like the psychologist this morning had told her, never being able to bury Sean had kept him somehow alive for her, a secret she kept locked tight in her heart.

Pain sliced through her numbness, more terrible than when she'd found out, just like everyone else in the country, that Sean had been murdered.

She'd heard it on the six o'clock news.

The world swayed in front of her eyes.

Belle's eyes were open when Jack caught her in his arms, but he instantly knew that she was totally unaware of his presence. By the time he'd sat her on the leather couch in the sitting area of his office her eyelids were fluttering closed. He did the only thing that he'd ever learned, through a lifetime of involvement in sports, that cured lightheadedness. He ruched up her skirt around her upper thighs and pushed her head down between her knees. He heard her gasp.

"Breathe, Belle," he ordered tensely.

She instantly knew that voice. In that position, in her weakened state and with Jack's strong hand on her neck, she had little else that she could do *but* breathe. She inhaled painfully. A few tears spattered onto Jack Caldwell's expensive-looking Oriental carpet. After a few deep cycles of breath she felt recovered enough to sputter, "Let go of me!" His hand stayed on her like a vise, keeping her down.

"Breathe a little more."

Anger blazed in Belle at his calm, domineering attitude. She utilized all of her considerable patience, cultivated through years of doing psychotherapy, and took several more deep breaths to satisfy the smug Jack Caldwell.

"Let me sit up, Jack," she said after a moment had passed. "I'm okay now."

"Slowly," he insisted when she tried to rise jerkily.

He briefly noticed the cascade of Belle's lush blonde hair as it fell around her shoulders, the wetness of her cheeks. If he had noticed the fury in her golden brown eyes, he would have had warning. But he didn't, so he was thoroughly shocked when her hand flew up and she slapped his cheek hard enough to sting.

"You *knew* who Sean was all along! How dare you make me suffer like that, you bastard." The fact that he merely blinked in reaction to her attack infuriated her. But his hand snapped up, quick as a snake, when she pulled her hand back to slap him again. He stilled her striking palm in midair.

"Don't ever do that again, Belle."

She exhaled shakily when she saw the anger in his eyes and heard the coldness of his voice. Her lower lip trembled but her chin rose in defiance. "Why didn't you tell me that you knew Sean Ryan?"

"When? The other night when you were psychotic, calling me by his name? Or a few seconds later when you were throwing me out of your bed?" Jack asked quietly enough, but his rising anger showed clearly in the way he jerked her captive wrist, forcing Belle to lean closer to him.

She flinched when she saw the hard gleam in his blue eyes. Their faces were only inches apart. His breath on her was warm and even while hers must have been striking his face with choppy, ragged gasps.

"You should have said something about knowing him, and you know it!" she accused.

Jack jerked his head in the direction of the broken frame and photo on the floor. "How was I supposed to know that you were talking about *that* Sean Ryan, especially when you just dropped it on me from nowhere like a thunderbolt? You didn't say his full name until the end of the night. Sean is a common name, you know, and besides…you were too busy tossing me out on my ass for me to clarify politely." She glared up at him while he took a slow, calming breath.

"I'll tell you what I know," he said. "I would have the other night, as well, if you'd given me the courtesy of three minutes of being in your presence after having just taken your virginity. I met Sean Ryan while we were in college at Yale. We became friends, and remained good friends even when we went to different law schools, and after I took the path of working in private practice and Sean chose prosecution. Even when our careers took us to different cities across the country, we stayed friends. I loved him like a brother. My parents and sister loved him that way too. Haley, my sister, asked both of us to be her daughter's godfathers and guardians. Sean's parents took me into their home and hearts, just like my family accepted him like he was my brother."

"You knew Sean's parents? You were Sean's friend?"

"That's right," he said grimly as he studied her face. "And I'll tell you something else, Belle. Sean didn't keep much from me. We told each other confidential things about our work, consulted each other, knowing that one of us would never betray the other's confidence. We talked about our concerns in regard to our families. We even told each other about the women in our lives—the ones who were worth telling about, anyway. But Sean never said a thing about you."

He watched closely while her lower lip trembled. She looked so lost. He ground his teeth, hard. It was obvious how much his statement hurt her.

"You're lying," she whispered.

He released her wrist. "About which part exactly?"

For a few seconds Belle's forearm just hung in the air. Then it sank slowly into her lap. She saw his point. Was she accusing him of lying about being Sean's best friend? Or was she saying that he was a liar when he asserted that Sean had never mentioned her to him?

A thought occurred to her.

"He never mentioned *you* to *me*, either," she rebounded heatedly. Anger rose fresh in her when Jack just shrugged and leaned back on the couch and watched her with a heavy-lidded impassivity.

"How long did you know him?" he asked.

"We were together for three months before he was…" Her voice trailed off.

"I talked to Sean the night before he died. He talked a lot about his preparations for the Tariq Sahid trial. But he never mentioned anyone special in his life."

Belle glared at him mutinously. Still, she hadn't missed the look of regret on Jack's face when he mentioned talking to Sean the night before he died.

"And as far as him not mentioning me to you," he continued smoothly, "a few months isn't exactly a long period of time, is it, to reveal all the details of your history to each other? Did you talk about your closest friends to him?"

"I don't remember," Belle said evasively after a moment.

Jack smirked. Belle felt like slapping that expression right off his handsome face. The realization of the full extent of her feelings of hostility and aggressiveness toward Jack Caldwell stunned her a little bit, but her awareness of her emotions didn't make them dissipate any.

"I'd guess from what I've learned about you and Sean so far, you remember all right. Knowing Sean, you were too busy getting to know each other in other ways besides talking about schoolyard buddies and your horoscope signs." Jack shook his head in vague puzzlement as he studied her face. "Why he never got around to fucking you is the real mystery here. I'll have to make sure I thank him for it in the afterlife."

Belle's ears rang. Had he really just said that? The way that his blue eyes gleamed as he watched her told her point blank that he had. Belle practically choked with rage.

"You...you..." Her brain short-circuited. She couldn't think of a curse word that adequately described her hatred of Jack Caldwell.

"For your information Sean and I were waiting until I'd been on birth control long enough for it to be safe. He, *unlike you*," Belle emphasized her point with a hard poke of her finger on Jack's silk tie, "was a gentleman. He cared enough about me to think about the future, to not want to get me pregnant or diseased. Sean wanted it to be special when he took my virginity. He would never have got me off on my kitchen counter and then screwed me so hard and so selfishly that I could barely walk the next day," she finished aggressively with a final thump on his chest.

She finally took in the look on Jack Caldwell's face. She gave a sharp yelp of alarm and tried to back away from him but her recognition of the monster that she'd created with her words came too late. The next thing she knew she was lying flat on her back on the couch, her arms pinned over her head with six feet and three inches of hard man pressing her down into total immobility. Jack's eyes were so sharp and incising Belle wondered in a panicked fancy if a gaze alone could cut through flesh. If it could, Belle thought she knew what Jack would get rid of.

Her tongue.

"For someone who was being tortured so much you were certainly enjoying yourself, Belle. Your pussy pulled so hard on me while you came that just the sensation alone would have sucked every last drop of cum out of me, even without stroking you," Jack breathed out with ominous quiet as he lowered his face to within an inch of hers. A moan escaped her throat, the sound striking him as incredibly sexy. His gaze focused on her mouth. He took in the way her pupils dilated with rising arousal. One thing about Belle: she loved the dirty talk. "And as far as Sean being a gentleman, he's welcome to the title. I'd still choose to be the one who got to fuck your brains out so selfishly. The one who's going to do it again," he added grimly before he covered her mouth in a punishing kiss.

She squirmed under him in nominal protest only briefly. It took her about two seconds to realize that she loved the feel of him. Besides, he was offering her an outlet for all this wild, pent-up energy inside her. Heat bloomed where his hardening cock pressed into her sex. Her tumultuous emotions, her thoughts of Sean and her blinding fury, were all fused and distilled into a powerful lust for the man on top of her.

She couldn't help but feel a stab of triumph when she craned up and began to slide her tongue sensually next to Jack's, and felt him hesitate momentarily in surprise. She arched her back and rubbed her breasts against him wantonly to assure him that he wasn't mistaken. Belle suddenly had a dark, urgent need to fuck her way into the oblivion of orgasm and this man . . . yes, *this* man would give her what she needed.

Jack paused, stunned, when Belle almost immediately succumbed to him, tangling her tongue with his, squirming and undulating beneath him, pressing her breasts and belly and pussy up against him tightly and then rocking against him with subtle circular movements that had him seeing red. Christ, she was like an inferno beneath him. He envisioned what he'd tried to ignore earlier when she had been faint and he'd pulled her skirt up over her legs. Her nude stockings weren't being held up by elastic this time but by delicate, lacy white garters. Jack could feel the outline of those garters on his thighs as Belle rubbed up against him like a cat in heat.

His mental comparison of her to a cat made the nasty thought arise that Belle was hankering for a fuck right now and any tom would do.

Or any dick, for that matter.

He was going to get this woman to want *him* if he had to die trying. When he ripped his mouth away from hers and she surged up toward him to reclaim him Jack admitted grimly that Belle likely would be the death of him. If it were possible to die from wanting, that is. Her lips and cheeks were flushed red with passion and her eyes were already glazed with the mindless desire that that most men were never fortunate enough to ever witness in their lovers—or if they *were* lucky enough, not without spending considerable time and patience in achieving it.

He still held her wrists behind her head so her straining movement toward him forced her to arch her back, granting him access to the mind-boggling sight of her full breasts poking up, stretching tightly into her silk blouse, the nipples already stiff and peaking.

"What's wrong?" she asked thickly once she finally took in the fact that Jack was withholding his mouth from her. She bit her lower lip in frustration and clamped her legs over the backs of his thighs. Her skirt bunched up around her hips. She groaned with satisfaction as she rubbed against him and felt the stiffness of his cock.

"Don't you want to fuck me?"

Jack ground his throbbing erection on her despite himself. If she'd been one hundred percent seductress when she'd said it, he probably could have abstained. But instead she'd been fifty percent seductress and fifty percent vulnerable. The combination made his cock surge and thicken with almost unbearable lust.

"Loaded questions tend to have loaded answers, honey."

Belle's eyes widened with arousal at the sensation of him sliding a very large, thick cock beneath the material of her skirt, directly on her clit. Her thighs tightened around him, demanding more. Despite the fact that they were clothed, a few more strokes like that and Belle was going to be quivering in orgasm.

"Wha...Jack?" Belle murmured in confusion when he abruptly moved off her.

His eyes were banked flames as he watched from where he sat next to her reclining body. He casually grabbed her ankle and moved her leg upward to rest on the back of the couch so that he could lean back all the way.

"I'm glad you know it's me, Belle."

She stared. "Of course I know it's you. I don't think that

you're Sean anymore. I haven't really, not since the other night."

"I wasn't talking about being taken for Sean Ryan. I was referring to the fact my cock is real. I'm not battery operated." He saw her look of surprise. For a few seconds they just stared at each other in the silence.

"Things are going to be challenging between us, aren't they?" Jack eventually said with a quick grin.

"There isn't any 'us', Jack."

One dark brow rose sardonically. "Oh, right. There's your wet pussy, my hard cock and Sean Ryan's ghost. Did I get all the players right?"

Her eyes narrowed. "You're *baiting* me, Jack. You have been all along. Why?"

Jack gritted his teeth. He'd do well to recall that Belle was a smart woman and a trained observer of human nature to boot.

"Maybe it's just as simple as the fact that I want you, and despite what I said the other night, I'd like you to at least have a vague, shadowy interest and knowledge of who I am instead of just being the convenient flip-switch to your orgasms."

"You're not *that* good," she told him mockingly.

Her lips clamped together with irritation when he slumped back further into the couch, completely uncaring about her verbal stab—her outright lie. Jack Caldwell *was* that good.

"Who's baiting whom now?" he murmured.

She sat up on her elbows. She dimly realized that her skirt was wrapped up around her waist and that one of her thighs was splayed outward, her knee bent and her high-heeled shoe resting on the floor beside the couch while her other black pump was tucked between Jack's thighs, where he'd placed it absently when he swung her leg over his head.

Logically she should have been concerned about having a conversation with Jack with her legs spread wide and her panties likely already damp with arousal. But she wasn't. Most of her awareness clamored around the enigmatic man who sat next to her and leaned his head back on the couch, his long legs open and relaxed, looking for all the world like he was considering an after-lunch office snooze. What kind of a game was he playing?

"So that's it? You won't have sex with me?" she asked irritably.

Jack kept his head on the back of the couch but rolled it in order to peer over at her. "I just told you that I want you, Belle. My balls are in your court." He tried not to smile as she mulled over that response. God, she was a beautiful woman.

"But I said that I wanted you…"

Jack shook his head slowly from her first uttered word. "You said you wanted to fuck. You didn't say you wanted me."

She glanced down over his body slowly. Covetously. He was wrong. She *did* want him. "What-what do you want me to do?" She watched in growing amazement as he repositioned himself, bringing the knee closer to her up on the couch and putting his elbow on the backrest. He rested his cheek on his fisted hand.

"You could seduce me," he offered hopefully with a smile that managed to be both funny and smoking hot at the same time. Belle shut her thighs slightly to counter the sharp ache at their apex. *Two points for that smile, Jack Caldwell.*

"How would you like me to seduce you?" The widening of his shapely lips required her thighs to clamp tighter.

"Every man wants to be seduced a little differently. That's the whole point. You'll have to get to know me a little bit to succeed."

"I want to succeed," she said quietly, flushing slightly at her admission.

Jack's eyes darkened and his smile faded. "Nice beginning then, Belle."

She floundered around for what to do next. What would Jack Caldwell most want her to do to seduce him? Her mind went back to the last time he'd made love to her. She recalled how masterfully he'd seduced her, how hot his eyes had burned when she'd told him what she was wearing beneath her clothing, how his face had gone rigid with need when she admitted out loud that she would take him into her body.

"I think…I think you want to be in control," she began softly. "I think you like it when you tell me to do something and I do it because…" Her voice faded.

Jack's total attention was on her. "Because what, Belle?"

"And I do it, because it turns me on to do for myself, but also because I know how you'll like it," she whispered.

"God you're sweet."

Inexplicably, tears stung her eyes at the starkness of his statement.

"So since I'm relatively inexperienced, this is how I'll seduce you right now." Her tongue slid over her lower lip nervously. "Tell me whatever it is that you want me to do… and I'll do it."

His smile was darkly sublime. "Anything?"

She considered putting some limits on it but then she noticed the intensity with which he was watching her. Instead she just nodded.

Jack's smile gentled. "Belle?"

"Yes?"

"You're doing an excellent job of seducing me," he said.

She laughed.

SIX

THE SILENCE SEEMED to take on a life of its own as they stared deeply at each other for the next few seconds. When Jack finally spoke he didn't ask her to do anything like she thought he would. He just asked her a question.

"Why did you let me take your virginity the other night? Why did you let me come inside of you?"

"I could ask you the same thing. You could have used a condom. You could have pulled out before you..." She paused in her defensive response when she noticed the way his right eyebrow drew up in amusement.

Oh. So this was his first demand of her—to be honest. Good Lord. She'd thought he was going to ask her to suck his beautiful cock or bind her hands and have his way with her or something *doable* like that. This was going to be harder than she'd thought.

"It's a good question, actually. I ought to be shot for being so irresponsible. I-I let you because I find you to be very attractive. I have ever since that day in the park."

"Go on," Jack encouraged. "Be honest, Belle."

She tried not to scowl at his practical dismissal of her

answer. "It was partly because you reminded me of Sean," she finally said quickly, knowing he wouldn't find that answer seductive, but he'd asked for honesty after all. He surprised her by simply nodding casually.

"Everyone used to think we were brothers. When we were in college people would confuse us sometimes."

Hundreds of questions about Jack and Sean's relationship clamored into her awareness at that moment. She was a little surprised when not one of them was the next thing that came out of her mouth.

"But you're different too," Belle said slowly. Feeling unsettled, she pulled her legs inward and readjusted her skirt over them as she nestled in the corner of the couch.

"You seem harder than Sean. Your eyes are harder. Your... ways are harder."

"For instance?"

"Sean would never have made those comments like you did earlier. The ones about thanking him in the afterlife for leaving me a virgin and how you didn't care if you were a gentlemen as long as you got to fuck me," she replied hotly. She frowned when he laughed.

"Yeah, you're probably right about that. Sean was always a nicer guy than me."

"And Sean would never, *never* have screwed me so hard knowing full well I had never had a man that way."

Jack just shook his head with a patient air as he studied her. "I didn't realize that you were a virgin until you were squeezing the life out of my cock. I'd been watching Clay Rothschild paw you all night like you were his personal property, and you didn't seem to mind. And what's more I *did* take it easy with you. Trust me, fucking you slow was good. It was more than good. It was *you* that set that wild pace and I still have the nail marks on my ass to prove it." He leaned forward slightly and captured her chin, forcing her to meet his eyes. "Remind me to show you later," he added ominously. "Now, two things, Belle. One—stop looking away. Any lawyer will tell you it makes you look guilty, and two—*answer the goddamned question.*"

She felt her heartbeat escalate at his tone. There was no amusement in his voice now. "I did it because I wanted you so much it silenced every rational thought I had."

A ghost of a smile touched his lips. "There. That wasn't so hard was it, honey?" he asked softly.

"*Yes.*"

His grin widened. Belle watched him warily. Did he have any idea how potent that smile was? She scoffed at the undoubted naïveté of her question. He'd probably had women eating out of his hand since he was thirteen years old using that smile.

"Tell me what you're thinking," Jack demanded with sudden intensity.

She frowned. "I was thinking that it's not fair. Your smile."

He paused at her unexpected answer. Abruptly his hand whipped out and grabbed one of her calves, tugging on it until he retrieved a foot. She yelped when he gripped her ankle and pulled, sliding her bottom down the couch toward him, close enough so that he could sink the hand on the back of the couch through her hair.

"Lots of things aren't fair, honey. Like the fact that just watching your curls swinging around your shoulders makes me hard as a rock, or the way I almost came in my pants the other night just looking at the color and texture of your naked skin. It's not fair that just the thought of fucking your sweet little pussy has made me have to jerk off more times than I can count in the past few days, and it's *certainly* not fair that you kicked me out of your bed when all I wanted to do was to make love to you again and again, and then sleep soundly with the knowledge that you were secure in my arms."

She swallowed hard. At the end he'd nearly been shouting. It looked like Jack Caldwell could teach her a thing or two about the value of honesty as a genuine aphrodisiac.

"I'm sorry about that," she murmured. "For asking you to leave, I mean. I was so confused. I can't say that I'm not still. But for what it's worth I want you to know that I am sorry."

He sighed. His fingers caressed her hair softly. "And I'm sorry that I hurt you that night, sorry that I made it so—what was it?—so that you could hardly walk the next day?"

Despite herself, she glanced downward.

"Belle?"

She looked back up into his face. "That wasn't exactly the truth." She colored intensely when she saw way his brows drew up. "I mean...I was sore. But it wasn't that bad. The experience was well worth the little discomfort that followed."

"What if I got you pregnant?"

She blinked at his sudden show of concern and—dare she say it?--vulnerabity.

"I'm on the Pill."

"Why? When you weren't sexually active?"

"I told you that I went on it before Sean died. I never went off it. It seemed to regularize my periods, decrease my cramps." She watched him to see if he was turned off by talk of her period, but his eyes on her were steady.

"You're probably worried about me though. Whether or not I could have given you some godawful disease." He plucked one strand of hair away from the mass and played with the curl at the bottom. Belle leaned her head toward his hand. Jack's lips tilted up at the innocent gesture, just like his cock did in his pants. "I'm aware that you have no reason to trust me. But I'm completely healthy. I may be guilty of knowingly putting you at risk for pregnancy but I wouldn't knowingly harm you," he said quietly.

"I believe you," she murmured.

"*Why?*" he asked with an incredulous smile.

"Because of that advice you asked for at your welcome dinner. I know you were talking about yourself, Jack. If you haven't been with anyone since losing your wife and you were monogamous with her…" Belle's voice trailed off when she saw how inscrutable his expression had become. She floundered around for another topic, something that would make him less formidable, less cold.

"Anyway, you didn't hurt me. There *was* one thing though, something I didn't expect." She saw that she'd piqued his curiosity and since she was curious herself—she didn't have any girlfriends that she felt comfortable enough asking—she asked him shyly, "Not just the next day, but for two days afterward, your…you know. It kept leaking out of me at random times. Is that normal?"

Jack's sharp bark of laughter took her by surprise.

"I'm not an expert on it, honey, but I might have heard a time or two that it does happen. To be honest with you though, I've never heard of it happening for two days following." His hand dropped to the side of her neck and he caressed her soft skin with light fingertips. Once again Belle leaned into his touch without seeming to notice. He dipped his mouth forward and spoke in a low, amused voice close to her ear.

"I can tell you a couple things that I do know for a fact though. I had a scalding orgasm inside you and it seemed like it lasted for a record-breaking length of time. And I wasn't satisfied until I dropped it at your furthest reaches. It's no wonder that it took awhile for it to find its way to daylight."

Belle's smile dissolved. "*Jack!*"

"Sorry, I didn't mean to embarrass you."

"I'm not embarrassed—" Belle began.

Jack's grin widened. "Oh. Not embarrassed? Turned on?" When Belle just stared at him wide-eyed his grin faded. "It's not a crime, Belle. All this talk about cum, fucking and your pussy has kept me consistently stiff for the past fifteen minutes. What about you?" His hand dropped from her neck, easing its way beneath the collar of her silk blouse to stroke her shoulder softly. "Are you wet, Belle?"

Her consciousness alternated between the intimacy of his low, seductive question and the feeling of his fingertips caressing her skin warmly, pausing to poke one long finger under her bra strap to slowly rub the skin beneath it.

"Yes," she finally managed thickly.

He dipped his head toward her face. "Wetter than you were before we started talking? As an outside observer—a purely objective one, of course—I can tell you that you had a nice, maybe…half-inch-round spot of cream leaking through your panties. Then you decided to shut your legs to me so I haven't been kept apprised since."

Belle just stared at him. She knew that her expression was probably some strange mixture of mortification and amusement. Jack's laugh was so warm that it didn't prepare her for what he said next.

"Scoot back on the couch, honey, and open your thighs. Let me see for myself, since you're not following the rules of the game and refuse to tell me."

"I'll tell you," she volunteered quickly. "I'm wet…wetter."

His right eyebrow rose in subtle challenge. "It's too late now, Belle. Your refusal has got me curious. Lean back and lift your skirt up to your waist."

When Belle couldn't think of anything to say to refute him she scooted back until her upper back leaned on the armrest. She didn't know why she was being so squeamish about his request. She'd been spread wide in front of him just a few minutes ago. Not that she'd realized that he'd been taking in so many details, but still…

She pulled her lined linen skirt up around her waist. "Like that?" she asked.

His face became stern. "No, not like that Belle. Do I have to spell it out for you? Spread your legs so I can see your pussy. Spread them wider than they were before. Leave the heels on," he ordered sharply when she reached for her pumps.

"I don't want to poke a hole in your leather couch."

Jack rolled his eyes as he leaned forward. He grabbed her right ankle and tossed it over the back of the couch. He pushed her left thigh wide until her high heel was flat on the floor, her knee bent.

Then he just stared.

Belle found herself squirming as he pinned her with those blue eyes.

Her hips moving restlessly finally broke through his intense focus. "It's no wonder you were shy about showing me. You're panties are soaked clean through. Take them off."

Her breath came in short, uneven gasps. She worked her panties over her garters and her legs. She paused in the action of dropping them to the floor next to the couch.

"Give them to me," Jack said.

She hesitated. She could feel the panel of the underwear. He was right. Her cream was thick on it. How mortifying. But for some reason, his manner with her was making her more aroused than she'd ever imagined. Her hand shook a little when she dropped the beige silk into his hands. His gaze was melded to hers but Belle couldn't stop herself from dropping her eyes and watching him rub the slick silk slowly. It felt like those two long fingers were stroking her pussy. She moaned hen he casually, but deliberately, raised the silk and inhaled deeply.

"Spread your thighs wide again," he ordered pointedly but distractedly as he continued to rub her panties, this time keeping them near his face. His nostrils flared to catch her scent. "You're sweet. Why would you want to hide that from me?" he asked with what appeared to be genuine puzzlement.

"It's usually private, that's why."

He shook his head. His fingers continued to caress the creamed silk. "Trust me, Belle, I probably already know your taste and scent better than you ever will. After the next half hour I'll be able to pick your wet panties out of a sample of a hundred of different women's underwear." He tossed the scrap of silk down on the couch between them like a gantlet. "My advice is that you start to include me into your definition of private, at least within the confines of sex, and you'll be a hell of a lot more comfortable."

Belle didn't know if it was the overwhelming intimacy of his words or the wetness that flooded into her sex that made tilt her head away from him in shame. She expected him to admonish her but when the silence stretched long and her exposed sex continued to weep and tighten with arousal Belle sought out Jack's eyes again. To her surprise his gaze was compassionate.

"Are you all right?"

Belle nodded. She realized that her eyes were filled with tears. What an unexpectedly powerful emotional experience this was.

"Do you want to stop? Anytime you want to say the word." Jack leaned forward intently. "I'll tell you a little secret, honey, and you remember it always. I'll still think you're an incredibly beautiful, sexy woman no matter what you do or say. I only want to see desire in your eyes, never fear or humiliation. Do you understand, Belle?"

She stared at him in amazement. "I understand," she murmured in a low, husky voice. Her thigh muscles smoothed, relaxing of their own accord, opening her further to his gaze. Belle thought she saw tension flow out of Jack too.

"Good." His hot eyes returned between her thighs. "The hair around your lips and clit is dark and wet. You're glistening like you've been oiled." Belle panted when he dropped his dark head and frustration skimmed his features. "Put your hands behind your thighs and push them back. I want to see all of you clearly."

Belle did what he said. She made small gliding motions with her hands along the back of her thighs while Jack looked his fill. Why hadn't she ever noticed how soft her thighs were, how firm? Her palms planted wide, her fingertips stretched toward her sex, coveting her own flesh.

"Look at me," Jack insisted.

She raised her head and met his gaze through her spread thighs.

"Do you want to touch yourself?"

Hr lower lip trembled just as her fingers stretched another few millimeters toward her sex. She nodded. To her surprise Jack's gaze looked doubtful as it flicked over her pussy and back to her eyes again.

"You'll light up like a torch if you touch your clit. It's red and swollen, honey."

Belle moaned desperately at his words.

"You can still touch yourself, but only where I say. Dip your finger into your pussy. It deserves to be called a honey pot. You're creaming out of it," he muttered distractedly.

Jack wasn't likely to watch this from a distance. He inched closer to her on the couch, his hot eyes never leaving the sight of her sinking her elegant, manicured forefinger into her pussy. Her moist flesh clung greedily even to that slender invader. His groan of excitement matched hers as she plunged deeply then increased the tempo of her strokes.

"How does it feel?" Jack asked with a voice that he hoped passed for steady.

Her pussy began to pump upward to meet her downward stroke.

"Good. But I need more, Jack. I need to be filled."

"Two fingers then, but only for a few strokes. Do you understand?" he asked sharply when she almost immediately shoved her second finger in to join her first. Jack leaned down to breathe in her scent, to watch with fascination as her creamy flesh clasped tightly around her fingers, to see how her hips thrashed upward as she finger-fucked herself. When he saw her fingers move up toward her clit Jack grabbed her wrist and pulled her hand away. He couldn't help but give a small grin when her hips continued to pump upward for a few strokes.

She was so amazing, so sensual. He couldn't wait to have her. But first...

"I'm sorry, honey," he murmured when he saw the confused look on her beautiful, sweat-dampened face. "There's just one other thing."

Belle blinked twice to bring him into focus. "What?"

He let go of her hand and palmed the backs of her smooth thighs, rolling her back even further. "The other night when I touched your ass, you went very stiff. Why? Does it disgust you?"

Belle shook her head rapidly. "No. Not disgust. I'm not used to it that's all."

"Sean never touched you there?"

Belle shook her head again.

"Look at me."

Her gaze flew up to meet his.

"I want you to dip your first finger one more time in your pussy—only once, honey," Jack added warningly. "And then I want you to slide that finger into your asshole. I'll spread you."

Belle's tongue flicked over her lower lip with anxious arousal. She wanted to do what he said but—

"Jack, you're not going to…"

Jack shook his head and grinned wryly. "No, Belle. Ass lubricant isn't one of my standard office supplies, believe it or not. I'm not going to fuck your ass. Not now. I just want you to get more comfortable with me, okay? I want you to *show* me how much you want this."

She nodded uneasily. She sank her finger so quickly into her pussy that Jack almost missed it. When her hand traveled downward he widened her ass cheeks, readying her as best he could for her finger, as tiny as she was. Jack glanced up, wondering at her hesitancy, but he realized that she wasn't sure where she should go. He leaned down and placed just the tips of his forefingers gently on each side of the tiny pink rosette, bracketing the entrance for her. He nodded his head, made temporarily speechless as Belle pointed her moist finger directly into herself and pushed.

"Do it the other way, Belle. Push up with your ass instead of down with your finger," he ordered tensely.

Belle whimpered when she felt his breath mist the sensitive skin between her cheeks, lightly stimulating her asshole. Her ass slid with surprising ease onto the first inch of her finger when she followed his instructions. She paused, curious at the sensations emanating both from her finger and ass. She tensed her butt muscles and took the rest of her finger into her.

Jack's eyes glowed with intense arousal. "How does it feel, honey?"

She trembled and tensed. She didn't know if it was because of the sensation of fingering her ass or the stark intimacy of Jack watching her so closely while she did it but she was going to explode at the lightest touch on her clit. She pushed her finger in and out once and was rewarded by hearing Jack growl deep in his throat.

"In my ass it feels full, sort of strange…maybe better than I thought it would." She bounced on her finger once again. "On my finger it feels…"

"What?" Jack asked in a voice that didn't even sound like his own. He crept closer to her while she considered, aligning his mouth with her drenched clit.

"I-I guess I can understand why men like it so much. Ass-fucking, I mean. It feels so smooth and muscular and tight," she murmured. She glanced down and noticed that Jack's mouth was centered over her pussy, but his brilliant blue eyes were watching her face intently.

"You're so sweet. Do you want to come?" he murmured huskily as he glanced down at the reddened bundle of sensitive flesh that swelled out between her labia.

"*Yes*," she whispered emphatically. Her hips surged up meet his mouth but Jack backed away slightly.

"I'll make you come, but finger-fuck your ass first. Let me see you do it good and hard."

She rammed her finger into her ass without a second of doubt. Her entire body clenched in desperate arousal. She would have done anything at that moment to come. "Like that? Ah God. Please, Jack. *Please*…"

"It's nice to hear that, honey," he whispered gruffly next to her pumping hand. "Belle. Belle. Look at me."

She focused on him through wild eyes. "Please Jack," she begged miserably.

"I'm not trying to torture you. Just listen. Remember

where we are. These walls are thick but you can't scream." He watched as she glanced around her dazedly, taking in her surroundings as if she was seeing them for the first time. She glanced back at him and nodded.

"Good girl," he muttered before he abruptly slanted his head and sucked her clit between his lips and parted teeth. He waited patiently while Belle tried her best to muffle her shout of pleasure, the result being a series of sharp, muffled whimpers. When he became sure that the first blast of orgasm had passed he created more suction then bit at the ultra-sensitive flesh gently. Belle arched off the couch and screamed. *So much for caution.* He loved the sound of her abandonment. He held her to him tightly to keep up the pressure that she obviously enjoyed so much.

She couldn't have stopped the scream that left her lips then anymore than she could have stopped her heart from beating. Her body convulsed as wave after wave of orgasm suffused her. She became vaguely aware that her hand continued to pump her finger into her ass. Had that stimulation, along with her intense arousal and Jack's masterful finale stroke, been responsible for the orgasm that seemed to encompass her whole body instead of just her sex and brain?

She drew air thickly into her lungs for long seconds before she became aware that Jack was watching her.

"Okay?" he murmured warmly.

She nodded. "That felt…incredible.

Jack hesitated in asking her to stand. The couch belonged to the law firm, not to him personally. But his priority was Belle and she looked worn out. People spilled coffee and such on couches all the time, right? Of course, he didn't think that cum would make the same kind of stain on leather…

Belle's gaze flicked up at him in renewed interest when he stood and removed his suit jacket then slid his leather belt through the clasp. "Turn over, lift your skirt and put your ass in the air, Belle," he ordered thickly. He wondered if she read his urgency because she positioned herself quickly. Jack had time to appreciate her as he removed his pants. Belle's ass pleased him. She was firm but just fleshy enough to make his mouth water. And that uniform color of her skin…

He stroked his stony cock once from root to tip in anticipation.

Belle glanced over her shoulder anxiously when the couch sank with Jack's weight behind her. She bit her lip to hide a groan. God he was gorgeous. He was still wearing his crisp white button-down shirt but his cock jutted out lewdly beneath it. He was enormous with need, ruddy and straining. Seeing him stroke the considerable length of his cock with his hand made her sex clench with more excitement than she thought possible after the orgasm she'd just had. Jack put his hands on her hips and repositioned her bottom so that she tilted slightly toward the front of the couch.

"Now put your arms out and touch your nipples to the couch. Yeah, just like that," He kept his right foot on the floor, bending his knee, while his other knee was on the couch behind her. He pressed the head of his cock to her narrow soaking channel.

"I hope you're not sore anymore because I'm going to have to fuck you hard, honey," he warned softly.

She shook her head and her hair skimmed over her back, falling forward over her shoulders. "No, Jack. I'm ready for you." Her cheek pressed to the couch but she glanced up at him as he towered over her. "Do it hard—"

Her whisper was cut off at the sensation of him grabbing her hips and thrusting into her with one firm, long stroke. Her eyes opened so wide she must have looked like she'd just been revealed the mysteries of the universe. Jack gave a deep groan of animal satisfaction and proceeded to set a hard pace. Her body quaked with each of his thrusts into her, causing her sensitized nipples to press and scrape against the leather of the couch. It felt so intense, so overwhelming. He just kept pounding her, crashing their flesh together until Belle knew she could no longer bear the friction.

Jack paused, cursing under his breath when he felt her climax drawing him deeper, clasping him like a rhythmic, milking fist. Sweat beaded on his face, neck, chest and belly with the effort that he needed to expend to keep his seed inside of him for just a few more strokes instead of coming deep right that second. Miraculously, he survived her climax without ejaculating.

"Come up on your hands, Belle," Jack managed to get out between panting breaths.

She heard him as if from a distance. She was both satiated and aroused at once, a bizarre and sublime state of being. Jack continued to move in her, creating that powerful friction. Her arms shook when she braced herself on them like he'd requested. She felt Jack slow slightly at the same time as she felt him lengthen inside of her.

Her vagina contracted, pulling him deeper, her body language telling him how much she wanted him to continue his relentless fucking. "You have the most incredible pussy," he muttered thickly. He kept one hand on her smooth hip as he thrust into her with short, stabbing strokes, the other hand trailing over her silk blouse along her spine. "You pull me deeper into you, tease me…"

She groaned, flinging back her head. "That's because I want your cum deep inside of me again, Jack."

Bull's-eye, Belle. He wound her curls between his fingers and pulled. Her throat stretched back in an elegant arch. He pulled her back on his cock in the deepest of thrusts.

Seduction complete.

He clutched her to him while he came.

Had he told Belle not to shout? Because as orgasm rocketed through him, Jack hadn't the slightest control over what came out of his throat. The first waves were so powerful he temporarily blacked out...peaked at nirvana, no doubt. When he came to awareness his low grunts of incredulous pleasure were coming in the same rhythmic shudders that racked his body.

He became aware that Belle's chin was on her shoulder and that her face was tight. She was pressing her ass firmly against his belly, clearly trying to get the pressure she needed in order to come again.

The feeling of Jack throbbing in her felt even more powerful than it had the night he'd taken her virginity. God, if it kept getting better and better each time, she would probably end up forsaking working, sleeping and eating and spend all of her time trying to get Jack to fuck her. The thought would have been funny if another orgasm hadn't been just within her reach, staying tantalizingly within a hairsbreadth of her grasping body. Jacked reached around and gave her swollen pussy a firm little swat before he rubbed her clit hard. Orgasm slammed into her.

She cried out in shocked ecstasy.

Jack watched her between heavy eyelids as she came, saw her look of surprise, felt her kick up his waning spasms of orgasm with the fresh ones of her own. He wished he could eat up those sexy, uneven cries that skipped past her parted lips while his fingers nursed her through her orgasm. When she finally slowed he wrapped his hands around her waist and brought her down on his lap as he sprawled in the corner of the couch.

Minutes passed. Their loud gasps slowly quieted. Neither

spoke. Belle murmured with contentment at the feel of Jack's fingers in her hair and the soft, warm kisses he pressed into her neck. He glanced up with vague irritation when he suddenly felt her stiffen. He liked it better when she purred like a kitten.

"Were we too loud? Maybe we should get dressed."

He pressed his mouth to her neck once more. "You *are* dressed, Belle." She wriggled in his lap. Jack groaned. He still nestled deep inside of her flesh. To his amazement his nerve endings were far from dead. "Calm down, honey. If the entire Chicago Fire Department came to get us out of here, Tom would hold them off single-handedly."

Belle turned toward him, eating him up with her gaze. His dark hair had spilled forward onto his forehead. His blue eyes seemed to glow with satiation. Her eyes outlined the hard line of his jaw, the sexy shape of his lips. She started when she felt him quicken inside of her.

"If you keep looking at me like that we're going another round on this couch. I don't mind either way, but I thought you might like to do it the next time in a bed. My bed. Come and stay at my house tonight."

"Jack, I can't…"

"Why not? It's Friday afternoon. If you have to go back to work right now I'll pick you up afterward," he said levelly.

"It's not that. I took the afternoon off because I had some things to take care of." One of which—talking to Jack about the fact that Sean had wanted to keep their relationship secret —she'd never accomplished. "But I have to take care of Ellie and—"

"Ellie is invited too. She'll like my place. It's up north, right on Lake Michigan, totally secluded. We can cook out on the terrace and take the dogs for a walk on the beach. Copenhagen will worship me forever for bringing the female of his dog dreams into his lair," Jack said with two up-thrusts of his eyebrows and a lascivious expression. "In fact, forget just spending the night. The invitation is for the whole weekend. Monday is Labor Day so it's a long one. Come on, Belle," he urged. "Don't tell me you have anything planned that could be more exciting than trying to keep Copenhagen from humping Ellie. Don't get any ideas about stopping me from humping you, though—"

Belle snorted with laughter and his crudeness. "You're right, you know. If Ellie and I did come out there she'd probably end up pregnant and I'd end up…"

"What?" Jack asked intently, his playful smile fading.

She looked at him soberly. "I'd end up screwing up my life, most likely. Getting hurt. Falling for you and never really knowing if it was with you or your likeness to Sean," she whispered softly.

Jack waited two heartbeats, three, then four.

"I am different from Sean, Belle. Surely you've started to realize that."

She glanced away in discomfort. "You're different. It's true. But there are times when—"

"Belle?" Jack asked harshly. She met his eyes anxiously. "You're not still harboring some kind of delusion that I'm *actually* Sean Ryan are you?"

She shook her head.

"Good, because that was really strange." Jack grimaced when he saw her embarrassment. "Do you like me? Do you like spending time with me?"

She was caught in the trap of his eyes. "Yes. Very much."

"Then spend more time with me. See what happens. We all have memories that get in the way of our futures. But it doesn't mean we should run from something that seems good just because there are similarities to the past. Good is good, right?" When he saw her hesitation he pushed, "You aren't the only one with memories. I have them as well. I have to deal with them too."

Uncertainty showed clearly on Belle's face but so did longing. Longing won.

She nodded her head slowly. "All right, Jack. I'll come."

SEVEN

BELLE HAD WANTED to stop by her office at the group
practice to pick up some files before returning to her condominium, but there was no way she was presentable profession-
ally, even for a brief visit. She'd cleaned up in the luxurious
bathroom attached to Jack's office, but her panties were still
damp and nothing but a thorough shower was going to
remedy the condition between her thighs.

After her shower she dressed in jeans and a knit top. She
fed Ellie and played with her for a few minutes distractedly.

She really needed to pack for the weekend. But despite the
shiver of anticipation that the thought of spending so many
hours with Jack Caldwell inspired, she delayed. Instead she
wandered into the small second bedroom that she used for a
den. For several long moments she just stared at her computer.
Once…twice…three times she raised her hand to the
keyboard only to let it drop.

Why can't I let it go?

The thought was elusive, almost too wispy to survive
among all those other bulky facts and impressive-sounding
psychological explanations for its existence. Now Belle knew

there was another reason she wanted to hang on to the idea. She'd been furious at Jack Caldwell when she'd first seen him today and within a matter of minutes she'd been begging him to fuck her. She'd exposed herself to him because he'd told her to, she'd finger-fucked her own ass while he'd watched because he'd demanded it, and she'd obediently stuck her butt up in the air and allowed him to fuck her frenziedly in a public workplace because *he* had wanted it.

And so had she. So much so, that the truth overwhelmed her.

What's more, just sitting there thinking about it was making her wet all over again, Belle realized with growing mortification. Either Belle had to accept the fact that she was some kind of a sex-starved nymphomaniac or...

"*He's Sean,*" Belle whispered suddenly, desperately, as though she feared that the fragile ghost of a belief was about to meet its demise and a last-minute rescue was required.

Her heart actually seemed to cringe in her chest when she heard the words. She was an expert on madness. She *knew* it was crazy to keep thinking that Jack Caldwell was Sean. She'd seen the picture. But no other man had ever been able to turn her into such an uninhibited creature of pure, unleashed sexuality save Sean. There were other things, the disturbing similarity of their eyes, their bodies . . . even their cocks.

Her spine stiffened with sudden determination. She was about to spend three nights with Jack. It was the perfect opportunity to give her obsession the final burial it required, to finally put Sean's ghost to rest.

Her hands finally rose to the keyboard, accessing a search engine. She typed in the words Ellsworth and Burke. The law firm's website immediately popped up. She clicked on a heading for "employees". Joanne...Joanne S-something, wasn't it? Yes. There it was. Joanne Swindon. She'd been in two of

Belle's psychology classes at Northwestern. They'd gone out to movies, dinner and the occasional bar several times with mutual friends during their undergraduate days. She'd thought the name Ellsworth and Burke had sounded familiar, just realizing within the past twenty-four hours why. Her good friend Sheila Livingston had mentioned in passing that Joanne had landed a cushy position there after graduating from law school at the University of Michigan.

Belle clicked back to the Ellsworth and Burke homepage and picked up her cell phone.

———

At a little after seven o'clock that evening Belle opened her front door and stared at Jack with surprise.

"Did you check to see if it was me first?" he asked with a dark scowl.

She gave him a wry look. "Jack, if you're so concerned about safety issues, why don't you explain to me how you keep getting up here without security calling me first? That *is* the way it's supposed to work."

He rolled his eyes but seemed distracted as he studied her. "You haven't got any security in this building. You've got a napping location for a bunch of geriatrics. But that's not how I got in tonight. I was talking to this really nice lady who lives on the thirty-sixth floor, Marsha Gilman—do you know her? Anyway, that old guy just buzzed me in with her."

Belle had to laugh. She was reminded of her earlier thoughts about the unfairness of his smile. Marsha Gilman had undoubtedly been the most recent victim of it. Her gaze wandered over him appreciatively. He was wearing the same dark suit that she'd seen him in earlier, although his handsome blue silk tie was currently neatly knotted. No one would ever

guess that he'd worn that crisp white shirt that looked so delicious against his dark skin while he'd fucked her into oblivion
in his office this afternoon.

"No I don't know her. You'll have to introduce us sometime," she said sarcastically. Her eyes hadn't really stopped
their warm tour over him as she leaned against the door.
Neither of them spoke for a few seconds.

"Are you going to let me in? Or are you just going to stand
there and experiment to see how hard you can get me with
your stare alone?" Her gaze rose from his crotch to meet his
warm stare. Jack felt himself thicken even further when her
stunned expression at his words softened into a wistful smile.

"That's either quite a compliment to me or a testament to
the magnitude of your horniness. I really don't know you that
well. Maybe you're inspired just as easily by Marsha Gilman…
or a stiff breeze, for that matter."

He laughed and stepped forward. Her hands encircled his
neck when he took her in his arms and bent to kiss her. It was
far from a traditional "hello" kiss. It was hot and deep and the
cadence of Jack's tongue instantly brought to mind what they'd
been doing together that afternoon. When he finally raised his
head and studied her the sexual tension in both of their bodies
had been turned up to high.

"It's a compliment to you, but it's also a testament to the
magnitude of my horniness, at least in regard to you. I
didn't realize how far I was from being finished with you
until you left today," he muttered quietly. He leaned down
and kissed her again, using his lips to leisurely mold hers.
Belle sighed at the slow, delicious burn that expanded in her
lower belly.

"Are you ready to go?" Jack asked eventually between
plucking and biting her lush lower lip. "Tom is illegally parked
out front."

"Tom?" Belle murmured in surprise, not sure if she'd heard correctly due to the befuddling effect of Jack's kisses.

He nodded. "He's not just my assistant, Belle. He lives with me."

Belle paled as she stared up at him.

Good God. Clay's comments about Jack and Tom rushed to the forefront of her awareness. The assertion was ridiculous to Belle. She knew that Jack wasn't gay, but why did he have a grown man live with him? Panic rose in her. Lord, what if… what if Jack was bi? What if Tom was his lover and he wanted to add a woman to make a trio? What if that's why he'd asked her to his house? What if…

Jack watched Belle's expressive face with initial puzzlement that segued to dawning amusement. "Been listening to Holloway & Croft gossip? Tom and I aren't lovers." His teeth flashed in his dark face as he considered the idea.

"Why does he live with you?" Belle asked with open-mouthed amazement.

"It's a long story but suffice it to say that Tom is sort of like my bodyguard." When he saw her continued confusion he shook his head, not really wanting to elaborate but seeing that Belle wasn't going to give him a choice.

"My mother is a very wealthy woman. When I was twenty-one years old the police discovered a kidnapping plot against me. It was thwarted and the guy who was going to try and bleed my parents for millions went to prison. But after that my parents insisted that I have some kind of protection: a bodyguard. A man named Christopher Aaron was hired to do it. As time passed and it became clear that I didn't really need protection, Christopher became more of an assistant to me. He became such an expert at assisting me with legal matters, since he more or less attended law school with me, that I didn't have any trouble convincing the law firm that I worked for to hire him along with me as an administrative assistant. It was a good cover for a bodyguard. Christopher passed away a while back and Tom replaced him. I know it sounds sort of odd, but it calms my mother down a lot to know that someone looks out for me."

"But Tom's not…you're not…"

"I'm not even vaguely interested in fucking anything with a cock. We probably won't even see Tom over the weekend. He has his own separate apartment and entrance." Jack's lips tilted with amusement as he watched her.

"He may not be my partner but he has become a good friend, which means he'll have no problem giving me shit for making him wait for so long. So do you think you could get your stuff so we can go?"

Belle blinked. "Oh sure, it's right here. Is it okay if I bring my computer? I might have to do a little work over the weekend…"

"Bring the kitchen sink if it'll make you happy. Just hurry up," Jack answered distractedly before he followed her to help her with her bag. A lush red silk scarf hung on a hook of the antique coat bench in Belle's foyer abruptly caught his eye. His hand whipped out quick as lightning and snagged it. He shoved it into his inner jacket pocket with a cat that ate the canary grin.

———

"Shit."

"What?" Belle asked Jack in surprise as she looked up from cutting her steak.

"It may have taken Copenhagen half of the night to figure out what Ellie means by all that butt wagging but I think the light in his pea-sized brain has lit up in a big way," Jack said grimly as he stood up from the table.

Belle glanced over to where their dogs were currently tussling on the family room floor. The canines had been enamored with each other since Belle and Ellie had arrived at Jack's house hours ago. As he showed her around the luxurious, sleek, modern structure of the lakeside house and later, while Jack grilled steaks, the two dogs had played and gamboled together on the large deck outside the patio doors of the family room. Jack had cut up an extra steak and split it between the dogs' bowls of Dog Chow— pointedly ignoring Belle's look of disapproval. Ellie and Copenhagen had sloppily inhaled their meals at the same time that Jack and Belle savored theirs. Since their arrival, however, she had been glad to see that their dogs's play seemed entirely innocent.

But that had obviously undergone a change while she and Jack had been entirely preoccupied with each other during their late dinner. Her eyes widened when she saw Copenhagen. She muttered the first thing that came to her stunned brain.

"Oh my God. Look at the size of that thing."

Jack snorted in amusement at such an elegant woman's stark exclamation, although he was in complete agreement as to its accuracy. Although Ellie seemed thoroughly excited by the newest development, Copenhagen didn't yet seem to fathom what he was supposed to do with the appendage that wagged between his hind legs with as much enthusiasm as did his tail.

Instincts must have guided the huge dog sufficiently however, to make him fully resist Jack's attempts to pull him away from Ellie. After several only semi-successful tries Jack muttered between desperate tugs, "It might be better to try and take Ellie away first. Do you think you could put her in the guest suite upstairs while I try to get Copenhagen into the basement?"

Belle tried but it was a harder request to fulfill than she would have ever thought. She hated to think it but her usually biddable, ladylike dog had been transformed into an ornery, horny-as-hell bitch. Belle was sweating with the effort of pulling Ellie up the stairs and getting her secured in the upstairs suite when she finally shut the door abruptly ten minutes later. She sagged against the door to catch her breath while Ellie whimpered on the other side.

Belle glanced up when she heard Jack's tread on the stairs. When he stepped into the dim hallway she saw that his dark hair was tousled from his wrestling match with Copenhagen. There was a considerable amount of dog drool wetting one thigh of his jeans and also on the white t-shirt he wore.

The realization made her laugh uncontrollably. Jack's look of annoyance was transformed at the sound of her laughter. Ellie made a howl of protest behind the closed door and then began to bat and scratch at it in frustration. Jack snorted and joined Belle in laughing.

She wiped away the tears that leaked out of her eyelids.

"It was your idea to get these dogs together, Jack," she accused humorously as Ellie began to claw and whine more vociferously. Anxiety joined amusement on her face. "God, Jack, she's going to scrape up that door."

"So?" Jack said through a broad smile. "Nothing she can do can't be fixed. The important thing is that she won't get out until she calms down a little bit. I hate to think of what havoc Copenhagen is wreaking in the basement. Best not to think about it," he decided as he grabbed her hand and stalked down the hallway.

"Where are we going?" Belle asked bemusedly, laughter still clinging around her lips.

"I'm drenched in a gallon of dog spit. I need a shower and you're going to take one with me," Jack said matter-of-factly as he led her into the master suite.

Belle didn't have time to voice her surprise before Jack pulled her into his huge, luxurious bathroom and yanked her shirt over her head. His hands dropped to the front clasp of her bra and before she knew it Belle was standing in front of him half-naked, her bare breasts swaying from his brisk movements. Jack didn't seem to be particularly enraptured with the sight of her though, Belle realized. He was busy unbuttoning the fly of her jeans with a look of concentration on his handsome face.

"I'm glad to hear it's just dog drool," Belle told him wryly as she kicked off her topsiders, endeavoring to seem as casual about taking a shower with Jack as he seemed about taking one with her. "I was starting to wonder."

He glanced up from shoving her jeans down her hips and ass with surprise. Then he laughed unrestrainedly. "Wondering if Copenhagen thought my thigh was a good enough substitution for Ellie?" he asked as he kneeled in front of her and pulled her jeans and then her panties over her feet.

"Well, there is…a lot of it," Belle finished after a slight gasp. The Jack Caldwell who had knelt was all brisk practicality but the same man who rose in front of her, lightly skimming her ankles and calves, was every inch the focused, appreciative male.

"Yeah," he agreed absentmindedly and let his hands drop. "I shouldn't touch you, my hands are dirty." For a few seconds his eyes roved over her with growing arousal. "You've got a gorgeous body, Belle," he finally murmured. "It's probably not much of a compliment for a woman as intelligent as you—maybe even an insult—but you're centerfold material. You try really hard to hide all that under your clothes, don't you?"

"It's not typically thought to be conducive to the therapeutic process to have my patients thinking about what's under my clothes."

He grinned. "I'm willing to bet a good portion of them do anyway, at least the men."

"Jack, that's not funny. I'm a good psychologist. Don't insult what I do by making insinuations about my sex or my body as it relates to my work. I wouldn't assume that your female clients are thinking about what you're packing behind the fly of your pants, or that if they *did* that it would affect your ability to do the job."

His grin didn't waver. He liked when Belle got feisty. "I have no doubt that you're a fantastic psychologist, Belle, and I never said a word about thinking your body affected your ability to do your job," he said with a friendly glance of reprimand as he whipped his t-shirt over his head and began to unbutton his jeans.

Her breath stuck in her throat when she took in the sight of his naked torso. The firm, delineated muscles of his shoulders and chest flexed with his movements. She couldn't help but drop her eyes in fascination over his flat, muscled abdomen as he lowered his jeans. Her eyes widened when he popped out of his briefs. He wasn't currently as stiff as she'd seen him in the past, but she'd apparently been wrong to think earlier that he was unaffected by her nakedness. Angela Winthrop's speculation about him having a cock as big as Zeus' flew into Belle's awareness.

If Angela only knew.

She frowned at her thought.

"What's wrong?"

"They do," she muttered sullenly.

"Excuse me?" Jack wondered, confused.

"Your female clients. They likely do speculate. Occasionally. Or a lot. About that," Belle finished with a nod toward his bobbing cock. "If they're not half-dead, anyway." When he turned around her eyes glommed onto his ass. Jack hadn't been lying earlier. Her fingernails *had* scored those tight, yummy butt cheeks.

Her was grinning as he turned on two of several surrounding showerheads in the steam shower. "You're the psychologist. You know it's only human to wonder."

She pursed her lips together with irritation when Jack proceeded to ignore her and stepped under the hot spray of the shower. Her irritation turned to lust quicker than a struck match flamed, however, as she watched the water make Jack's dark skin and hair glisten, the way his muscles rippled as he grabbed a bar of soap and lathered his chest and belly, obviously ridding himself of Copenhagen's dog drool without further ado.

She wouldn't have been surprised to learn that she was drooling as much as Copenhagen as she watched Jack rub his hands over the length of his hard, hair-sprinkled thighs, lather his crotch and then make three gliding, slow, deliberate strokes over the entire length of his cock. Her throat went dry. He'd lengthened a full inch in front of her eyes. Wetness and warmth flooded her. Had he really just done that? Belle felt like she was in the front row of a very erotic peep show.

Jack glanced out to where she was standing. "Okay. You can come in. All of the dog spit is gone," he called out cheerfully as he rinsed the soap off.

Belle joined him beneath the hot spraying jets. Jack slid the glass doors shut behind her to build up some steam. She glanced around the shower space. It was almost as large as her second bedroom and included a low seating area along one wall. "Is this shower designed for a hygienic orgy or what?" she wondered.

Jack shrugged. "Hey, I just rent this house."

"How is it that Copenhagen's drool got on your cock, Jack?" she challenged as she let him position her so that the shower spray hit her back.

"I was just doing that to turn you on," he said with a devilish glint in his eyes. "Did it work?"

Belle shook her head and laughed. He moved.

He palmed her entire sex and shoved his middle finger up into her pussy lightning-quick.

"Jack!"

She went straight from relative calm to moaning with arousal as he pumped into her at a steady pace, the flat of his hand giving her clit a sweet little slap with each damp upstroke.

"The answer to my question is yes," Jack murmured as he leaned down over her face, forcing her eyes to meet his. "You're already slick, Belle."

Her breath hitched raggedly when he thrust into her harder. He saw her face tighten with each upstroke. By her reaction, he'd hit her sweet spot. He lowered his mouth to within a half an inch of her opened lips. "I thought we went through this before, Belle. When I ask you if you're pussy is wet or if you're turned on, I want an answer from your mouth. I don't care if the answer is 'no fucking way, Jack' as long as you're being honest and as long as I can hear the answer. Okay?"

Belle moaned and nodded her head. When she saw the look in his eyes she said quickly, "Okay."

He grinned before he dipped his head and sent his tongue into her mouth. Belle thought she was going to liquefy at the sensation of him plunging into both places in her body at once. After a few moments he broke the kiss and reached down with the hand that wasn't occupied. Belle clutched at his shoulders for balance when he draped her thigh over his forearm and lifted one foot off the floor, pushing her knee into her, exposing more of her sex. She panted audibly when he added another finger and increased the tempo of his finger-fucking yet again, causing his palm to make wet, staccato slapping sounds against her pussy.

Jack watched her face steadily as he thrust into her repeatedly, his palm creating intermittent suctioning little slaps on her clit. "I can feel how erect your clit is," he said after a minute of stroking her deeply. "Are you about to come, honey?"

"Yes. Oh God, Jack, *yes*."

He touched his mouth to hers in a gesture of focused tenderness, wanting to capture the sensation of the sexy whimpers that fell past her lips. "And do you want to? Or do want me to draw it out?"

"*Want to!*" Belle gasped.

"All right. But I want you to work for it a little," Jack murmured. He dropped her leg to give her balance. On his next upward stroke he flexed his biceps hard. His fingers reached high and his palm pressed sinuously over her clit with a hard, sustained pressure. She made a sharp cry that Jack stifled abruptly with his mouth as he kissed her deeply. She held onto him tightly. Despite the fact that both feet were presently on the floor, he was offering her a considerable amount of pressure with which to bring herself off, and she needed the balance.

"Show me how much you want to come, honey," he said softly against her lips after he'd closed their kiss.

Belle went up onto her tiptoes. Her thigh and butt muscles clenched and she bucked up against his hand wildly. Her delicate features pulled with agonized pleasure when she came. After the spasms of her orgasm had quieted, she glanced up at him, breathless. Jack was studying her with eyes lit like glowing embers.

"Nice?"

"Very," she murmured breathlessly. When she considered the way she'd been humping his hand so desperately, she pressed her cheek into his chest so that he wouldn't see her blushing. "And I was thinking that Ellie was acting like she was horny as hell."

Jack couldn't help but grin as he turned off the two front shower jets and turned on another one over the seating space. He grabbed Belle's hips, turning her back to him, and sat down.

"You crack me up, honey." His grin widened at his unintentional double entendre, since in their current positions it was as though he were conversing with Belle's beautiful ass. "How can you be both so embarrassed about your responsiveness, and so honest about it at the same time?"

When Belle tried to turn around Jack restrained her gently but completely by placing his hands on her ass and hips and not permitting her to move. Belle twisted in frustration, trying to get to him. His cock was long, thick and flushed with arousal. Her mouth watered.

"Jack, let go of me," she protested. "I want to touch you."

"In a minute, honey," Jack murmured. His eyes never left her ass. He stroked a length of silky inner thigh. "Right now I want you to bend over."

Belle hesitated, even though a fresh wave of desire shot through her. She backed up, following the subtle directives fom Jack's hands as he positioned her between his bent knees.

"Now spread your thighs," he directed huskily. "And bend over. Not like that, Belle. Put your hands just above your knees and arch your back. Stick your ass high in the air. Higher."

He felt his heartbeat thrum in his cock with increased speed and pressure as he watched her follow his instructions. "Put your pussy right up to my mouth. Hurry," he muttered tightly, "I can't wait to sink my tongue into you but you have to be right in front of me."

Belle glanced around to gauge the exact location of Jack's mouth where he sat behind her. She sent her tailbone up as high as she could, as if a string attached to the ceiling was hooked in her asshole and drawing her up. Her thighs tensed hard. It wasn't an easy position to hold but she forced herself to do it, eager for what Jack had promised.

Jack's cock popped up as if it had a mind of its own when he saw the fine tremor in her thighs and realized how much energy she was expending to hold her body in the way he'd directed. He pushed back the round globes of her ass cheeks, exposing her tiny asshole and the lush, swollen lips of her pussy. Leaning forward, he dipped into her sweetness.

Her clit literally sizzled when Jack slowly began to fuck her pussy with a long, stiffened tongue. She moaned low and long at the sybaritic, sensual sensation of him alternating between tonguing her thoroughly, applying a hard suction, and then laving her clit again with short, fast strokes.

Jack turned his face sideways and sent his tongue as deep as he could, drunk with the nectar of her, needing more. The fact that his cock was ready to erupt didn't pierce his intense focus as much as Belle's trembling thighs and her desperate sounds of mixed distress and arousal did.

"You can relax your thighs, honey," he directed. "I'll come to you."

Belle's eyes opened at the terrible absence of Jack's tongue. He had to repeat himself before she understood what he was saying. She let her thighs relax, panting heavily. Who would have known that it would take so much energy to keep oneself so tensely in an awkward position?

As soon as he noticed that her thighs were relaxed, he leaned forward and pressed back her ass cheeks even further with his hands. Not wanting to make Belle suffer any more he rubbed his stiffened tongue hard against her clit, agitating the nerve-packed flesh.

Belle exploded like a cache of fireworks.

It took her several seconds to realize that the high-pitched keening sound that she heard was her own scream. She was still in the first heady throes of orgasm when Jack pulled his heavenly mouth away. Belle's lips opened to cry out in painful protest but the next sensation that struck her was of him reaching a hard arm around her waist and pulling her down to his lap.

"Quit squirming. Take my cock," he ordered tensely.

Belle spread her legs and felt him place the smooth head of his cock at her entrance. He transferred his hands to her waist and sank her down the length of him in one long stroke, her ass cheeks clapping against his thighs with a wet *whap*. Her orgasm rocketed into new life at the sensation of his cock fully sheathed in her body. She quivered and rocked in mindless pleasure but snapped into awareness at the sharp, lashlike quality of Jack's voice.

"Fuck, Belle. Do you hear me? *Fuck* me you beautiful girl."

She gave a cry of surprise when Jack spanked her right ass cheek once, then twice, brisk enough to sting. It effectively broke through her post-climactic, insensate state.

"Now, Belle," he muttered grimly.

Belle immediately tensed her thighs and raised herself, only to sink back on him when she'd almost cleared the smooth, plum-sized head of his cock. His uneven shout of gratification was her reward. She felt how desperately he gripped her and pulled her back down.

She glanced back at his face. Her eyes went wide.

Every muscle in Jack's body flexed so hard, he looked like he was about to break. It was an unarguably arousing sight, but also a little awe-inspiring that so much power could be locked up in one individual. Her thighs tensed and her hips began to pump furiously as a result of what she saw. She fucked him singlemindedly, desperate to give him the relief he so obviously needed.

When he growled loudly and held her ass down on him, Belle braced herself to be the recipient of all that pent-up energy. He lifted himself off the seat and gave it to her with forceful jabbing thrusts as he came. The shout that followed sounded like he couldn't quite grasp how good it felt.

Belle struggled for breath at the sensation of his cock lengthening and jerking furiously in orgasm while it was embedded deep inside of her. Without realizing she was doing it, her first two fingers slid down over her slick clit. She rolled her hips in a tight circular motion, coaxing every last shiver of pleasure out of both of them.

"Sweet Jesus," Jack muttered a minute later. He came to full awareness at the sound of the shower running and water trickling down the shower drain. Belle was still sitting in his lap, his cock still embedded in her. She was leaning forward, belly to thigh. Her right arm hung slackly next to her, her fingers trailing loosely in the swirling water. He could see the sides of the firm, apricot-hued globes of her breasts.

Jack looked away with determination and studied the water as it jetted out of the showerhead above him.

Belle moaned at the sensation of Jack's cock surging in her vagina. Her head rose from her knees and she glanced back at him. The last sight that she'd had of him before he'd come made her eyes travel over his face and body with genuine concern.

"Are you okay?"

He nodded his head from where it rested against the marble tile of the shower. He found the look of worry on Belle's flushed face confusing but very endearing.

"Uh-huh. But it's entirely possible that a portion of my brain got incinerated with that orgasm though. I hope you don't mind that my IQ might have just been decreased fifty points or so."

He groaned in unexpected pleasure at the sensation of Belle giggling while he was deep inside of her.

"We'd be the equivalent of Copenhagen and Ellie. I'd be leading you around by your cock and you'd still be clueless as to which direction to point it."

Jack almost protested when she glided off the length of him but instead watched her with lazy appreciation as she washed and rinsed off her gorgeous body.

"If you wiggled your ass around as much as Ellie does for Copenhagen, I'd consider the brain cells a very good sacrifice," he murmured.

When he saw that she was done he leaned forward on his knees. "Go and get into bed, honey. I'll be out in a second."

"Belle?" Jack called when she opened the shower door. Steam billowed out into bathroom behind her.

She turned and met his stare.

"Lie down on my bed and open your thighs wide."

Belle nodded after a few seconds. When he called out her name again quietly she glanced back with wary eyes. The heartbeat in her neck already beat rapidly at what he'd just said.

"When I say wide, I don't mean a few inches. I mean *wide.*

Do you understand me?" Jack waited. He watched hungrily as her upper teeth ravaged her lower lip.

She saw the sudden gleam that entered his blue eyes. He lunged up with alarming speed. "I *understand* you, Jack," she squealed out between peals of laughter as she hurried out of the shower.

EIGHT

BELLE FOUND a comb in her purse and headed over to Jack's luxurious, wrought iron, king-sized sleigh bed. She peeled back the comforter before she partially reclined on her back. She groaned with pleasure. The shower and orgasms had made her very hot but the incredibly soft, high thread count cotton sheets were cool and soothing. Her mind worked as she drew the comb through her wavy hair.

She had to find a way to turn the tables on Jack. He always mastered her so easily when it came to sex. But if Belle wanted to test out if he really was Sean, she had to suck him. It was that simple. Sean's and Jack's cocks may look very similar but surely no two men had the exact same erogenous zones. And Belle's mouth knew every sweet spot on Sean's cock and balls.

All of her thoughts were silenced when she heard Jack shut off the shower. The cool air of the room felt comforting on her overheated sex when she spread her thighs wide and waited, her breath choppy and shallow with anticipation.

Jack paused when he came out of the bathroom a minute later

and stared. Christ. He was only a man but somehow he'd been granted the gift of heavenly delights. He knelt on the bed in front of Belle as if he were a worshipper at a sacred altar. His eyes ran over her again, taking in her lambent golden gaze, her voluptuous breasts, the smooth expanse of her belly, the erotic relaxation of her loose fingers and hands where they lay open on the bed next to her, the silken quality of her thighs, the delicate, sensitive, pink folds of her exposed sex. He thought of the title of a Courbet painting he'd seen once at the Musee D'Orsay in Paris of a nude woman lying back on a bed with her legs spread wide.

Origin of the Universe.

"Ah, honey," he whispered. "You take my breath away." He lowered his head down over her pussy until he was less than a quarter inch away from a pink lip. He inhaled her musky sweetness slowly. He saw Belle tighten at his proximity, at the feeling of his breath brushing her. "You're becoming more relaxed about showing yourself to me. That turns me on."

She moaned softly. Having firsthand experience with what Jack could do to her pussy made her forget about everything else but her desire to have his mouth on her. She flexed her hips, lifting herself toward him.

Jack moved back, just out of reach. She made a sound of frustration. "Tell me what you'd like, Belle."

"For you to put your mouth on me," she whispered.

"A request easily granted," Jack said. He lowered his head and began to devour her, sliding his tongue up and around her lips, nibbling the sensitive flesh, sucking her juices hungrily, agitating and torturing her clit, tongue-fucking her pussy. Belle entwined her fingers in his thick hair, thrashing against him, bucking her hips. A low keening sound vibrated her throat.

He held her steady for his mouth but his biceps and shoulders flexed with the effort of stilling her twisting, undulating movements as time passed and she became more aroused. Belle made a sound of protest when he withdrew his tongue from her honeyed channel. He palmed her and rolled her onto one hip.

Belle gasped when he spanked her exposed buttock three times, making loud cracking noises. Her eyes flew to Jack's in shock. "What did…?"

"That's for not keeping still, Belle," he said with a hard gleam in his blue eyes. "Are you going to be good?"

Belle nodded rapidly. "Yes. I'll try to keep still. Stiller," she added quickly.

Jack smiled at her quick addition and went back to eating her. He traced her glossy lips with his tongue, carefully avoiding her swollen clit. Then he slid two fingers into her. Belle started to beg.

"Jack… Oh, please," she muttered shakily.

"Please what?" He placed his lips directly over her clit, letting his breath caress her. She moaned at the sensation. He pumped his fingers into her hard then twisted his wrist.

Belle's hips jumped up despite her earlier promises. Her ass moved like she was on springs. "Please, *please* make me come," she cried out desperately.

Jack continued to finger-fuck her, liking the feeling of her clinging, tight little pussy pulling him inward too much to deny himself. But he didn't put his mouth back on her. "I was about to make you come, honey, but you broke your promise. Now you'll have to wait. Put your ass back on the bed."

Belle cried out in frustration but she relaxed her hips. "Jack, please. That's not fair." Her pussy was so wet that she could actually hear a lewd slurping sound as his fingers fucked her. Belle moaned and tossed her head on the pillows. She could sense her orgasm, teasing and beckoning, just out of reach.

"We already had the discussion about fairness earlier today, beauty. Now let's try once more." He lowered his mouth again until his lips were almost brushing the blood- engorged piece of flesh that protruded from her sex lips. "Tell me what you want."

"To come! Oh *please.*" She gritted her teeth at the effort but kept her hips still. Jack waited a few tense moments to see if she would keep her position, testing her by fucking her juicy pussy harder with his fingers.

"Good girl," Jack praised finally before he tongued the length of her clit and covered her with his mouth, flexing his jaws hard while he simultaneously shoved a third finger inside of her.

She exploded. She arched off the bed and screamed as pleasure blasted through her.

His nostrils flared with arousal. He growled deep in his throat as he continued to agitate her clit with his stiffened tongue. Belle must have liked the vibration he made because her scream kicked up a notch and the muscles of her pussy convulsed harder around his fingers.

Just when Belle began to sink back to earth again Jack took her clit between his lips and teeth and sucked. She shouted out in disbelief as the orgasm intensified and she found herself flying in a sexual stratosphere once again.

She opened her eyes slowly a few moments later. Jack was lying next to her, watching her face with an expression that was both tender and taut with arousal.

"Hi," she murmured huskily.

Jack smiled. "Hello. How are you feeling?"

"Like a very fortunate woman," she said with lazy content-ment as she curled up against him. Her eyes opened wide when she felt movement next to her thigh. She looked up at Jack in renewed arousal and vague embarrassment. "Jack, you're…"

Jack watched her with amusement but his hand continued to stroke the length of his cock. "I'm very turned on, Belle, and you looked like you were comatose. I thought I would take things into my own hand, so to speak. I'm willing to vacate the position, though, and turn it over to you if you're interested."

He watched her steadily as she stared. His cock thickened even more at the way her eyes darkened and her expression became hungry.

Belle knew she must be gawking but it was incredibly erotic to watch Jack pleasuring himself. When his hand lowered on a downward stroke, Belle couldn't stop herself from reaching for the delicious, smooth head of his penis, fisting him, rubbing her thumb into the slit where pre-cum had leaked out. Jack hissed and gladly turned things over to her.

"Jack?" she murmured after a moment.

"Ummhmm."

"Remember what you said today, about how you could pick my scent out of a hundred women's? Were you serious about that?"

Jack's eyes opened. Belle's stroke was magical. She wasn't pumping him furiously, she was caressing him, teasing him with her strong, little hand in a measured fashion that he loved. "I was being hypothetical to make a point. Surely you knew that," he said with a grin.

"I know." She gripped the firm head of his cock and squeezed, deep in thought. He stifled a gasp.

"But do you really think you could? Identify me that way?"

"I think I could. You're essence is unique, just like everything else about you." Jack's eyebrows drew together when she looked up at him searchingly. He stilled, suddenly recognizing her intensity. He had to crane his head forward to hear her words even though she whispered them fiercely.

"I think I could too. Recognize my lover's taste, his smell. Recognize his reactions."

Jack's bemused expression vanished when Belle leaned down to take him in her mouth.

"*Fuck*!"

Belle barely registered his grimly muttered curse. She was too disoriented from the feeling of Jack shoving her back on the pillows and coming up on his knees to loom over her. She quailed when she saw the tension in his jaw and the fury that glowed in his eyes.

"You lying little bitch."

"*What*?" she gasped.

"You told me that you didn't believe that I was Sean Ryan anymore."

"I don't. I mean, I—"

"Then what was all of that about before? You were planning on running a little experiment on me, a Belle March taste test, so to speak. All for the express purpose of identifying the *real* thing—Sean Ryan's cock, right? *Right, Belle?*"

Belle jumped at his shout. She just stared up at him wide-eyed and speechless.

"You of all people must know how nuts you're behaving," he accused.

Belle closed her eyes, too embarrassed to meet his gaze.

"Holy shit," Jack muttered when understanding dawned. "You *do* know how crazy it is. You know for a fact that it's an impossibility, but you refuse to let it go, don't you? You're holding onto the idea because of one reason and one reason alone—because you're damn stubborn, Belle."

Her eyes sprang open in rising anger. "I'm not stubborn. Just in love."

Jack shook his head. "You *were* in love." He dropped onto his hands and lowered over her face. "Sean Ryan is dead, Belle. Say it."

"No," she began to sit up but Jack pressed her shoulder down with one hand.

"Say it."

Belle stared up into blue eyes that seemed to pierce her soul. She swallowed a knot of emotion that clogged her throat. How could she say *it* with those eyes on her?

"He's dead," she finally whispered.

"Sean Ryan is dead."

Belle glanced up at him with fury. "Sean Ryan is dead," she repeated hotly.

For a few seconds Jack just stared at her. "I'm going to make you believe it, Belle. I loved Sean like a brother. But do you know how insulting it is? To know that you're fucking me, just because you think I'm him?"

A tear skipped down her cheek. "Jack, you're making more of this then there really is. I don't *really* think it, I *do* want to be with you. It's just . . . what are you doing?" Belle asked with amazement when Jack came off her slightly and scooped her legs up into the crook of his elbow behind her knees. His face looked determined and eerily hard as he began to stroke his cock back to full readiness. Belle tried to sit up and move away, wary of the wild anger that poured out of his eyes. Jack grasped her legs tighter, pressing the length of the back of them along his abdomen and chest. He shifted her so that her ankles went to the sides of his face.

"I'm going to fuck you. I'm going to fuck you the way that *I* fuck—selfish and hard, the way that your precious Sean never would. I'm going to fuck you because you've got a tight, juicy little pussy and I want to blow deep in it." Jack placed the head of his cock at her entrance. "I'm going to fuck you like you fuck *me*, Belle, just to get my rocks off."

"Jack, *wait*," Belle twisted her hips in protest but he brought his other hand down and stilled her.

She stared up into his face. There was anxiety in her gaze but he saw arousal as well.

"I really do want to be with you. I don't fuck you selfishly, Jack."

Jack's eyes narrowed as he studied her carefully. Her pussy clung to his cock tip, seeming to beg him to enter. He felt her clench hungrily around him, and ground his teeth hard.

"I'm still going to fuck you that way, Belle. Because *I* want to."

He waited until she opened her eyes and met his gaze. "I'm going to keep your legs tight together so that your clit won't be able to benefit from my downstroke. I'm going to fuck hard and come as fast as I can manage. I'm not going to get you off before I come. This is for me, not you. Understand?"

She nodded bemusedly.

He entered her with one ruthless thrust. She gasped. Her eyes rolled back into her head. Sweet Jesus. She thought he'd fucked her hard before, but that was a whispering caress compared to this. He was ramming into her like a freight train. She opened her eyes and watched him in fascinated arousal. He was watching her breasts as they swayed and jiggled at the impact of his pounding. His pectoral, shoulder and arm muscles flexed large and tight as he held her immobile for his thrusts. Her hips made small bucking movements that matched his punishing, primitive tempo, but she knew that even if she lay stiff and lifeless he would have fucked her with as much focus.

Her pussy was his to do with as he pleased.

His cock looked enormous between her legs, the veins popped and engorged with blood. He shoved her legs back and plunged deeper.

Belle groaned. Despite his insistence that this wasn't for her, she was going to come.

He finally dragged his eyes from the erotic sight of her bouncing breasts and acknowledged Belle's expression. From the sound of her groan and the look on her face, she was going to come. The knowledge rushed orgasm to his front door.

"Tell me whose cock is filling you up, Belle."

"*Jack's, Jack's,*" she chanted mindlessly as she tipped over the crest of orgasm.

Jack threw his head back and gave a guttural shout as he came. The orgasm scalded him. When he returned from the blackness of oblivion, Belle's orgasm was still milking him. He stroked once more. Both of them groaned at the impact.

He dropped down over her, feeling like he'd just been turned inside out.

It took several minutes for their breathing to completely return to normal. Belle watched Jack where he leaned over her. His head was bowed and his dark hair fell over his forehead. Unable to resist, she reached up and ran her fingers through his tousled hair. Her hand stilled when he slowly raised his head and pinned her with his magnificent eyes.

"I'm sorry," she whispered.

He closed his eyes briefly. He was the one who was sorry and his regretful expression said so.

"Will you stop, Belle?" he asked intently. "*Please.* I'm asking you to give up this obsession. How can we have a chance if you keep this up?"

Belle blinked back tears and looked away. "I'll try. But sometimes you're so much like him. I don't understand how it could be possible, but..."

Jack gritted his teeth at the sight of her tears. "That's because it's *not* possible. Belle, *look* at me." He waited until her moist golden eyes met his. "Would Sean have fucked you like I did just?"

Confusion skimmed her expression. "No. But…"

"Belle, you're making me crazy. Just let it go. If you keep it up I'm going to punish you," Jack said darkly. He sighed with regret when he saw the expression on her face but continued with stark determination.

"I'll have you on my terms no matter what it takes. And my terms are that you completely accept me and want me for myself. I'm not as nice a guy as Sean was. Don't make me prove it to you, Belle."

————

In the middle of the night Jack awoke with a start. He was alone. He and Belle had fallen asleep earlier separated in the huge bed. Both of them had been uneasy with what had passed. It hardly seemed appropriate to cuddle up together after Belle had revealed that she still thought he was Sean, and Jack had responded by giving her a cock pummeling.

His muscles tensed in preparation to leap up out of the bed to discover where she'd gone but then his bedroom door opened and a shadowy figure slipped into the room. He lay very still as he watched her cross the room and ease into the bed.

"Belle?" he asked gruffly.

She startled. "I didn't mean to wake you. I thought I'd better take Ellie and Copenhagan out."

"Are they all right?"

"Yes," Belle answered as she flipped the sheet over her.

"Are *you* all right?"

Belle glanced over at him in the darkness. "Yes," she finally answered.

The ensuing silence seemed to throb in Jack's ears. "Will you stay?"

She had asked herself that same question several times since last night. This whole affair with Jack was bizarre. She felt buffeted by so many emotions that she couldn't identify. And aside from all the Jack/Sean strangeness, she didn't know what to make of her sexual response to him. It was over-whelmingly strong. She craved it. But it was embarrassing too. Belle couldn't understand it. She couldn't understand herself.

She only knew that she'd set her feet on a path and she couldn't bring herself to turn back.

"Do you want me to?" she eventually whispered.

"Yes."

Jack felt her turn on her side to face him. He longed to reach out and hold her, but he didn't move.

"Why, Jack?" she whispered into the darkness. "You're right. My holding onto the idea that you are Sean is not only weird, it's very insulting to you. Why would you *want* me to stay?"

"I told you earlier today. You're the most gorgeous woman I've ever laid eyes on. Being with you is sublime. I want you for my own," he stated starkly.

"Oh," Belle muttered, dazed. She felt tears sting her eyes. Jack could say the damndest things. "I'll stay," she whispered.

She murmured in surprise when he slid across the bed and took her into his arms. Her initial stiffness faded quickly when she tentatively touched his chest then inhaled his scent, eventually letting it escort her into the realms of a deep dreamless sleep.

He woke up at dawn the following morning wondering why he felt so at peace. He opened his eyes and saw Belle's face resting on the pillow next to him and knew. He considered making love to her, nice and slow and hot. Instead he released her gently, got out of bed and grabbed some shorts and a shirt from his walk-in closet. She was probably exhausted. And sore.

He grimaced at that thought and let himself out of the bedroom quietly.

An hour later Belle exited Jack's bathroom fully showered and dressed. At the sight of the huge empty bed she paused, warmly considering the night of sleep in Jack's embrace.

She glanced over to where her laptop lay next to her carryall.

Let it go, Belle, she admonished herself.

She checked on Ellie first, but the room where the Irish setter had slept—or stewed—last night was empty, the door open. She didn't find Jack downstairs. She discovered a freshly made pot of coffee in the kitchen, however.

A loud bark drew her out onto the terrace after she'd prepared her coffee. It was turning out to be a beautiful Labor Day weekend. There wasn't a cloud in the sky, although it was cooler than usual for this time of year. Belle was glad she was wearing a loose cable knit sweater along with her shorts with that chilly breeze coming off the lake. She sat down on the stairs that led out to the beach, sipping her coffee and watching Jack play with the dogs, appreciative of the opportunity to study him while he was unaware of it.

He wore a pair of low-rise, long khaki shorts and a dark blue, short-sleeved, collared shirt. He was barefoot. His movements were the sinuous, easy ones of a natural athlete who was comfortable with his body. Belle wondered if he'd grown up vacationing on a beach because he looked strangely natural with the sand under his feet and the water in the background.

She recalled the picture of his parents on the boat and realized he probably had. Jack had that same grace as his parents, that casual elegance that likely was acquired from growing up privileged.

Belle felt a poignant stab of loss when she realized that her automatic thoughts had been fully accepting of the fact that he was Jack Caldwell. She waited for a moment and let the pain settle. Happiness surged up in her unexpectedly, the feeling strangely not incompatible with her sense of loss.

He noticed Belle's presence when Ellie dashed toward the house instead of fetching the ball that he'd thrown to her and Copenhagen. She looked up from scratching Ellie when he approached.

"You got up early this morning."

Jack shrugged. "I'm always an early riser." He tossed the ball up for Copenhagen, who caught it and rushed over to Ellie with it, as though to show off his accomplishment. He smiled at the low, sensual sound of Belle's laughter. "What's got you so happy this morning?" he wondered.

"It just seems like a good day to be alive."

His grin wavered and his eyes narrowed as he watched her. "That it does."

"So what are we going to do today?"

"Downtown Kenilworth is sort of nice. I thought we'd go to lunch. We could browse in some of the shops if you want to. They have this great old-fashioned butcher there. Maybe we could pick up something that looks good for the grill tonight, something for the dogs too. How about a walk right now though? It turns rocky a ways down but there's a pretty decent path that follows the water."

"Your place is amazing," Belle said a few minutes later as she glanced from the beach back to the solitary house. "How did you ever find it?"

"Believe it or not, pretty easily. I used an agent and got lucky for once. I'm considering buying it."

"Do you think you'll like living in Chicago?"

He glanced down at her. Her hair was blowing wildly in the brisk wind off the lake and a curl caught in the corner of her mouth. He brushed it away with two fingers before he answered. "It's looking promising."

Her eyes flicked over to meet his. His gaze was warm and steady on her. Before she knew that she was going to ask it she blurted out, "Jack, what were you doing that morning when I met you? In Lincoln Park? Isn't that a little far from home for you and Copenhagen to be taking a morning walk?"

His mouth flattened with tension. Something in her tone told him that this was related to her Sean Ryan obsession. When he answered her he hoped he sounded calm, despite his rising irritation. He was determined not to ruin such a promising day. "Yes. But it's not far from Diversey Harbor, where Copenhagen and I had spent the night on my boat. It had just arrived from Boston. I'd put it on the lake the day before I met you."

"Oh, I see," Belle murmured. The next few moments passed in silence. They watched the dogs run and play, nipping at each other and barking once in awhile.

"They really like each other," Belle finally said with a laugh, her moment of crisis dimming. "No more…incidents since last night?"

"Not that I've noticed."

"Well it's not like you couldn't notice *that.*"

Jack grunted in agreement.

"Listen, I wanted to talk to you about our dogs'…love affair," Jack said with mock soberness, pointedly ignoring her scoffing noise. "I was thinking, who are we to keep them apart?"

Belle looked at him incredulously. "Don't even go there, Jack Caldwell."

He gave her a wounded look. "What? I mean it. If they like each other and nature takes its course what's so terrible about that? We're going to keep seeing each other. I don't see how we can justify keeping them separated while we're upstairs doing exactly what they want to do."

Belle chose to respond to the simpler, not to mention sillier, topic of dog sex instead of commenting on his matter-of-fact statement that they were going to keep seeing each other. "Typical. You can't see it because you wouldn't have to deal with the consequences like Ellie and I would. What am I going to do with five or six puppies that will probably grow up to be almost as big as me if their daddy is any indication?"

He considered thoughtfully. "Five or six? Do you really think?"

"Maybe more. Besides, all thoughts of puppies aside, if you think I'm going to make it normal operating procedure to calmly eat my dinner while Copenhagen is humping my dog, you're crazy, Jack."

He started laughing so hard that he had to stop after a moment to try to catch his breath. She shook her head but her irritation was all for show. The hitch in her heart as she watched him wipe tears from the corners of his blue eyes was familiar.

And Belle knew she was in some *serious* trouble.

Later on that morning Belle's cell phone rang while Jack was upstairs showering. When she noticed the area code for the phone number she walked out onto the terrace and shut the patio door.

"Belle March? Is that you?

"Yes! Is this Joanne?"

"How in the world are you, Belle?" Joanne Swindon asked brightly. "I couldn't believe it when I got your message."

They spent the next few minutes catching up, finally getting around to Joanne's job at Ellsworth & Burke. Belle glanced warily at the closed patio doors. Jack would be downstairs any minute now.

"Listen, I have an unusual request. I'm dating a guy who's an associate at Holloway & Croft. His new boss is giving him a really hard time. His name is Jack Caldwell. I understand that he used to be a partner at Ellsworth & Burke. I told my friend that I would call you to find out if we could get any insight into his character, find out why he's being so hard on him," Belle said rapidly. She'd never been a particularly good liar.

"Oh, right. Jack Caldwell. That was so sad, what happened to him. I never worked with him directly. I'm in labor relations and Jack Caldwell was a partner in the mergers and acquisitions group. But I do know he was very highly respected by everyone. Of course, most of the women respected him *and* lusted after him. Have you actually seen him yet?"

"Uh…yeah. I know what you mean."

Joanne laughed. "Well anyway, all the lechery was definitely for naught, because Jack Caldwell was apparently gaga about his very gorgeous wife. I remember a friend of mine said she saw a picture of them in his office. She gave up all hope of ever getting a piece of Jack Caldwell immediately."

Belle managed to make some kind of noise of acknowledgment. Even though she'd suspected it from the story Jack told her about his "friend", hearing firsthand proof that he had been married before, and obviously deeply in love, left her feeling strangely heartsore. Did Belle *really* remind Jack of his wife? The lovely brunette woman in the photo in his office couldn't be more different in her appearance in comparison to Belle. .

She shook her head. It didn't make any sense.

"I'll bet the reason Jack Caldwell is so grumpy all the time with your boyfriend is that he's depressed or something. He never did come back to Ellsworth & Burke after the car wreck. Everybody in the car was killed except for him."

"Jack was in the accident too?" Belle asked, a shiver of alarm coursing through her.

"Yeah, he was hurt really badly. His was in the hospital for months, I think. Probably didn't have much of a will to recover after losing his wife. People here were wondering if he was going to come back, and for good reason. He decided to pull up his roots and leave. I hadn't heard where he'd gone until now. Anyway, it's really a sad story. Tell your boyfriend to hang in there. From what I understand, Jack Caldwell is a great guy. Really charismatic. I'm sure his moodiness relates to all he's gone through. He probably just needs a little more recovery time."

"Yeah, I'll tell him," Belle murmured. When she glanced up she saw Jack entering the family room in the distance. She spoke softly and quickly, "Listen, Joanne, I've got to run. I have a friend waiting. But just out of curiosity, do you recall when Jack Caldwell's accident was exactly?"

Joanne paused in thought. "You know, I think I do, because it happened during a holiday and I was out of town. I heard about it upon returning. It was Memorial Day weekend of last year."

Belle said her goodbyes to Joanne in a daze.

Sean had died on that same Memorial Day weekend.

NINE

"BELLE, why do you keep looking at me like that?" Jack asked quietly.

They were nursing coffee and dessert after a delicious lunch at a seafood restaurant in town. The lunch hour crowd had left, but Jack and Belle lingered. They'd managed to discuss everything from the presidential administration's latest blunder to whom *should* have won the Best Actor Oscar this year to the best brand of dog food. But he kept catching her giving him searching looks when she thought he wasn't paying attention.

"Am I looking at you in the same way that you're looking at me?" she asked with forced casualness as she sliced off a bite of the cheesecake that they were sharing.

"What way am I looking at you?"

"Like you're wishing you'd ordered a piece of me instead of a slice of cheesecake for dessert," she said as she popped the sweet morsel in her mouth.

An attractive woman leaving the restaurant glanced over when Jack laughed. Belle gave her a brief repressive look, but she couldn't say she blamed the woman for her appreciative glance.

She wished she could take a bath in Jack's deep, masculine laughter.

Belle grinned when he turned over the dessert menu and studied it in mock disappointment. "Damn, I didn't see that on the menu."

"Regular customers know that it's always available," she murmured. Something occurred to her and her seductress act fell flat. "Or in this case, the er…"

"Only customer?" Jack finished. His blue eyes were lit with warmth and humor as he watched her. His voice dropped in volume as he leaned across the table. "And are you going to let me be a regular one too?"

She studied him with speculative, narrowed eyes. "That depends."

"On what?"

"On whether or not you can keep up your patronage."

Arousal steamed up to join amusement in Jack's eyes. "Funny you should mention it. My patronage is considerably up right this second, honey." His smile widened when she choked on her coffee. He leaned over and murmured quietly. "For a woman who started off the week as a virgin, Belle March, you're becoming downright raunchy."

Belle sighed as she wiped her mouth with a cloth napkin. Her expression sobered. "I'm becoming worse than raunchy."

Jack's eyebrows rose when he heard her tone of voice. "That sounds like disapproval that I hear in your voice."

"That's because it is," she said evenly as she met Jack's eyes.

"You don't approve of great sex?"

Belle glanced cautiously around before she answered. There was no one in hearing distance. "I approve of expressing my sexuality in a healthy way."

Jack considered her for several seconds before he spoke grimly. "The conclusion being that the way you're expressing your sexuality with me isn't healthy."

Her mouth tightened as she watched him but she didn't respond.

"You're referring to last night, right? To that last time?" Jack asked pointedly. When Belle nodded he demanded quietly, "Tell me what you're thinking, Belle."

Belle looked down at the table, unable to meet his eyes. "I'm wondering what you think of me. If you think I'm...a freak."

"Because of the Sean thing?"

She frowned. "Maybe this isn't the best place to discuss it," she said evasively.

"There's no one around, Belle."

She gave him a fleeting look of irritation. "Okay. You can choose your definition of freak. Freak like I'm crazy, or freak like I'm some kind of a...perverted...slut...nympho..."

"Stop it, Belle."

Belle glanced up in surprise from her search for more to words to describe herself when she heard the anger in Jack's voice.

"I won't have you putting yourself down like that. You're an amazingly sensual, exciting woman. There's nothing wrong with the way you respond to me."

"If there's nothing wrong with me then how could I have come while you did what you did to me last night?" Belle hissed.

"Because you know that I would never really hurt you. I might make you a little sore sometimes from screwing you too hard, or I might make your ass a little pink from a spanking, but I would never cause you any serious harm. And every time I do cause you a little pain there will be pleasure too. I would never cause you pain for pain's sake. That doesn't turn me on. It makes me sick."

"But last night…you did that to punish me," Belle whispered.

"I suppose I did," Jack said with hard look. "I was royally pissed off to know that you'd been in bed with a different man than me the entire time." When he saw her expression, he exhaled slowly to calm himself down. That was a completely different topic from Belle's worries about her sexuality. He would do well to recall how inexperienced she was despite her natural responsiveness. "My point is that you trust me to not hurt you. For really serious things I'll tell you, just like I did last night, what I plan to do. And if you don't want me to do it I won't."

"I did say *no*."

"You never said no, Belle. And your body was saying 'yes' loud and clear."

Fury rose in her. "Jack, that's such a rationalization."

"I'll tell you what's a rationalization," Jack said, his voice growing in passion if not in volume. "It's a rationalization for you to call yourself names like slut and pervert instead of just accepting yourself for what you are."

"Oh? And what am I, Jack?"

"You're a submissive, Belle. One of the most natural, beautiful ones I'm likely to ever encounter."

Belle's eyes widened in shock. Long silent seconds passed.

"You didn't know?" Jack asked softly. "Don't answer. I can see that you didn't."

Belle swallowed heavily. "Jack, you're so wrong. I hate all of that stuff. Leather and whips and chains…"

Jack shrugged. "I'm not particularly fond of them either, Belle. Personally I'd prefer a nice, soft knot with a silk scarf rather than something as sophomoric as handcuffs in order to restrain you. Your skin is like silk, only silk should bind it."

"Jack," Belle murmured uncomfortably. Her furtive glance of the now-empty restaurant was guilty. Unaccountably at the thought of him tying her up with one of her prized Hermès scarves she flooded with heat. Belle felt like he'd reached under the table and stroked her pussy bull's-eye fashion.

"Do you see, Belle?" he asked with a deep voice gone hoarse with desire.

Belle blinked. "See what?"

Jack leaned forward. "You got hot just thinking about what I said. It's how you were born, how you were shaped. Belle, you're a psychologist. You know that not everything is black and white. There are degrees. I'm not into anything hardcore, like humiliation or sharing my lover. I don't belong to sex clubs or troll for submissives. I consider myself to have dominant tendencies, but that doesn't mean it's my total sexual identity or that I absolutely require it to get excited. Good, honest, straight sex is just fine and dandy for me a good portion of the time." He grinned wryly. "And that statement is exponentially true for you. I'd consider myself to be a lucky man even if I had to beg for a missionary fuck on hands and knees, as long as you let me do it in the end."

Belle couldn't help but give a small grin at his ridiculous assertion.

"Everyone's preferred spice is different when it comes to sex, honey. And what I want in the bedroom is a woman who is so certain of who she is that she's willing to give control to me for a suspended period of time, trusting herself to me, knowing that I won't harm her even when I might ask her to try something anxiety-provoking, believing deep down that I'll do my damndest to bring us both pleasure. I'm not an idiot. I know how much courage it took for you to spread your legs and show me your pussy while I watched yesterday. I could see the battle on your face. But when you did what I asked you weren't just submitting to me. You were submitting to your true desire. And that's very powerful, very pure . . . very arousing."

Belle couldn't take her eyes off him. Despite her anxiety at what he'd said his face and quiet, sure voice steadied her. Tears stung her eyes. "I'd always thought that I responded that way because I was so comfortable with Sean, because I loved him. If what you're saying is true, then I'm just…"

Pain passed fleetingly over Jack's otherwise impassive face. He reached across the table and grabbed her hand as a tear skipped across her cheek. "Ah, honey. You misunderstand. You're a unique woman. Just because I called you a submissive, don't take the label too seriously. The idea of you dropping to your knees for just any alpha male is laughable."

He hesitated. "I guess it's safe to assume that since you didn't know that you had submissive proclivities, you definitely didn't realize that Sean had dominant ones."

Belle glanced away with chagrin. Of course it was obvious when she looked back on it now.

"Don't get down on yourself, Belle. You're innocent, not stupid."

Belle furtively wiped a tear off her face. Her mind worked furiously as she considered what Jack had said. She thought of her historical sexual behavior, and considered her preferences in this new light.

"It's true that I've always been very attracted to masculine, confident…powerful men. The only problem is they're pretty rare."

Jack breathed deeply with relief. Belle didn't appear to be so plowed over anymore. Instead she looked thoughtful, like she was mulling over a complex problem. "The end result being that you've managed to remain a virgin for almost twenty-seven years. Men were probably intimidated by you, Belle. Your beauty and the way you carry yourself have likely been a natural screening mechanism for your desires. If a man wasn't strong enough to take you, he wasn't strong enough to have you."

"Or I just flat-out didn't want him," Belle added with a roll of her eyes, thinking of Clay. "There was another man, though," she continued hesitantly. "Other than you and Sean, I mean. It was in college. He was a professor who I had my freshman year."

Jack looked stern. "When you were eighteen years old? I'm not going to like this story, am I?"

Belle glanced over warily when the waiter entered the room but Jack made a motion that must have indicated that they wanted privacy because he just nodded politely and exited. "No, it wasn't then. It was when I met up with him three years later at a party. We started an affair, but it was admittedly strange."

"What do you mean?"

Belle looked at him uncertainly. She was more than a little embarrassed by her behavior back then. But she supposed that Jack's assertions this afternoon threw light on the matter. "I hope you don't think poorly of me. I was young. I regret it now more than I can say. I still can't believe I did it."

"Did what?" Jack asked gently. Belle's discomfort was clear, but so was her obvious need to tell him about this affair with her college professor.

"Became involved with a married man," she answered starkly. "It was all pretty sordid. But at that time it was the most exciting sexual thing I'd ever done."

"What did you do with him?"

Belle bit her lower lip. "Not much really. He said that he'd feel less guilty about cheating on his wife if he didn't have intercourse with me. So…he taught me how to suck him. And that's all I did for him, whenever and wherever he wanted it," she whispered.

Jack watched her steadily. "And you liked it?"

She nodded, her cheeks flushed.

"Why?"

"Lots of reasons. But I mostly got turned on by his way with me."

"You submitted to him," Jack said grimly after a moment. "The stupid bastard didn't know what he had right in the palm of his hand. Here's to the asshole's ignorance. Serves him right for fucking around with one of his students," Jack said. He held up his glass of ice water in a quick salute.

Belle smiled wanly. "That's what Sean said too." Her subsequent glance at Jack was anxious. He squeezed her hand.

"It doesn't make me upset when you talk about Sean, Belle, especially when I hear that *too*. Makes me know that you're seeing us separately…more clearly."

"Are you okay with all of this, Belle?" he asked after a moment.

She shrugged. In truth, she longed to ask him about his marriage, about his wife. Was that the kind of sexual relationship he'd shared with her? It must have been if Jack had been as happy in his marriage as Joanne indicated, and as grief-stricken by his wife's loss as he'd covertly revealed to Belle. But she couldn't think of a good segue to the topic, especially since Jack had never truly admitted that he'd been married and lost a wife.

"I'm a little shocked. I just want to think about it some more," she said.

He nodded slowly. "You can talk to me about it. Any time

you want. I'm not trying to define you or our relationship in stone."

She reached out and caressed his forearm him with the hand he wasn't holding.

———

They had fun spending time together in the sleepy downtown for the next few hours. They browsed in a bookstore leisurely and compared favorite authors. In a women's boutique, Belle held up garments that she liked and Jack stood back and nodded with approval or shook his head with a *you've got to be kidding me* expression on his handsome face. He seemed to share her taste for elegant, clean-cut lines, but he was most eagerly approving of soft, shimmering, sensual fabrics like silk. Belle smiled to herself. Jack Caldwell was such a sybarite. To her surprise he had a better eye for color than she, choosing shades that highlighted her skin and hair color with unerring accuracy.

Belle couldn't believe it when he stopped the saleswoman and asked her if they carried lingerie. He followed the employee to a rear portion of the boutique then proceeded to reverse their earlier routine. He'd hold up items he liked with a gleam of amusement and arousal in his blue eyes, giving Belle veto power. She nodded for almost all of his choices, but shook her head when he held up a clingy, insubstantial black bra and thong set.

"Why not?" he demanded.

"There's no support whatsoever in that bra, Jack."

"You don't need support. You're very firm. This material would cling to you like a second skin," Jack said huskily, imagining what she'd look like.

Belle laughed. "Jack, trust me. Women my size don't wear

bras like that. I'd probably give myself a black eye if I hit a bump in the road. I'll bet they don't even carry it in my size."

Jack held up a 34D triumphantly. Belle scowled. How did he know her bra size?

She shook her head again.

"Please, Belle? For me?"

"Humph," Belle responded with mock dismissiveness, secretly swayed by the mischievous glimmer in his blue eyes. It was sufficient for Jack. He transferred the bra and panty set to his other hand.

By the time they walked out the door Belle was carrying a handled bag with one of the blouses that Jack had liked, the black bra and thong set and a classy but sinfully sheer champagne-colored negligee that both of them had agreed on wholeheartedly. Jack had wanted to buy more but Belle wouldn't let him. They finally had settled on the three items as a compromise.

Afterward they decided to get ice cream at a sweet shop. While they were standing at the counter deciding on their choices, Belle gave a happy cry. "Ooh, look! They have old-fashioned cherry sticks." She held up one of the dark red-and-white swirled candies and immediately peeled back the wrapper. "Forget ice cream. This is what I want. My mom used to let me drink my hot tea on Christmas morning through a cherry stick."

She sucked between her lips and smiled at the memories the flavor evoked. She mistook his dazed expression of lust for noncomprehension and explained.

"See, if you put the stick into your hot tea and suck hard enough it'll form a hole in the candy stick. Then you can drink your tea through it like a straw and it makes it cherry flavored."

When the attendant asked what type of ice cream he

would like, Jack reluctantly forced his eyes from the sight of Belle happily sliding the red stick between her full lips. The vision was enough explanation for the sudden erection, but all of that talk about sucking hard enough to drill new holes didn't seem to help things either.

As the attendant began to ring up their purchases, Belle waved her stick. "Just the candy stick for me."

"What are these?" Jack asked the man behind the counter as he pointed to a box of candy sticks packaged differently than the others.

The man glanced over his spectacles. "Oh, those are a new flavor. Eucalyptus and menthol. The Japanese make them. They're all-natural and are supposed to be really good for a cold. You got to watch them though. The Japanese make them a lot stronger than we make our cough drops."

Jack nodded with polite interest. "Can I get a box of them? And the cherry too."

Belle looked surprised. "Are you getting a cold?"

His eyes twinkled. "It doesn't hurt to be prepared."

As they walked slowly down the street later, hand in hand, they passed a barber and Jack glanced in the window and slowed. "Would you mind if I got my hair trimmed? I could use it and this place is completely empty. It shouldn't take ten minutes."

Belle told him that she would run across to the antique store and return in a few minutes.

She met his gaze and they shared a smile when she returned to the barber a while later. Jack was in the barber's chair with a smock covering his shirt, chatting casually with the man who was trimming him up. Belle stood in front of a magazine rack and leafed through the choices, not really interested in finding anything to read, mostly just mouthing her candy stick idly.

The back of her neck tingled with heightened awareness. She glanced over her shoulder several times to look back at Jack, realizing that his gaze was responsible for the prickly sensation. Although he was talking casually to the barber his eyes were glued to her. His stare was downright steamy.

Belle's mouthing movements on her candy slowed, becoming more sensual. She liked the way his nostrils flared slightly at her actions. It did something to her to know that Jack was essentially restricted to that chair. She could tease him a little bit, and there wasn't anything that he could do about it. He'd be forced to just sit and watch.

Jack was barely aware of what he was saying to the barber as he watched Belle, standing across the room with her back turned to him, occasionally turning to watch him with her chin on her shoulder, her eyes enormous in her face. He could easily read the expression in her whisky-colored eyes from this distance. What he saw there made him tense with expectation.

Belle March looked like she was about to do something downright naughty.

He watched, mesmerized, as she held her stick of candy at the tip and slowly sucked it in and out of her tightly pursed red-stained lips with a rhythmic fucking motion. He almost groaned out loud. God, what would it be like to have her cherry red lips wrapped around his cock while she sucked a new hole for him and his seed, along with all logical thought, erupted down her throat? He began to sweat as she continued to torture him.

Belle couldn't believe she did it. But when she saw Jack's face tighten as he watched her suck her candy, she felt compelled. She suddenly dipped her knees, arched her back and shook her jean-clad fanny at him, quick and precise, the ass equivalent of what Samantha on *Bewitched* used to do with her nose.

His eyes bugged open. Jack couldn't help but be reminded of his comment about her wagging her ass like Ellie had for Copenhagen yesterday. His gaze flashed up to her smug, sinfully sexy grin, which was still wrapped tightly around the cherry stick. He suddenly knew for fact that she'd been thinking the same thing when she'd done it.

He grabbed the smock and jerked if off him in one motion.

Belle's expression went from self-satisfaction to wide-eyed disbelief in a split-second. Jack was up out of the chair and tossing a fifty-dollar bill to the shocked barber before Belle could take a breath. When she took in the expression in Jack's eyes she made a sound somewhere between a choking laugh and a yelp of panic.

Before she could think rationally about what she was doing she ran out of the barbershop and onto the street, well aware that Jack was coming after with a grim expression on his face. Her heart thumped wildly in her chest and her breathing was choppy as she gasped with laughter. She shouldn't have glanced over her shoulder, because it slowed her down. Jack's hand snaked out rapidly and grabbed her elbow. She shrieked.

"Quiet, woman," Jack admonished as he pulled her into an empty store alcove. He nudged her until her back was against the wall and pressed his body into her.

She took in Jack's dark expression, but also saw the way his well-shaped mouth tilted up in one corner. He was as amused as she was and taking pains to hide it. She snorted with laughter.

"Think you're pretty cute, don't you?" The grin at the side of his mouth twitched in spite of himself when she laughed even louder. He loved seeing her like this. The mixture of innocence and sensuality in her intoxicated him.

"You should have seen the look on your face," she said between giggles.

"Well you should have seen the look on yours. Thought you were going to get away with all that cock-teasing, didn't you?"

Her eyes widened. "I was just having a little fun. Where's your sense of humor?" She gave a startled cry of surprise when Jack abruptly grabbed her shoulders and turned her around. Belle found herself pushed against the wall of the alcove with Jack's large, hard body pushed into her backside.

"Jack, someone will see," she whispered urgently as she scanned the empty street of the sleepy downtown business district. There was an open hardware store across the street, although Belle couldn't see anyone near the window.

"They might," he agreed with an ominous calm. "Maybe you should have thought of that before, when you were shaking your butt and asking for this." He ground his erection into the furrow of her ass. She moaned at the sensation, all traces of humor vanished. Jack dropped his head, nuzzling her soft curls. "If you're going to tease, honey, you have to be prepared for the consequences."

"The consequences?" she asked breathlessly.

"Umm-hmmm," Jack vibrated next to her ear before he pressed his mouth over her, hot and insistent.

Belle shivered at the impact of his heat on her ear—or at his words. She couldn't be sure which. "What-what kind of consequences?"

"You'll have to wait and see. But I promise you this. Unlike Copenhagen, I know *exactly* what to do when a female of the species issues the kind of challenge that you just made in that barbershop."

TEN

BELLE KEPT HEARING Jack's threat in her head when they sat down to supper later. When Tom O'Sullivan had knocked on the patio door in the early evening to have a brief word with Jack after they'd returned home, Belle had immediately glommed onto him, asking him to stay and have a drink on the terrace. Although she'd been excited by Jack's dark promise, she felt nervous about it as well. She figured that if Tom were there, Jack wouldn't have a chance to put any of his plans in motion. Jack's knowing, amused expression when she attempted to lasso Tom into staying made her realize Jack knew exactly what she was doing. After a quick glance at Jack, Tom said he'd take a rain check on her offer.

"How about a walk?" Belle asked with excessive enthusiasm after she and Jack had cleaned up the dinner dishes that evening. She'd temporarily forgotten her nervousness over a lovely, romantic dinner out on the terrace. After it had grown dark they'd watched a fireworks display that several northern suburbs set off at the lakefront to celebrate the holiday. But her anxiety had crept up on her again in the last few minutes.

Jack shook his head as he leaned against the counter. "Nope. It's time for you to pay the piper, Belle."

"And how am I going to accomplish that, exactly?" she asked warily.

"Go up to the bedroom, strip bare, lay down flat on your belly on the bed and wait for me."

She stared at him. His tone of voice sounded almost casual, but the dark gleam in his blue eyes told Belle he was completely serious. She opened her mouth to say something, anything. Jack quirked his right brow up in subtle challenge.

"Okay," she finally said doubtfully.

"Belle," Jack stopped her when she turned to go. "Tom was on me for not turning on the security system last night. I wanted you to know it was on, so that you don't trigger it by accident. I'll take out Ellie tonight."

She thought she must have misunderstood Jack when she was still lying on the bed alone fifteen minutes later. She'd almost gotten up three different times, only to restrain herself at the last minute. Her hips moved restlessly. The air-conditioning kept the duvet cover beneath her naked body very cool. Her nipples felt rock hard and sensitive pressed into the soft, chilly surface. Her skin began to pebble. She called Jack a few choice words and started to scoot off the bed when she finally heard his tread in the hallway.

She twisted her head to see him when he entered the room, carrying one of the shopping bags from their outing today. Belle watched him as he circled the bed and began to calmly remove items from the bag and place them on the bedside table.

"Are you cold, honey?" he asked politely when he noticed her goose bumps.

"Uh…yes," Belle admitted, most of her attention on what he was putting on the table. Two boxes, which she recognized as holding the candy sticks he'd bought today, a red silk scarf.

And a bottle of lubricant.

Her eyes widened in panic.

Jack paused as he opened up both boxes of candy. "What's wrong?"

Belle had to force herself not to jump off the bed. "Jack, I don't think—"

"Remember what I said. I'll tell you what I'm planning to do beforehand, and you can stop me then if you don't want me to do it. And I'll stop. But you have to wait until that moment. You can't say 'no' before you're there, Belle."

He sat down next to her on the bed and began to run both of his hands over the pebbled skin of her back, ass and thighs, warming her. "Okay?" he murmured after her goose bumps began to smooth.

"Okay," she whispered, her gaze intent on his face.

Jack smiled. "Good. Then turn over."

Belle's eyes opened wide in disbelief when he unfurled a red scarf and kneeled down over her.

"Jack, that's *my* scarf!"

His grin was devilish. "Oh, so it is. I borrowed it yesterday. Thought it might come in handy. And I'll be damned, it *has*. Grab one of the posts with both hands. I'm going to tie you up."

Belle stretched up to reach one of the bars of the wrought iron headboard. She felt like the pulse at her throat was going to jump free of her skin as she waited while Jack secured her arms above her head with the soft scarf. She watched him inspect his handiwork as he knelt back on his heels. The thought struck her that she was glad he hadn't bound her feet, because when his gaze slowly raked her body, her thighs clamped together to still the stinging ache in her sex.

"Struggle against it a little bit, Belle. See if it holds."

She acquiesced, curious to know herself. When she saw how hot his eyes turned when she twisted her arms and shoulders, making her breasts sway and bounce she stopped. Her eyelids narrowed. "You knew it would hold, Jack Caldwell," she accused.

He just gave her a friendly grin, stood and began to undress.

"What . . . what are you going to do?" Belle asked, experiencing both anxiety about the possible answers to her question and rising arousal at watching Jack unbutton his shorts.

He didn't answer until he was completely undressed. Belle's eyes feasted on him. She couldn't help but feel that Jack was doing his share of teasing when he removed his shorts and briefs before his shirt. His cock bobbed and waggled just beneath the hem of his shirt, making Belle turn her head, frustrated with the slight obstruction. When he whipped his shirt quickly over his torso his cock and balls swayed with the movement. Belle unconsciously licked her lower lip, just as hungry for him in this partially aroused state as she might have been if he'd looked like he was capable of pounding nails with his cock.

He grabbed one of the cherry sticks from the box. "First of all I thought we'd see whether you were just being a cock-tease today or whether you would actually follow through on the promises that your sweet mouth was making. Scoot up on the pillows, honey."

Belle wiggled her hips and slid her wrists up the brass post until her upper back was firmly supported by the pillows against the headboard. Jack straddled her body. He slowly unwrapped the candy as he held her gaze. His thumb lowered to press into her lush lower lip. Before Belle suspected what he was going to do he plunged his first two fingers into her mouth.

"Show me how strongly you can suck," he rasped.

Belle immediately closed tight around him, vacuuming his long fingers into the back of her mouth. She saw his eyes darken with desire.

Because he enjoyed the sight so much, he fucked her with his fingers. Her suction only intensified. *Christ, she could probably suck my fingernails off*, he thought in dazed lust. He withdrew his fingers and quickly replaced them with the candy stick.

"Suck, Belle," he ordered in a gruff whisper. She clamped tightly around the candy, her eyes fixing on him with a wide-eyed stare. Jack slid the red stick back and forth between her pursed lips, enjoying the sight, pushing deeper and deeper each time. When she craned upward with her neck, he put his left hand behind her head and held her up while his other hand continued to slide the stick of candy into her mouth.

When he withdrew the candy she made a sucking, slurping noise that made his cock pop up like it knew exactly where it wanted to be. He trailed the damp candy stick around her lips, rubbing her, staining her mouth a dark, luscious red. She stared up at him with eyes shiny with lust.

"You've proved that you can suck hard," he murmured. "But can you suck deep?"

She nodded quickly.

"How deep?" Jack asked almost distractedly as he continued to stain her lips.

Her reddened tongue flicked rapidly against her lower lip. "I probably could suck you down to your balls if you gave me enough time," she whispered.

Jack stopped what he was doing despite himself. His eyes were brilliant, fiery crescents as he studied her through narrowed eyes. "Are you teasing me again, Belle?" he asked softly.

Her hair shimmered across the pillow when she shook her head adamantly. "I can. Let me. I want to taste you so bad."

His expression went hard.

"I'll decide what the consequences are for teasing," he said. He readjusted the stick of candy so that it formed an extension from his thumb and forefinger and slid it between her lips again. Belle sucked in four or five inches immediately, without him pushing. Jack studied her throat and pushed further. He paused when he saw her gag. Belle stilled her reaction admirably. He could just imagine what it would feel to have the head of his cock buried in her throat while it vibrated around him.

He readjusted the angle to slide down her throat, his thumb and forefinger sliding into her warm, wet mouth along with the stick of candy. Jack withdrew once, all of the way, then slid the first the candy and then his fingers between her reddened lips once again.

He groaned at the erotic sight.

"Enough," Jack said a little harshly when he withdrew the candy completely. She was killing him.

"I can do better if you untie me and let me control the angle."

God, she wanted to suck him. She stared hungrily at his engorged cock. It waved at her tauntingly from where it angled up from his groin when Jack leaned over to set the candy aside. He looked heavy and hard and delicious.

Talk about a cock-tease, Belle thought in frustration.

"If you did any better at sucking, I would be creaming up your belly and breasts," he told her grimly. Without warning he dipped his sticky fingers into her mouth, wordlessly demanding that she clean him. Belle readily removed the residue of sugar with a warm, firm, fluttering tongue. Jack closed his eyes and breathed deeply in order to gain a semblance of control at the sensation. When he realized how poorly his attempts were working at calming himself, he removed his fingers and untied her.

Belle yelped when he flipped her over briskly. He held her waist up and propped two thick pillows beneath her belly and hips, forcing her ass to stick up in the air. Belle acquiesced when he told her to grab a pole on the brass headboard again and he retied her hands with the scarf, but Jack could tell she was bristling.

"Why won't you let me suck you?" she demanded irritably.

"You're supposed to be getting a lesson in the consequences of teasing." Jack straddled her left thigh and spread his hand wide over one cheek of her firm ass. "Have you learned anything yet?"

Belle stilled at the touch of his hand. Instinctively she pressed her clit against the pillows beneath her to still the sharp ache between her thighs. She hated to admit it but all of this tying up business had her hotter than she ever recalled being. "Not to do it anymore?" she asked as she pressed her flushed cheek into the mattress.

"That's not the lesson," Jack murmured as though disappointed, but she heard the amusement in his deep voice. He began to move his hand in a tight circular motion, rotating the flesh of her ass. "I'm going to spank you now, Belle. Not hard and not too many times. You haven't been *too* bad. I think ten times should be enough to give your ass a nice blush."

She gasped out loud when he lifted his hand and smacked a buttock. It stung more than the times that he'd spanked her casually before. She squirmed when he spanked her other cheek briskly, keeping his palm on her ass and rubbing her firm flesh for a moment before he lifted and landed another stinging smack.

"Keep still, or you're going to earn more," he murmured.

Belle's eyes clenched closed. It was humiliating to think of him calmly spanking her ass while she was tied up, naked and helpless in front of him. But her pussy seemed to love it. She felt liquid warmth rush through her sex. Her thighs pressed together desperately. Her nipples tightened against the soft bedding. The cracking noise of Jack's palm on her ass joined the sound of her heart beating excitedly in her ears.

After a few moments Jack paused on a downstroke, rubbing her ass cheek.

"Just two more left, honey. You're ass is coloring up nicely. Are you getting wet?" he asked quietly.

"Yes," Belle admitted, embarrassed but recalling what Jack had told her about responding when he asked.

"Spread your thighs more so I can see."

He stared as Belle spread her legs, and her sex was revealed like a blooming exotic flower.

"Ah, honey. You're so deserving of your name." He absorbed the vision of her, salivating. He roused after a moment and raised his palm. She moaned as he soundly spanked her firm, taut flesh two more times.

She pressed her heated face into the comforter when Jack caressed her bottom soothingly. "Jack, you're killing me," she said in a muffled voice.

His response was a harsh bark of laughter. "If I'm killing you, you're brutally murdering me, honey."

Belle turned her face to the side and watched as he leaned over her. They groaned in unison when Jack's dense erection brushed over her ass. Her escalated breathing stilled when she saw him pick up the bottle of lubricant and one of the menthol and eucalyptus candy sticks he'd bought in the sweet shop.

"What are you going to do?" she asked anxiously. She waited for a tense moment but she only heard him removing the wrapper of the candy and then the anxiety-provoking sound of the flip top of the bottle of lubricant opening. "Jack? I don't know if I'm ready to…"

"Calm down, Belle. I'm not going to fuck your ass. Not right now anyway."

Belle strained her neck around to see what he was doing. Her eyes widened at the sight of him smearing a very thin coat of lubricant over first inch of the candy stick.

"Jack, you're not thinking about—"

"I'm going to put this in your ass," he finished for her levelly.

"*Why?*" Belle asked incredulously.

"Because your ass is beautiful, especially now that it's pink from your spanking, and it'll turn me on to watch this glide in and out of your little asshole. In other words, *because I want to, Belle.*" His gaze rose to meet hers in a silent challenge.

She slowly shut her gaping mouth. "All right," she whispered.

He smiled grimly and spread back one ass cheek. "Push back, honey," he ordered when he pressed the end of the stick to her hole. Belle complied. He slid the stick in and out, dipping it farther and farther into her ass each time until only an inch of purple-and-white candy remained popping out of her. He twisted and jiggled it before he lifted and plunged it back again with one firm stroke. Belle tensed her ass cheeks and pressed her hips into the pillows.

"Relax, Belle," Jack encouraged as he began to fuck her with the thin stick in a rapid rhythm. "It's sliding in easily. It doesn't hurt, does it?" He paused on a downstroke.

"No. Oh… *Oh God*."

Jack withdrew the stick of candy when he heard her unrestrained, loud moan. "What is it?" he asked in alarm.

Belle panted. She wiggled her hips in the pillows. "It was starting to…burn."

"In a bad way?" Jack wondered.

"No! Jack, *put it back*," Belle said. Her desperation distantly surprised her, but she couldn't help herself. The menthol from the candy stick made her ass simmer with an erotic heat that had begun to affect her sex too. Jack reinserted the stick, pressed her ass cheeks tightly together and held it in her hole for a few seconds. The he began to slide it in and out in earnest.

"You knew it was going to do this, didn't you?" Belle accused raggedly as she begun to buck up against the invading stick of candy and ground down to get pressure on the pillows. Her clit sizzled. Her asshole burned with a slow tingling heat that seemed to activate nerves in her pussy that she didn't know existed until now.

"I was hoping but I didn't know it would have quite this effect. Leave it to the Japanese," Jack said half in amusement, half in awe. His eyes were glazed with lust as he watched Belle ass-fuck a piece of candy as if her life depended on it. He blinked in amazement. "Christ, honey, your ass is so hot. You're melting it like it was a piece of ice."

But he might as well have been talking to the wall because Belle was trembling and crying out with the first waves of orgasm. He sank the candy stick, since she seemed to love the heat, and shoved one finger into her wet, quivering pussy.

His jaw clenched tight with barely restrained arousal when he felt how juicy she was. He kept his finger high up in her, appreciating the feeling of her muscular walls rippling around his finger, pulling him in. Her juices wept around his knuckle.

When he wiggled his finger Belle moaned louder. The tiny contractions of her pussy intensified before they slowly began to diminish.

Jack slid the candy stick from her ass. When he leaned down over her a few seconds later he caressed her neck, which was damp with perspiration. "Okay, Belle?"

"Yes," she murmured between gasps for air.

"Do you think you've learned your lesson about cock-teasing yet?" he asked warmly as he brushed her curly hair aside to cool her neck.

"That if I tease you I'll get a stick of candy up my butt?" Belle asked testily.

He laughed. Belle shivered at the feeling of his breath on her damp neck.

"No, that's not the lesson," he said through a grin.

She snorted in amused frustration. "Well, maybe I don't get your damned lesson, but I sure understand the true meaning of ass candy now," she muttered. She couldn't help but smile at the sound of his unrestrained, deep laughter.

"Hmm... Since you're so stubborn, I guess we'll have to just keep trying,"

He sighed with mock resignation, untied her wrists and tossed the scarf aside.

"Stand up next to the bed, honey," he requested gruffly. When he came up next to her he faced her away from him with his hands on her hips. "Bend over, Belle. Spread your thighs," he directed, his voice becoming thick with rising lust. When he flicked open the top of the lubricant bottle again he saw Belle tense and peer over her shoulder but she didn't say anything or move from her position.

"Why are you so worried about getting fucked in the ass?"

"Are you going to?" she asked breathlessly.

"You're forgetting that the final decision on that would be

up to you." He smoothed some lubricant onto his middle finger and spread her ass cheeks. "I'm just going to put my finger in you right now. Push back."

Belle pushed. Jack clenched his eyes shut at his first sensation of her ass. She was so hot. No wonder she'd melted that candy like it had been stuck in a furnace.

"I'm going to make you come now, Belle. I want you to start to associate your ass being penetrated with pleasure, not embarrassment."

"But—" Belle gasped convulsively when he pressed two fingers into her pussy. She tried to speak but couldn't release words, overwhelmed as she was by being fucked rhythmically in both places.

"You were saying?"

Belle pumped her hips and breathed raggedly while she spoke. "It's not that I'm embarrassed…not a lot, anyway. That candy and your finger are a lot smaller than your cock," Belle managed eventually before she gave a deep moan. "Maybe you've never noticed but you're huge, Jack."

"It would take some doing, but trust me Belle—it'll work. But not tonight." He removed all of his fingers from her. Belle cried out in protest but Jack ignored her. He tenderly massaged her tiny, puckered asshole, teasing her until Belle pressed up on him eagerly, begging for penetration without words. The finger slid into her ass at the same time as his cream-soaked fingers pinched her distended clit in a rapid, ruthless rhythm.

She screamed as a powerful orgasm crashed into her. She thrashed and moaned desperately as Jack's fingers pressed and glided against her clit with mind-blowing pressure. His other finger rammed into her ass with force as she came, his palm making a sharp slapping noise against her butt cheeks when his finger completely sank.

His hand dropped away from her pussy but he continued to slam his finger into her ass as her orgasm abated. He gripped his aching cock and slid his fisted palm down the length. He didn't think he could take this torture a second longer.

"Wag your ass and show me what you've wanted all along, Belle," he ordered with tense desire.

Belle sent her tailbone up and wagged. Jack managed to take about two seconds of watching a sight that could probably drive men stark raving mad. He stilled her come-hither fanny abruptly, growled deep in his throat and sank his cock into her in one long hard stroke.

He set an unapologetic, furious pace from the onset.

Belle gasped, shocked anew by the sensation of Jack being inside her, stretching her to her complete limit, filling her. She had to bend her knees to steady her balance. Otherwise, even with his hand holding her to him, the sheer force of him would have bowled her over. He continued to finger-fuck her asshole. The feeling of being stimulated and filled in both places felt indescribable. Her entire sacrum pulsed with a sexual energy that was ready to explode up her spine again at any moment. When Jack changed his angle and began to make precise stabbing strokes downward with his cock Belle began keening in a high-pitched, desperate wail.

Jack heard her cry and recognized it as mirroring his own impending small death.

"Come," he muttered thickly, increasing the strength of his thrusts despite the fact that Belle looked to be straining to keep upright with the impact of him crashing into her from behind. "Come and you'll take me with you."

Not only his words but also the stark need in his voice made her explode with his next crashing downstroke. He shouted out in exhilaration at the sensation of her coming, milking his cock like a silken fist. He jabbed into her hard and deep, ejaculating at her furthest reaches. A groan ripped his throat. The pleasure was harsh. Indescribable.

"Oh my God, Belle," he groaned a moment later between gasps of air. "Fucking you really is sublime."

Belle made an incoherent sound between heavy breathing. He glanced down, taking in the way her neck hung so limply. He withdrew from her regretfully, giving her bottom a caress. Her hair tickled his chest as it settled when he helped her rise.

"Lie down, honey. I'll be right back."

He took her into his arms after he finished washing up. For long minutes they touched and stroked each other silently. Eventually Jack murmured lazily next to her neck, "Did you ever learn the lesson about cock-teasing?"

Belle sighed when he kissed her sensitive skin with his open mouth and caressed her with his rough, warm tongue. "The only thing I learned is that you must want me to tease you again if that was the consequence."

Jack smiled. "I knew you'd eventually learn, honey."

ELEVEN

THEY MADE love for a good portion of the night. When Jack got up around four a.m. to take out the dogs, Belle fell asleep. He awakened her an hour later, his cock hard and pulsing where it lay next to the back of her thigh.

"Again, Jack?" she whispered with sleepy amusement.

Jack moved up behind where she was curled on her side, sleeping. "I keep thinking about you with that candy stick in your ass. It's driving me crazy. You can go back to sleep if you want to," Jack murmured as he playfully nipped at her ear. "I'm just looking for a quickie."

She grunted with amusement. As if she was likely to sleep while Jack fucked her. "How romantic."

She felt Jack's smile against her neck.

"Are you too sore?"

Belle's breath caught when she felt him nudge her pussy. The head of his cock felt smooth and steely-hard against her tender, sorely abused flesh. And yet liquid heat flooded her tissues.

"I am a little sore," she admitted. "But I think it would be okay."

"Sweet Belle," Jack whispered as he slid into her. Belle was shocked when she came again as he made love to her. She'd wanted to give Jack pleasure but she hadn't thought herself capable of more orgasms on top of the innumerable ones that she'd already had that night.

But once again Jack Caldwell stretched the limits of what she knew about her own sexuality.

Belle slept until almost ten the next morning. She vaguely recalled Jack kissing her hours ago before he'd gotten out of bed. After she showered she found a note downstairs from him in the kitchen leaving instructions for disabling the elaborate security system, saying that he'd taken the dogs with him and gone into town to get gas and run a few errands. He'd told her yesterday that he'd bought the four-door pickup truck out in the driveway specifically for jaunts with Copenhagen. Belle supposed that's what he'd used to chauffeur around both large dogs.

She smiled thinking of how cute the three of them must look. She felt a little sad that she'd missed going with them.

The time on Jack's note, however, made her realize that she might have enough time to get on her computer and do some research before he got home. Jack had given her the password when he'd shown her around on Friday night.

It was surprisingly easy to find articles on the Internet about him and his family, especially once she learned his parents' names. There was a score of newspaper and magazine bits about Alexandra Caldwell, mostly concerned with charity events and social activities. Alexandra Caldwell, or Alex, as some of the more familiar society reporters referred to her, was the only child of Jonathan Flager, who in turn had been the only child of Alexi Flager, the oil baron. Allied Shared, the name of the Flager conglomerate, had expanded long ago to everything from computers to satellite technology.

"Jeez," Belle murmured with amazement when she saw the company's vast holdings and realized that Jack and his sister were the sole heirs to all of it.

She clicked randomly on an article about a special event being given at the Flager Newport mansion and was shocked anew. It was another unexpected picture of Sean and Jack. Both of them had pretty young women on their arms and all of them were dressed in formal attire. According to the inscription under the picture the event had been Jack's twenty-first birthday celebration. She breathed deeply, trying to calm her racing heartbeat as her eyes jumped between the images of the two men.

At least she didn't pass out this time. That was progress, wasn't it?

She forced herself to click away from the picture and began to read an extensive biography of Alexandra Caldwell. She was absorbed in a portion about an annual equestrian event sponsored by Alexandra for charity when she heard Copenhagen bark. Frustration filled her as she hastily shut down the computer. She hadn't even gotten to one article about Jack and his wife's car accident.

Jack was in the midst of grabbing a second sack of groceries out of the back of the cab while the dogs frisked and jumped on him and generally got in his way. He shooed them off of him distractedly, but his gaze caught and snagged on Belle. The sight of her walking across the front lawn wearing a white halter sundress that was sheer enough to show the outline of her hips and legs with the sun shining through robbed him of breath. Her hair looked like it had recently been brushed and shone golden in the sunlight. Her feet were bare in the thick grass. She looked fresh and natural and as sexy as an unmade bed. Instead of picking up the other sack, he set the one he held back down.

When she got within striking distance he pulled her into his arms. He devoured her mouth, thinking how delicious she was, how it seemed like he was starved for the taste of her after being separated from her for only a few hours.

"Hmmm, what was that for?" she asked dazedly when Jack raised his head a minute later. His blue eyes were warm as they wandered over her features.

"Because I couldn't help myself," he murmured huskily next to her lips before he kissed her once more and sank his fingers into the soft waves of her hair. "You looked like a man's dream come true walking across that lawn just now."

"As long as you're the man in question."

"No other, honey."

For a full moment their gazes held.

This time *she* reached up to kiss *him*. Jack groaned as she speared his mouth, traced his front teeth delicately then rubbed and teased her tongue against his.

"You should take care," Jack murmured as she licked and nibbled his lips hungrily a second later. "You're sorely at risk of ending up right back in bed."

"How do you know that's not exactly where I want to be?"

"Maybe I was thinking about the fact that I wanted to give you at least a few hours of recovery time. Don't tell me you're not sore after last night."

She sighed and desisted in her seduction. "I'm a little tender," she admitted.

She yelped when he smacked her ass briskly and turned to grab the groceries again. "Hey, how did you know I wasn't sore there?" she asked with fake irritation as she reached for one of the bags. Jack kept both of them in his arms as he slammed the truck door shut with his foot.

"Hell, honey, I was practically playing patty-cake when I spanked you. You didn't think that actually hurt, did you?"

Belle was about ready to refute him hotly when she saw the amused gleam in his eyes. "Patty-cake *my ass*, Jack Caldwell." She tried not to let her grin show when he laughed at her. She followed him as he headed to the house with the groceries. "You didn't make me sore or anything but when you were doing it, it stung."

"It was supposed to, Belle. It wouldn't have been much of a spanking if it didn't," he replied calmly. He saw her open her mouth to make some undoubtedly smart aleck remark. "Enough about it, Belle," he said warningly as his blue eyes sliced over to her. "You're getting me hard just talking about it. And I did make a promise to myself that I was going to leave you be this afternoon."

He shook his head when Belle passed him with a sniff. He could have sworn she swung her ass an extra inch in each direction as she sashayed down the hallway after the dogs, telling him firsthand what she thought of his noble ideas.

And it *was* pure torture keeping his hands off her for the rest of the afternoon. The day was hot and humid with little of the cooling wind coming off the lake that had made the day before so mild. They fixed a picnic lunch with the supplies that Jack had bought in town and ate it on the beach.

They laughed as they watched Copenhagen slosh around, procrastinate and stall in the shallows before he finally let his feet leave ground and treaded water energetically. He barked at Ellie as he dogpaddled, seemingly requesting that the Irish setter join him.

"She's never swum before, has she?" Jack asked quietly a moment later.

Belle shook her head. Ellie was standing at the edge of the lake, alternately creeping forward into the water and then hopping backward anxiously when the light waves hit the shore. Jack stood up abruptly from the spread blanket where they'd been lolling lazily.

"What are you doing?" Belle asked in surprise when he tossed off his t-shirt and began unbuttoning his cargo shorts. He unceremoniously hooked his thumbs into the waistband of his boxer briefs and jerked them down. "Jack? You can't take off all of your clothes out here."

"Who says? It's my beach."

"But…" Belle's protest died on her tongue as she watched him saunter down the beach as insouciant and as beautiful as a Greek god would be as he strolled around Mount Olympus. He soothed Ellie with his voice and with his hand. He took her by the collar and walked side by side with her until they'd breached the waves, which seemed to be the source of Ellie's skittishness. When the water reached Ellie's neck and her feet were still on ground Jack sank down into the water until he was at the Irish setter's level. He moved just ahead of her and cajoled her gently with his deep voice. Ellie made a whining noise of frustration when Jack clapped once in a request for her to come to him. Copenhagen chimed in with a loud bark.

Finally instinct took over and Ellie launched forward. She gave a triumphant bark as she paddled toward Jack and was rewarded with his laughter and an exuberant ear scratching.

Belle hadn't even realized she'd stood and walked toward the beach until she saw her dog splash forward with blind trust toward the man in the water. Jack abruptly stopped his horseplay with the dogs when he took in the sight of her standing at the edge of the lake.

"What's wrong?" He couldn't quite interpret the expression on Belle's face but it made him wary. He wondered if he'd imagined it a second later when she smiled brightly. Jack had thought the sun was out before but he knew he'd been wrong.

Her smile was like the sun breaking cleanly and completely through clouds that he hadn't realized existed until now.

"Is Tom here?" she called out.

"No. He left a little bit after I got home."

She immediately reached around her neck and untied the halter of the sundress she wore. Jack watched in awe as the top fell down and her breasts were bared. They swayed gracefully at her movements. She slid the zipper at her waist down and stepped out of the dress carefully. Underneath she wore only a pair of white silk panties. He felt his cock lengthen and stretch despite the coolness of the Lake Michigan water when she stepped out of her panties and tossed them on top of her dress. He waited for her to come to him but it was a trial to be patient.

"It's cold," she said with a grin when the water lapped around her waist. Her nipples pulled tight and hard.

He smiled. None of the classical Italian painters had ever portrayed such a pretty water nymph.

"Come here and I'll warm you up," he replied, his voice thick with sensual promise.

Belle took one look at those piercing eyes, so light in his otherwise tanned and shadowed face, and dove in the water, taking a few necessary strokes to get to him. His round, dense shoulder muscles felt warm and wonderful beneath her chilled fingers.

"Are you touching bottom?" Belle asked incredulously when her feet tried to find the bottom and failed.

"Uh-huh." Their faces were close together when he leaned his head down. "Just hang on. You're not heavy. I think these keep you pretty buoyant."

"*Jack*," Belle said with a puff of exhaling air that turned into a purr. He massaged her breasts in his hands. The sensation of his warm caress in the cool water was wonderful. He plucked at and finessed her already tight nipples until she pebbled further. When he pinched her lightly Belle moaned and shifted her hips. Her eyes flew to his as her lower belly brushed up against the solid length of his penis. Jack clenched his jaw tight, stifling a growl of arousal.

"Do you swim well?" Jack asked in a gravelly voice.

She nodded her head.

"Come on then. Let's swim out away."

"But Jack…" Belle removed one of her hands from his shoulders, intending to stroke his cock. Jack grabbed her sinking hand.

"You said that you were going to warm me up," she reminded him.

"I wasn't lying at the time. You looked so gorgeous I forgot my promise not to touch you until later. But I wasn't *completely* dishonest. Exercise will warm you up."

She couldn't help but return his grin. Before he could say another word she pushed off, utilizing the denseness of his chest. She sensed him by her side as she swam and occasionally caught sight of him a few feet away as she breathed.

She was a good swimmer but she knew her limit. At some point she paused, treading water. They'd gone quite a ways. Jack got about ten feet ahead of her before he noticed she was no longer by his side. When he surfaced momentarily Belle waved for him to go on if he wanted. As she'd suspected, he had been attenuating his strokes to match hers. His continued pace was much more rapid than Belle could have ever managed. She wasn't surprised to notice that by the time she got back to where the dogs were, he wasn't too far behind, even though he'd ventured far beyond her. She still breathed heavily when she sat down on the blanket and Jack dropped down next to her.

"That was a good idea. It felt good," Belle admitted after a minute of catching her breath.

"Yeah, it did. You're a good swimmer."

"Not as good as you are, but I do like to swim." She stretched back on the blanket. The hot sun felt marvelous on her wet skin. "It wore me out a little."

Jack caressed her damp waist longingly. His hand looked dark next to her skin. "Don't you burn easily, honey?"

She opened her eyelids a crack and examined Jack's naked glistening body with obvious appreciation. "We can't all be bronzed gods."

He grinned. "The goddesses are usually milky white. I like your skin a hell of a lot more. Peaches and cream. Still, you are pretty fair." He leapt up. "I'll go see if I can find some sunscreen."

Belle must have fallen asleep while he went inside. She opened her eyes when she heard his deep voice urging her gently to turn over. She complied drowsily. The sun's heat and her strenuous exercise would have put her back to sleep quickly, but the combined effect of Jack rubbing lotion onto her back and shoulders sent her into a content slumber with regretful immediacy. The thought struck her before she crossed the path into complete unconsciousness that his sensual massage was not something to be missed lightly.

She started up from a delicious deep sleep sometime later at the sound of a masculine voice—a voice that definitely wasn't Jack's.

"When did we make this into a nude beach?"

She squeaked and grabbed her dress in a panic. She draped it over her torso and shielded her eyes to stare up at Tom O'Sullivan's amused face. He gave her a friendly wave. She returned the wave weakly. Out of the corner of her eye she noticed that Jack was slowly raising his head. He looked like he'd fallen asleep too, and was now completely grouchy about the interruption of his nap.

"Go *away*, Tom," Jack said shortly before his dark head dropped back on the blanket. He opened one blue eye and realized Belle was awake. He sighed in frustration when he saw her panicked expression. "Tom, turn around for Christ's sake. You're making Belle uncomfortable."

"I have to talk to you about something, Jack. In private. Now."

Jack's stare was stony when he looked up at Tom. Belle was too mortified to take in the uncharacteristically clipped, businesslike tone to Tom's voice, let alone notice that Jack definitely had.

She gave an incoherent excuse and dashed past Tom toward the house.

———

Belle opened her eyes slowly to the sound of Jack murmuring her name and gently stroking her neck and back. She stretched lazily as she turned toward him.

"I'm sorry. You must think I have a sleep disorder or something. I can't believe I went back to sleep again."

"It's okay. We were up all night and the swim and the sun got you even sleepier. I just woke you because I forgot to tell you we have dinner reservations tonight at seven thirty."

It was on the edge of Belle's tongue to ask Jack how dressy the restaurant was. She'd only brought one dress but it was a classic black sleeveless one that she was sure would work for just about anywhere. But then she noticed the way that Jack was studying her so soberly.

"Is something wrong?" she asked.

His hand fell down to the bed from where it had been

stroking her neck. "Have I done something that made you feel uncomfortable about asking me questions about my background?"

Belle stared at him in confusion. His eyes looked especially brilliant in his suntanned face as he regarded her seriously. "Of course not. Why would you say that?"

"I know that you were looking at articles on the Internet today about me and my family." When he took in her expression, he shrugged. "I told you Tom was my bodyguard, Belle. It's his job to know this stuff."

She made a sound of indignation. "To eavesdrop on me? What… He can tell where I searched because I used your network?"

Jack shook his head wearily. "Believe it or not, it's not on *this* end that he knew. It's on the other end. He has access to a pretty sophisticated program that pulls out patterns and anomalies of hits to any websites that are associated with my family or myself. Random hits don't show up as meaningful. It's the pattern of the number of times and the source that creates a red flag."

"But I just did it once," Belle said.

"Tom said it didn't show up as a pattern but as a singularity, because the search was coming from my own home network. If you want more of the details ask him," Jack said with sudden irritation. "The thing that I want to know is, why you just didn't ask *me* if you wanted to know something. I've been wondering why you never ask me any questions about my life. I was starting to get insulted."

A thought seemed to strike him. He frowned darkly. "Wait a second. This doesn't have anything to do with your Sean Ryan delusion, does it? You're not looking for ways to fuel it, are you?"

"No, it doesn't. And I'm *not* delusional. I'm just a little confused about the way that I feel about you, that's all. If you want to know the truth I wanted to find out more about your . . . well, your wife, to be honest. You're so secretive about her."

There. She'd said it. Belle fully expected Jack to become guarded and elusive but he shocked her by just shrugging.

"I didn't realize I was being secretive about Madeleine. Where did you get that idea?"

She made a scoffing sound. "*Please*, Jack. You told me that story about the *friend* who was suffering so much after the death of the love of his life. I told you at the time that I knew it was *you* and not a friend. And I was right, wasn't I?"

He watched her impassively.

She shook her head at his continued denial.

"Fine. Whatever. If you don't want to talk about your wife that's your business. But don't act like you're shocked that I would have to go to another source because I was curious. Because despite what you just said you *have* made me feel uncomfortable about asking you."

She started to sit up but Jack stilled her with a hand on her shoulder. Belle stared up at him warily.

"You're right," he said after a pause. "I can see your point. Go ahead. Ask me anything about Madeleine that you want."

Belle gave an exasperated sigh at his unexpected carte blanch. But after a moment she realized that he looked entirely serious. She bit her lower lip anxiously.

"Do you just want me to tell you about her?" he asked quietly after a long silence.

Averting her eyes, she nodded her head.

Jack took a deep breath and lay back on the pillows.

"I was married to Madeleine for seven years. I met her in Paris when I was working on an international corporate merger. She was supposedly the second in command to the

Vice-President of Finance of the French corporation, but the VP of Finance was an idiot compared to her." Belle peered over at his profile at the wistfulness she heard in his deep voice.

"We fell in love almost immediately, but it only solidified as we worked on the merger together."

She braced against the wave of pain that swept over her. *Great.* Madeleine Caldwell was not only beautiful, she was smart *and* French. How could she compete with a French accent?

You were the one who asked for it, Belle reminded herself.

"I-I think I saw a picture of her," she murmured awkwardly. "In your office." Jack glanced up at her dazedly but then nodded his head when he realized what she'd meant. "She was very beautiful."

He nodded again. "Inside and out. People were put off by her at first because they couldn't figure out her angle. But Madeleine didn't have any angles. She was just incredibly kind."

"I know about how she died, Jack," she whispered after a moment. She rolled on her side to face him. Despite the growing dimness in bedroom she could see his light eyes watching her steadily. She hesitated briefly, but her hand seemed to have a will of its own. Her fingers caressed his scar gently. His eyes seemed to glow in the shadows.

"I'm so sorry," she whispered. It pained her to think of him suffering so much.

"She shouldn't have died," he said grimly after a moment. "I still feel responsible. Despite the fact that everyone keeps telling me that it was just the cruel randomness of circumstance, I know the truth."

"You were driving?" Belle asked, her eyes wide with compassion.

Jack nodded. "A guy blew a red light and hit the passenger side. He was killed instantly, but so were Madeline and the friend that I told you about before, my bodyguard, Christopher Aaron."

"And you?"

Jack took a deep, steadying breath. "They say I died too. There in the hospital. But I made the return trip back."

Belle's eyes darkened with alarm. "You were *dead*? And they revived you? God, Jack. That's…that's…awful…and…and incredible. Are you glad?" she whispered cautiously after a moment.

He ran his hands through her curling hair. "I wasn't, Belle. I was pretty pissed off about it. I was pretty pissed off about my entire life. Does it sound too farfetched to say that I am now though?"

"Glad you're alive, you mean?"

He nodded. "I've been given a whole new life. At first I just wanted my old life back. Desperately."

"And now?"

Jack put his arms around her. When he spoke his breath caressed her ear. "I'm starting to love this one. Do you think that you could too, Belle? Come to love your life again? After Sean?"

Tears burned in her eyes.

"Yes. I think maybe I could, Jack," she whispered against his chest.

TWELVE

JACK KNOCKED on the bathroom door later that evening and opened it when Belle told him to enter.

"I'm going to shower…in …the…" His words drifted off into silence when he saw Belle. She was sitting on a vanity stool, brushing her hair. She'd showered earlier in preparation for going out that evening. He recognized the bra and thong set that he'd bought for her. A pair of black, lacy, silk thigh-highs encased her long shapely legs. And the real kicker—no pun intended—was a pair of three-and-a half-inch black heels that had tiny sexy straps that encircled her elegant ankles.

"Jack?" Belle turned around to face him instead of watching him in the mirror. "You were saying?" she asked when his eyes finally moved from her breasts to meet her gaze.

"You could have given me fair warning," Jack muttered as he came into the bathroom. Belle watched in bemusement as he put his hands on her shoulders and spun her so that she faced the mirror again. He stood directly behind her and caressed a curl, his eyes burning her with an unwavering stare. "I was right. That bra does fit you like a second skin. Your breasts defy description in that thing, honey."

She smiled at him in the reflection. "It fits all right," she said by way of concession. "You weren't supposed to see me until tonight. You ruined my surprise."

He looked pleased. "Did you dress like this for me?" he asked in a rumbling growl as he sank his fingers into more of her hair. He groaned at the feel of the dense silk caressing him.

"Who else?"

His blue eyes pierced her lambent gaze. After a moment he glanced downward in deliberate appreciation over her body, lingering on the way back up. While he stared his fill he pressed closer to her and let her golden hair fall across his crotch. "Belle? You know how I said that I wasn't going to touch you this afternoon?"

She nodded.

"Well it's six thirty. It's the evening now."

She smiled. "We'll be late for dinner."

"Do you care?"

She shook her head and her curls flowed over his hands. His smile widened.

"God, I love your hair, Belle." He fisted two handfuls of it. "You seduce me with it every second that I'm with you."

"I don't mean to," she said in an amused murmur.

Jack's eyes gleamed in the mirror. "No? Well then, maybe I should fuck it and you before dinner."

Belle stared at him for a moment before she laughed. "Fuck *my hair*?"

He smiled good-naturedly at her reaction but he was already unfastening his shorts, a determined look on his face. "You think I'm kidding?"

Belle shook her head dazedly when he lowered his shorts and briefs. When he stood she blinked at the feeling of his cock standing at attention at the back of her neck. "I know better by now than to ever think you're kidding when it comes to sex, Jack."

She smiled when she saw his rakish grin widen in the mirror. *He'd have made a great pirate.* "What should I do?" Belle asked, interested but also vaguely confused.

"Nothing, really. Just sit there and be my sex object. You don't mind, do you?"

She burst out with laughter. "Jack, you're so…"

"Okay, if it'll make you feel better to do something, brush your hair like you were when I came in a minute ago. Umm, just like that," he growled a few seconds later. He thrust his naked cock into the cloud of her hair as she brushed it. He closed his eyes at the exquisite sensation of having his sensitive flesh surrounded by pure silk. Her curls straightened from her brushstroke, and then coiled back into their natural spirals, swaying around him seductively.

When he opened his eyes he took in her expression in the mirror. Her eyes shone and her cheeks had become flushed. Her dark pink lips were parted just enough that Jack could see her red tongue dart over the bottom ridge of her small white teeth.

"Do you want to see me better while I fuck your curls, honey?"

Her gaze flew up to meet his. She nodded.

Jack shifted so that she could see his cock over her shoulder in the mirror. He fingered one shimmering ringlet efore he wrapped it idly around his cock, just beneath the thick ridge below the head. "Look at the way it coils around it," he said thickly. He abruptly grabbed a handful of her ringlets greedily and plunged into the bounty, the first four or five inches of his cock buried in his tight fist lined with silky curls. He groaned and pumped.

"Christ, it feels good."

Belle's breath came rapidly as she watched him in the mirror. She'd thought watching him stroke himself was the most erotic sight she'd ever seen. But this was downright triple-X rated. In typical Jack fashion he didn't demonstrate a trace of inhibition or shame. He'd said he wanted to fuck her hair, and he was doing just that while she watched. And if the sweat that began to shine on his tanned, taut belly and the glittering expression in his blue eyes was any indication, he was enjoying the hell out of it.

He let the ringlets in his hand fall to swish across his cock, only to grab a fresh fistful in order to subject it to his thrusts. He caught Belle's eye in the mirror.

"Would you let me come in your hair, Belle?" he asked thickly a minute later as he held her gaze steadily. His cock pumped rhythmically in and out of a fist of her curls.

"Yes," Belle murmured, wide-eyed.

His white teeth flashed in his tan face. "I'm not going to, honey. But it turns me on that you would say yes." His nostrils flared with arousal. "Are you getting turned on at all by this or are you just humoring me?"

Belle tried to shake her head but she couldn't because of the way Jack was gripping her hair. "*Not* humoring you, Jack. I'm turned on."

He slowed his movements for a second but moved his fist up on his cock so that he could thrust a little further. "Spring your nipples out of that bra," he demanded as his gaze sank to her breasts and he began to thrust again.

She pushed down the tight fabric so that her breasts spilled over the top of the cups. Jack groaned and his strokes grew more rapid when she ran her fingers over her nipples, pinching lightly. She moaned. Her nipples darkened and pulled tight. She watched in the mirror as her fingers plucked at them until they became distended.

"You're killing me," Jack mumbled darkly. His eyes were glazed with lust. Belle felt a surge of power accompany her arousal.

"Would you like me to touch my pussy?" she asked him in the mirror.

"*God* yes."

Belle opened her thighs wide. Watching him was causing a simmering, pressurized burn to build in her. She lifted the practically nonexistent material of the thong to one side and slid a finger into her pussy. She gasped raggedly at the sensation.

"You're wet, aren't you?" Jack rasped, but he already knew the answer. He'd seen the way she glided so smoothly into herself.

"Yes. Very."

Jack continued to thrust into her soft ringlets but his eyes were like spotlights on her moving hand in her lap.

"I want you to make yourself come while I watch." He noticed the shadow of anxiety in her expression. "What, Belle?"

She hesitated before she answered. What she'd just been admiring about Jack—his uninhibited, raw sexuality—wasn't a quality that she associated with herself. "I'm not sure if I can with you watching," she said uncertainly. "I've never done it before."

He look amused. "Well I've never fucked a woman's hair either."

"You haven't?"

"You inspire me, honey," he muttered tightly. "Your hair drives me crazy."

"Obviously," she murmured wryly. But in all fairness watching him was driving her a little crazy too. She felt hot, horny, even a little raunchy. She ran her tongue along her lower lip when she caught the sight of the thick, smooth knob of Jack's cock poking through her hair. She knew that he was probably spreading droplets of cum in the strands.

Her fingers pulled at the black thong, exposing her whole sex.

"I can do it," she said breathlessly as if in a flash of insight. And she suddenly knew she could. Her feet tingled inside of her heels with a sexual tickle, and her clit sizzled, demanding attention.

"Good," Jack said, his expression that of a satyr. He filled his other fist with her hair at the same time as he thrust his cock more rapidly into the one lined with soft, coiling curls.

She groaned. Her first two fingers were making tiny, very fast circular motions on her slick clit. Jack's brief look of pure lechery had inspired her. She reached up, using the mirror as her guide, and took a heavy testicle into her hand.

Jack's face went rigid. He gasped. "Christ, Belle," he shouted harshly. Since Belle held him securely he could no longer thrust. Instead he pistoned his fist down over his cock.

She moaned when Jack tugged at her hair. Her breath came in short choppy gasps as she brought herself closer and closer to orgasm. She caressed his tautly drawn balls with knowing tender fingers. Her eyes met his in the mirror.

"I want to suck you so bad that it's starting to feel like a physical pain, Jack."

He didn't know how to respond to that, made mute with monumental lust. His balls shrank away from Belle's fingers. To make matters worse, Belle closed her eyes and started to shake and whimper in orgasm.

He'd never moved so fast in his life. He pulled her up and ripped viciously at the material of her brand-new panties, only aware of them as an obstacle to his need. The shout he made when he bent Belle over the vanity and sank mightily into her sounded like it had been torn clean out of his soul. His face pulled with agony at the sheer pleasure of being encased in her tight, convulsing channel. He thrust once, twice, three times.

And then he was right there with Belle as his climax shuddered through him with mind-shattering, prolonged shocks of sexual release.

Their gasps and pants echoed off the bathroom walls. Jack eventually raised himself from his slumped position over her.

"That was interesting," he said wryly when he caught her eye in the mirror.

She saw the glint in his blue eyes. She started to laugh, her reaction kicking up when Jack joined her unrestrainedly.

Belle realized that her breath had never flowed so unrestrictedly, so freely—and that neither had her joy.

THIRTEEN

"YOU'RE NOT EATING MUCH. I thought great sex was supposed to stimulate your appetite. Should I be insulted?" Jack teased after the waiter had cleared and brought them coffee. But his humor existed side by side with genuine concern. Belle had been preoccupied since they left for dinner. It surprised him a little because she'd seemed so happy and carefree after their sexual experimentation in the bathroom earlier. He'd started to believe that he was getting through to her, that she was beginning to care for him. For the past few days he'd allowed himself to hope that Belle could let go of Sean, leave him in the past where he belonged.

He wanted to be the man in Belle's present and future. He wouldn't accept sharing a place in her life with a ghost. It wasn't natural. And it wasn't healthy for her. She'd slowly begun to let down her guard, to let him in. What they'd done last night in bed and this evening in the bathroom took a genuine level of trust.

So what had happened between then and now?

"Belle?" he prompted when she didn't respond about her

lack of appetite. He reached forward and touched her hand. "What's wrong? Why are you so distracted?"

Jack's touch brought Belle out of her reverie.

"I'm not sure," she said.

"Maybe you're miffed because of your panties," Jack suggested, trying the lighthearted approach. For a few seconds he thought it had worked when she smiled warmly.

"If anything I'd be miffed because you insisted that I not put on any other ones. I feel indecent sitting here with nothing on under this dress."

He grinned. "But only you and I know about it. Or the fact that you can be, at times—indecent, I mean."

Belle gave a small shake of her head and smiled as she looked into his mischievous eyes. "I *used* to be decent. Before I met you."

He leaned forward and spoke very quietly. "Are you feeling vulnerable because of the way we've been making love recently?"

Belle went very still. Her large eyes searched Jack's face. "Making love? Is that what you would call it?"

His lips flattened into a thin line. "You wouldn't?"

She studied the tablecloth for long seconds. "You always call it fucking," she finally said in a hushed voice.

He gave a small shrug but his pulse began to thrum more rapidly in his neck. "If it offends you I'll stop. You didn't answer the question, Belle. Do you think I'm making love to you or do you think I'm just using you for my own pleasure?"

She bit her lower lip. "I think you're making love to me. And I think I'm making love to you." Her gaze flicked up to meet his. "Maybe that's what's bothering me, Jack."

The waiter chose that moment to bring the bill. After he gave his credit card, and they were alone again, Jack glanced back at Belle. "Why should that bother you?"

"Something's not right," She said slowly.

A chill passed through him.

"This is all about Sean again, isn't it?" he asked after a long pause.

"*Is* it, Jack?"

She said it so quietly. Her words richocheted around inside his head. For a several full seconds they stared at each other.

The waiter returned with the receipt and his credit card. Belle saw how hard Jack's expression was as he left a tip and signed the bill.

The silence on the way home was horrible. Strangling. Belle honestly didn't want to argue with him. She was having a wonderful weekend. That was the problem.

It was *too* wonderful.

She'd gone and done just what she'd feared doing the most. She'd fallen in love with the apparently furious man in the driver's seat next to her.

When they'd pulled into the driveway and Jack had turned off the engine he turned to her quickly, before she could get out of the car.

"Do you want to know what I think is happening here, Belle?" Without waiting for her to answer he plunged on irately, "I think you've started to let me in. And it's scaring you half to death. What you must be thinking about yourself right now… I mean, what kind of a woman would let a man that she's known for a week spank her or fuck her ass with a candy stick or brings herself off while he watches?"

He leaned over until his face was inches from her face. "What kind of a woman would *love* it?" he asked with ominous softness. "Those are the questions you're asking yourself, aren't they?"

Her breath started to come more rapidly, but she held herself erect and returned Jack's furious stare with a growing anger of her own. "Maybe. Or maybe I'm just wondering how you *knew* I would like it so much."

Jack shrugged but he didn't back off an inch. "The same way every man on the planet ever finds out anything sexual about a woman. You pray for luck and take a chance. The fact of the matter is you're upset at yourself for letting it happen," he challenged, his voice growing louder. "And the only way you can rationalize or make sense of it is by believing in the *crazy* idea that I'm Sean. That would make everything right and good and pure for you, wouldn't it? Because if noble, savior of the downtrodden, ethics was his middle name *Sean Ryan* ever fucked your hair, then hair-fucking must be one of the least known ten commandments. But if you let *me* do it... Hell, it causes you so much stress that you tip over into psychosis."

Her eyes shone with fury now. "You know what? You're *absolutely* right. How I could have *ever* thought there was a trace of similarity between you and Sean is the real mystery here. You don't hold a candle to him."

"You should know, since you're the one who can see his ghost more clearly than you can see me."

She opened her car door and lunged out. "I'm getting my things. I'm leaving."

Jack cursed viciously and nonsensically as he slammed the car door and followed her. Neither one of them spoke as he opened the front door and began to deactivate the alarm. He grabbed her hand when she flew past him toward the stairs.

"Belle—Copenhagen, damn it, get down! Belle, *wait,*" Jack growled out in mounting frustration when the enormous dog ran to greet them and enthusiastically jumped on Jack's hip, temporarily unbalancing him. "Belle, just a—Christ, *down,* you fricking horse!"

Belle took advantage of the distraction of Copenhagen and

lit for the stairs, determined to get her things and then call a cab if Jack refused to take her to her condominium. She kept hearing his words in her head, the memory frothing her already chaotic emotional state. Something struck her, and she halted so abruptly she almost pitched forward on her high heels. She spun around slowly to face him.

"You *lied*," she said.

His brow furrowed. "What the hell are you talking about?"

"That day . . . in Lincoln Park. You said that you grew up a city kid, that you didn't know any horse's names except for the name of a famous horse from a book you read about Napoleon and Wellington. *Copenhagen*."

"So?"

"I knew there was something that I read today that was bothering me, but it didn't hit me fully until now. Your mother is an accomplished equestrian. She sponsors a charity equestrian competition every year in Newport."

His expression turned stony.

She took several steps toward him, her eyes unwavering on his face. "Don't you *dare* try to tell me that you never knew any horse's names when your mother likely keeps a stable full of horses at every house you own. What kind of game are you playing?"

The silence pulsed in her ears.

"I'm so far from playing a game with you, Belle. Why can't you see that?"

But she wasn't listening. "Or maybe you weren't lying then. Maybe you've been lying about everything else," she continued. "Little truths come through that way, don't they, despite all attempts to hide them? Just like that comment you let slip the first time we made love. Or like the fact that Ellie trusts you so much, just like she did Sean. They say animals know these things."

"What *things*, damn it?" he grated out bitterly.

Uncertainty shadowed Belle's face momentarily, only to be replaced by a fanatic fire in her eyes. "Ellie senses it just like I do. She knows you. From before."

Jack shook his head slowly as he came toward her, narrowing the space between them. "How can that *be*, Belle? How can an otherwise rational, intelligent woman believe something so nonsensical? The first time I ever laid eyes on you was that morning in Lincoln Park."

She shook her head adamantly. "No. You're lying, I just can't figure out *why*. The first time you ever saw me was in the condominium elevator a year and a half ago."

He paused, shocked anew to hear her say it despite the fact that he'd known where she was going with this all along. It alarmed him. It infuriated him.

It made him more than a little desperate.

"Look at me, Belle. *Look*, goddamit. I'm not Sean. I'm Jack. Why are you being so stubborn about this? Why are you acting so crazy?"

"Fine," she said slowly, her focused gaze never leaving his face. "I'm crazy. If you were really a complete stranger to me until a week ago, don't you think it would be unusual for you to want to be around me? Most men couldn't run fast enough at the prospect of becoming involved with a mentally unbalanced woman."

He spread his hand on the side of her neck. Her eyes were filled with turbulent emotions but it was the pleading he saw in their golden depths that made him want to shout out in wild frustration.

"I *am* like other men, Belle. I want you so bad it's like a fire in my gut. But if you persist in this obsession, I'll have no choice. You're right. No sane man would actually choose to be with an unbalanced woman. What's more important to you? To feel like you're right? Or to be with me?"

Her eyes widened with surprise. "That's not fair. You haven't even bothered to explain why you lied about not knowing any horse's names. You haven't told me how it was possible…"

"And I'm never going to," he exploded so abruptly that Belle started in alarm. "Why should I have to explain myself? This is all on you. You either decide to trust me, or you don't." He brought his face close to hers so their breaths mingled and their gazes melded. "It all comes down to trust either way, Belle. Whatever you believe, you'll have to trust me, won't you?"

Long seconds passed. She went entirely still beneath Jack's magnetic stare. A strange brew of charged emotions seemed to thicken the air between them. His hand on her neck felt hot, insistent.

He was right. It all came down to whether she could trust this flesh and blood man standing in front of her…*this* man. No matter what the truth was.

"Belle?" Jack breathed out quietly.

She reached up and put her hand on his neck in a gesture that mirrored his. "I do trust you. But *why*—?"

She ceased her questioning abruptly when for the briefest moment—a moment so fleeting that Belle questioned whether or not she'd actually seen it—Jack's face collapsed with pain.

"You might be insane about Sean Ryan, but I'm clearly insane when it comes to you. I want you to know deep down in your soul that I'm different from him. You have to believe that he's dead." Jack shook his head wildly. Christ, he'd even risk pushing her away if it forced her to finally see that Sean Ryan and Jack Caldwell were two separate men.

Belle gasped when he swept her up into his arms and headed for the stairs. "Jack? What are you doing?"

His face looked cold and determined. "I told you the other night that I was going to punish you if you persisted with this." His gaze abruptly pierced her, fire and ice at once. "And that's what I'm going to do."

When she saw his expression she decided to forget about reasoning with him. She'd just make a break for it the first second she could. Some measure of her thoughts must have shown on her face because he smiled grimly. "You didn't think I was serious about it, did you? You're about to find out just how serious I was," he muttered as he kicked the bedroom door shut abruptly in Copenhagen's surprised face.

He crossed to the far side of the bedroom and retrieved the red Hermès scarf from his bedside table. Belle shouted in surprise when he tossed her face first onto the large, soft bed. She immediately began to scoot away from him but Jack caught her ankle, then her calves and pulled her back easily.

"Put your hands behind your back so that I can tie your wrists," he said.

"Jack, you can't expect…"

"I *do* expect it. I expect you to take your punishment. I expect you to remember what I promised you about what we do in bed. I expect you to trust me with no *buts* about it."

Belle's heart seemed to pause in her chest when she glanced over her shoulder at the man who stood over her. He was obviously furious and emotionally overwrought. For a moment, she wavered. But then the truth crowded to the forefront of her awareness again, impossible to deny.

Impossible, *period.*

She trusted him, even at this tension-filled moment.

She eased her breasts down onto the bed and put her hands at the small of her back. He made quick work of binding her wrists. He sat down next to her on the bed. His hands weren't ungentle when he pulled her across his lap, centering her ass directly at the top of his thighs. He shoved her elegant little black dress up to her waist.

He smoothed his hand over a firm ass cheek. "What am I going to do?"

"Spank me?" she asked shakily, her chin on her shoulder.

"That's right. More times and harder than last night. Because tonight you're being punished. For what, Belle?"

She moved restlessly on him. His hand caressed her bottom tenderly, creating a soothing sensation compared to the sting that she knew would come. Her heart started to beat rapidly in anticipation.

"Because I keep believing something that's not possible?"

Jack raised his hand and smacked her once. Belle gasped in surprise and squirmed on him. Jack put his other arm at the curve of her back, stilling her. "I'm going to spank you good and hard because you're stubborn, Belle. Do you understand?"

She nodded her head, her hair spilling around her.

Jack spanked her again briskly.

"Yes. I understand," she said quickly.

He fondled her for several seconds, gauging her reaction. When Belle moaned shakily in anguished arousal, he heard.

He began to spank her in earnest.

She closed her eyes tight as if to shut out the erotic smacking sound of Jack's hand against her flesh, to erase the image of what she must look like in his lap while he spanked her, her dress pushed up around her waist, wearing nothing underneath but her lacy black stockings . . . to block out *everything*: the straining tension of her turbulent thoughts and longings.

She wished she could banish the low moans of excitement that rang in her ears, moans that she knew to be her own. If

Jack was doing this to derail her crazy beliefs, it was working. Only the moment existed. Only him.

Only them.

She began to raise her ass an inch off Jack's lap, offering herself up to meet his lusty downward stroke.

But then she became aware of what she was doing. Wasn't this part of the problem? How she just couldn't accept the part of herself that got so turned on when he did things like this in bed? That's what Jack believed. He'd said the only way she could rationalize her intense, wholesale reaction to him was to believe he was her former love.

She opened her eyes and twisted her head, glancing back. The little that she saw made her sex simmer. Jack looked grim and determined, but his face was also drawn tight with desire. He liked spanking her.

A lot.

Jack felt her eyes on him and met her gaze. He continued to stare at her as he steadily smacked her ass, first one cheek then the other, for five or so more strokes. Then he paused and rubbed her flesh, not tenderly like before but palming her possessively, kneading and squeezing her ass. "Does it sting?" he asked.

"Yes," Belle whispered, her eyes still locked on his gaze.

"I'm sorry, honey. But I'm going to have to spank you more. Head down," he ordered as he gently pushed her forehead into the mattress.

She cried out sharply in surprised arousal. At the same time that he'd pushed her head down he'd abruptly stuck his hand between her thighs and begun to press and glide his first two fingers against her clit. His slipped his last two fingers inside her pussy and thrust in and out. She saw red. She ground her hips downward on his pleasuring hand. She gasped and fought to get air into her lungs.

And then he pulled his hand away.

"Jack!"

"You really like this don't you? To get your ass spanked? You get so wet when you're turned on. That must have been why I got in you with such relative ease on the night I took your virginity. Your pussy is small, but it fills up with such warm, sweet cream."

She pressed her heated cheek into the cool duvet cover and bit her lower lip to prevent moaning like crazy at his gruff dirty talk.

He palmed a round buttock. "I'm giving you ten more. And I'm not going to go lightly on you. Do you understand, Belle?"

"Yes," she answered raggedly.

Despite her agreement her ass popped off Jack's lap and she yelped when he landed a resounding smack. "Jack!"

He paused. "Yes?"

Belle glanced at him, round-eyed.

"Only nine more, honey. Can you take it?" he asked her quietly.

"I think so," Belle admitted truthfully. She tried to force herself to breathe as he cracked off the final spankings. When he was done she felt like her ass was on fire. She moaned softly while Jack caressed her sizzling hot, tender flesh.

He leaned over toward the nightstand and retrieved the bottle of lubricant. "Let's see if you're as hot on the inside as you are on the outside."

Belle's ears focused on the sound of the plastic bottle popping open. She squirmed in Jack's lap in the silence that followed, when she knew he must be lubricating his finger.

"Keep still, honey," he said in response to her wiggling ass.

He spread her ass cheeks with one hand and pushed the first inch of his finger into her. His lubricated finger felt cool and exciting inside of her. The hand that was holding apart her bottom grabbed hold of a blushing cheek and squeezed, urging her upwards. "Come up on me," he said hoarsely.

She complied, and within seconds he was finger-fucking her ass smoothly. Belle moaned louder and pumped her hips more forcefully. Jack growled. His second finger pressed to her hole.

"Try to relax," he ordered gently. "Don't resist it. Push back on it. Good girl," he murmured when his second finger gained entrance. "Hold still now."

Belle whimpered as he stroked her so intimately. Once again her entire sacrum was on fire, tingling with sexual energy.

"How does it feel?" Jack asked after a moment.

"It feels good. In a...bad kind of way," Belle admitted between pants.

He added some force to his finger-fucking and she gasped in response. "Do you like getting a little nasty with me, Belle? Do you like getting your ass spanked and fucked?"

"Yes. God...yes," she groaned.

"Because that's what I'm going to do in a minute. I'm going to fuck your ass."

"With your cock?"

"Yes."

"Because you're punishing me?" she wondered uneasily.

"No, Belle. I'm going to fuck your ass because I want to. And you're going to let me," Jack said darkly.

FOURTEEN

SHE GRITTED her teeth as Jack continued to finger-fuck her, preparing her for much larger faire. Now that she knew that was what he was doing she felt an added edge of anticipatory excitement. Despite her uncertainty about his promised action she ground herself down into his lap, seeking a much-needed release for the sexual pressure that continued to build in her. The realization struck her that she thought she might be able to come just by him finger-fucking her ass.

"You're turned on, aren't you?" Jack asked.

"Yes."

"If you take a third finger I'll let you come." He moved the hand that wasn't fucking her down, just a hairsbreadth away from her swollen clit. "Don't move down, Belle. Only move up, onto my fingers," Jack warned.

Belle could only nod in agreement. Speech had abandoned her. Her body was stretched on the precipice between tension and release. She did what Jack said and took his thumb along with his first two fingers slowly. Her panting became shallow and rapid. Sweat beaded her brow.

"That's it," Jack murmured thickly. He moved his hand up

on her clit and supplied the pressure that Belle needed. She tensed impossibly further until she shattered and shouted. As she was transported with climactic pleasure Jack carefully drew out her orgasm at the same time as he continued to work her more strenuously with his fingers. By the time her tremors had stilled she took him freely, bobbing her ass up to meet his firm downstrokes.

Jack gritted his teeth at the exquisite sexual torment of it. He knew he wouldn't be able to last much longer. He sat Belle up on the bed and rose to attack his own clothing.

She watched him with a dazed focus.

When he stood before her naked, his cock stiff and heavy, he saw the look of uncertainty that trickled onto her delicate features. He waited for a moment and her eyes eventually traveled up to meet his.

Her uncertainty faded, leaving only trust and desire.

He reached behind her and untied her wrists. Belle held up her arms as he whisked her dress over her head. Her bra was the last thing that he tossed aside. Jack inspected her for a long moment.

"Lie down on your belly and reach for one of the bedposts," Jack rasped.

Once she lay prostrate he quickly tied her wrists securely with the scarf. He piled some pillows beneath her hips to lift her ass in the air. He stifled a groan at the sight of her. Her ass was still pink from her spanking. He loved the way she was so firm yet nowhere near skinny. Belle had plenty of rounded, full flesh to take a brisk spanking. He kneeled behind her and caressed her right ass cheek then let his hand trail down over her thigh. Her stockings were always silk, undoubtedly purchased at the finest of boutiques. That turned him on more than he could say. He caressed her firm calf then trailed his fingers over her sexy high heels.

"Jack?"

"What?" he asked.

"What are you doing?" Belle asked as she tried to look behind her. She trusted him but the suspense was killing her.

"Trying to think about something else for two seconds," he admitted. "I'm extremely turned on, Belle." He picked up the bottle of lubricant from the bed and poured a generous amount directly on himself. Belle strained around again. "I'm lubing up my cock," he told her, recognizing that the lack of information was increasing her anxiety.

"Oh," was all she could think to say to that statement. Her breathing started to escalate once again in anticipation. "Will it hurt?" she asked cautiously after a moment.

Jack heard the tremor in her voice and his hand motion stilled. A muscle ticced in his cheek from tension. "I can't guarantee that it won't. But I've prepared you well."

She nodded. "Okay," she agreed shakily.

Despite the tension that corded his muscles, Jack smiled. He separated her ass cheeks and leaned forward. When he pressed the thick head of his cock to her ass he had to close his eyes at the erotic sight. "Take me, Belle. Just like you did my fingers," he whispered unevenly.

Belle's pussy quickened to life at the feeling of Jack's broad head pressed against her. Curiosity and lust overshadowed her anxiety. She pressed up while he held himself steady. She gasped loudly when she felt the bulbous head of his penis slide into her. He felt enormous. She wriggled slightly, liking the pressure.

Enormous and good.

Jack clenched his teeth in restraint.

"Hold still, Belle," he commanded firmly. She relaxed beneath him and he sank another inch.

"Stop," Belle muttered faintly into the bed.

He immediately ceased moving. She was so gratifyingly tight that she was making the skin of his cock wrinkle back at the point of entry despite the fact that he was as hard as stone and stretched taut as a drum. And her heat. God her ass was hot. He closed his eyes again, knowing the sight wouldn't help his control any. He forced himself to focus on counting his inhalations and exhalations. After a few seconds he felt Belle's tension lessen.

"Okay?" he asked.

Belle nodded. Before she could second guess herself she surged up on him, making more of his cock hers. She trembled. "Ah...you're huge, Jack. But I think...I think I might be able to take you," Belle said with slowly dawning realization.

"You'll not only take me. You're going to take it hard."

Belle twisted her neck and caught his eye briefly. She moaned at the sight of him. He looked like he was about to explode with tension. His torso was totally ripped with tight, defined muscles. He was motionless but he wasn't calm. *Calm like a bomb*, she thought in excitement flavored with anxiety. Knowing how much energy he was expending to rein himself in paradoxically gave her strength. She moved up on the thick stalk of his cock, stretching herself impossibly further. Her breath left her throat in jagged puffs of air. His cock stuffed her so....

"*Full*. Oh my God, you're filling me up, Jack."

Jack's eyes were like glowing blue crescents as he watched their mating bodies. The need to sink into her to the hilt pounded at his brain with a savage tempo. For the first time he began to suspect that Belle was right. She was too small for him to be subjecting her to this. But the desire to be encapsulated in her heat, to make Belle his in this primitive way nagged at him relentlessly. He propped himself on one arm and reached between her and the pillow.

She felt like a bug pinned by a needle. She couldn't decide if the safest path was to tell Jack to pull out or to push forward. Besides, he was so intent, so angry with her. He'd tied her up. She was helpless to resist him. He was going to fuck her in the ass for his own pleasure whether she agreed to it or not.

The thought made her arousal pitch exponentially.

The sensation of him in her was strange but also darkly erotic and very stimulating. When she felt his knowing fingers slide against her clit she moaned and trembled. She wasn't only a bug pinned by an extremely large needle, she was a bug about to pop.

"Come, Belle," Jack breathed harshly into her ear.

He slid two fingers in her pussy, pinched her clit and vibrated her. Belle tilted over into orgasm. The stimulation on all of her sacral pleasure centers, the feeling of him pulsing and throbbing deep in her ass, the pressure on her clit and the sliding actions of his fingers in her pussy all combined to give her the most violently explosive climax she'd ever experienced. She screamed and thrashed and temporarily lost consciousness.

And when she came back to full awareness Jack's balls were nestled cozily in the flesh of her ass cheeks. She moaned. Her fingers clutched desperately to the brass post. But all the while she was aware of Jack's harsh, irregular breathing intermingled with an occasional hissing curse. Belle slowly began to relax as her body accommodated him.

"Are you all right?" he asked after a moment.

"Yes," she said with quiet assurance.

"No pain?" he asked tautly.

"No," she whispered.

Jack groaned deeply and clenched his eyes shut when he heard her response. "I'm not going to go easy on you. You need to learn." He withdrew once and sank back into her, gasping at the cruelty of the pleasure. "I want you to know who's fucking you this way. I want it stamped forever in your brain like it will be on mine. There's only room for me, Belle—*Jack*."

He flexed his hips and pumped.

She cried out sharply at not only the sensation of him taking her ass as freely as he would her pussy, but at his words. She gripped the bedpost and held on for dear life. God it felt nasty. It felt *good*. Her hips began to move in rythym with his thrusting cock. Her arousal became so intense she automatically sought relief for it by grinding her clit into the pillows with Jack's repeated, demanding downstrokes.

He grabbed her hips and added the force of his arms to his thrusts, serving her ass to his hungry cock. A series of sharp cries skipped out of Belle's throat. He increased his tempo and strength until he was fucking her without an ounce of restraint. But even in the midst of his almost orgiastic pleasure the dark need to make Belle acknowledge him remained. He fisted her curls with one hand.

"Who does your pussy belong to, Belle?"

"You…Jack."

"And who does your ass belong to?"

Belle whimpered as he tilted his angle, grounding down on her harder. "It's…yours."

"Say my name."

"*Jack*. I'm yours."

He abruptly held her steady and came down on top of her. He reached under her to apply pressure. His face contorted with pleasure and emotion.

"You're *mine*, beauty. Come with me," he ordered savagely against her ear. He sank his teeth briefly into her neck in agonized lust.

A tortured shout ripped through his throat at the same

time as what felt like a gallon of cum exploded from his cock in one concentrated blast. He was blinded by the intensity of the pleasure, his body convulsing seemingly endlessly.

She clamored for air. She felt him stretch impossibly longer inside her body. The sensation of him climaxing was stronger, more acute, in her ass than it ever had been in her pussy. She could actually feel his pulsations and the jets of warm semen. She pressed herself to his fingers, gave herself utterly to the experience, falling yet again into a shattering orgasm. Their shouts intermingled. She felt his hot mouth on her neck, seeking her insistently. Belle turned and their mouths came together in a kiss of deep mutuality and joining.

Their mouths broke apart eventually, both of them gasping harshly for air, both of their hearts beating wildly in their chests. His forehead sank into the mattress beside her head.

After long tense minutes his out of control breathing finally began to slow.

He shut his eyes tightly. He sensed Belle's gaze on him but he couldn't bring himself to meet it. His abrupt curse was crude and furious.

"Jack?" Belle murmured, confused, when he abruptly lifted his upper body off her. Was he still that angry with her? She gave a shaky gasp of surprise when he slid out of her. She'd been so worried about him causing her pain by making love to her in that way, but in the end it was his final withdrawing stroke that evoked the worst hurt by far.

She lowered her arms and twisted around to see him when he briskly untied her. When she repeated his name he didn't turn around. Instead he stood and reached for his clothing.

"I'm going to ask Tom to take you home," Jack said as he pulled on his pants.

"What?" she asked blankly. She couldn't compute what he was saying. The knowledge of what was actually happening came sluggishly. When it finally penetrated, pain and panic came with it.

He didn't speak for several seconds. He retrieved his shirt from the floor and headed toward the bedroom door.

"Tom will be waiting for you downstairs once you get your things together."

FIFTEEN

TOM EVENTUALLY FOUND Jack out on the beach sitting in the sand when he returned after midnight. He plopped down next to him. Neither of them spoke for several minutes as they contemplated the vast blackness of Lake Michigan. Tom finally glanced over when Jack lifted a glass to his lips and drank deeply.

"You're going to wish you didn't pour all that bourbon down your throat in the morning."

"That's the least of my worries," Jack said dully. He shifted uncomfortably. "Was she…was she okay when you dropped her off?"

Tom's mouth fell open incredulously. "You're kidding, right?"

Jack grimaced and looked away.

"Why don't you just tell her, for Christ's sake?"

"No," Jack said with firm resolution, but the fire that usually accompanied his determination was gone. He felt empty. Burned into a hollow husk.

"Stubborn bastard," Tom murmured with irritation. "So what the hell did you go through it all for? All those surgeries?

The uncertainty about whether or not the procedure would even work? Remember? I'm the guy whose job it is to tell you if I have the tiniest doubt. And I *don't*, Jack. There isn't the slightest buzz that would make me worry. Don't you trust Belle?"

That statement brought the fire back. "Of course I trust her. This isn't about that!"

"Then why can't you just tell her the truth?"

Jack's mouth flattened into a thin angry line. "Because the truth always finds a way to ears that want to hear it."

"It's safe, Jack. Do we have to have every expert in the country notarize a statement that it was a completely random accident? Because that's what it was. You were no more responsible than I was."

"You don't know that for sure. What are the chances that it was a coincidence, both things happening so closely together?" Jack stared unseeingly into the inky blackness. He'd thought and said the same words hundreds of times in the past year and a half, but the truth was his belief in them was faltering. He uttered them now more by habit than anything else. It was just that the risk of being wrong in trusting what Tom said was too great…

"No. I *won't* put Belle back into contact with something so potentially dangerous. It was wrong of me to do it before. I refuse to do it again. This was never part of my plan."

"Plans are made to be changed, Jack. You couldn't have guessed that she would react this way. Seems to me like you're a damn lucky man, and you're spitting in the face of your good fortune."

"Don't you even begin to talk to me about my good fortune, Tom," Jack growled ominously.

A trace of regret crossed Tom's face. For a long moment the two men stared each other down in the darkness. Eventually Jack transferred his gaze to the lake, willing himself to calm. He knew that he was just taking out his frustration on Tom because he was a handy punching bag.

"It would have been safe. If *only* she could have just accepted me. Who would have ever guessed that I would curse the woman of my dreams for her ability to love a man beyond death—to love beyond reason?"

Tom sighed and slumped back in his chair. "Especially when *you're* the man that she loves so irrationally," he murmured under his breath.

"You're wrong, Tom," Jack muttered bleakly. "Belle has been wrong. I *am* a different man. Sean Ryan would never have treated her this way."

Why the hell couldn't he have just left her alone? Now Belle would hate him, despise him.

And he'd have to suffer with that cancerous knowledge every day that he lived another man's life.

––––––

"Belle?"

She immediately recognized the voice. She considered not even turning around. The hand on her elbow made her pause though. She was on inner Lake Shore Drive right before it became Michigan Avenue. Plenty of people were around and she didn't want to make a scene.

"Clay," she said coolly in acknowledgement. "What can I do for you?"

"Giving me the time of day is a start. It's probably more than I deserve after the way I treated you a couple of weeks ago."

"*Probably?*"

"Okay, definitely," Clay amended with a charming grin. "Have you been getting my flowers?"

She scowled. She recalled the first time she'd returned from work on the Tuesday after spending the weekend with Jack and the doorman had informed her that the flower arrangement on the counter had been delivered for her. Of course she'd assumed that they'd been from Jack, some attempt at an apology for the way he'd treated her.

Not that two dozen roses would have been sufficient by a long haul. But it would have been a start.

Palpable disappointment had surged through her when she read the card that accompanied the flowers. It was an apology all right, but not from Jack. Clay had sent her flowers almost every day now for the past week. Her doorman's elderly wife had been the regular recipient of them.

"I've been meaning to call you about that, Clay. *Please* stop sending them. It's pointless," Belle said as she resumed walking.

"*Pointless*? Isn't that a little extreme?"

Belle glanced over at him in distracted surprise. "Extreme? No. It's actually very accurate. You must be spending a fortune on those flower arrangements and there's absolutely no point to it."

Clay shrugged nonchalantly as he walked beside her. Belle frowned when she noticed how insouciant and confident he appeared.

"Well if the money is all you're concerned about, don't be. I'm going to be getting a huge bonus from a project that just went through. That is, I will if Jack Caldwell doesn't completely crack up before then."

Belle's pace slowed. "What are you talking about?"

Clay's expression lightened at her apparent interest. "Last Friday Angie Winthrop and I were in a meeting with Jack

Caldwell and Bob Scalini, who's the CFO for Mendex, and James Forrester, who's the CFO for Avitech. They're in the midst of a merger and it's a huge account for us. Caldwell landed it because of some work he did for Scalini while he was in Boston.

"Anyway, Scalini and Forrester have been stalled over an Avitech tax liability and things were getting pretty heated between them. Angie and I were trying to smooth things over as much as we could, but Caldwell was just sitting there, cold as a February Lake Michigan breeze, staring out his office window. All of a sudden he turned around and said, 'None of this fucking matters'."

Clay grinned at Belle broadly. "Can you believe the nerve of the guy? I know I was down on him before, but after working with him for a while, I'm starting to think he's a genius."

She stopped in her tracks in front of a department store window. "Why did Jack say that?"

Clay shrugged. "Hell if I know. The guy's a loose cannon. But it worked because Scalini respects him so much and he was so struck by Jack just laying it on the line like that, that he agreed to the terms on the spot." Clay laughed delightedly.

Belle stared sightlessly at a pair of gold high-heeled shoes on the mannequin in the store window. Her voice sounded far away when she spoke. "He wasn't talking about the terms of the merger. He was talking about his work. Jack doesn't like practicing that kind of law…anymore."

"What? How do you know that?" Clay asked in surprised amazement. Something seemed to occur to him. "Did he tell you that the night of his welcome dinner at the Shanghai Terrace"

Clay rushed to keep up with her when she began walking again, this time with brisk resolution. When he saw her fixed expression he added pleadingly, "Belle, I'm sorry for that thing I said about you and Jack that day at Holloway & Croft."

"You mean when you asked if I was letting Jack fuck me?" she asked calmly as she reached the corner and raised her hand to hail a cab.

"Yeah. That was out of line. I was really pissed off. Belle?"

She opened the door of the cab that stopped smartly in front of her. "I have to go," she said distractedly.

She got into the backseat of the cab and gazed up at a stunned-looking Clay. "You were right, though. I was letting Jack Caldwell fuck me, and loving every minute of it. So I guess the term 'frigid' as it applies to a woman is largely based on the man she's with, don't you think, Clay?"

She slammed the cab door shut. The cab immediately pulled away. The cabdriver met her eyes in the rearview window.

"Hope he can find his balls back there in the street," he murmured in amusement. "Where to, young lady?"

"Holloway & Croft at LaSalle and Jackson. And hurry, would you?"

———

Jack stared at the legal document on his desk rebelliously. How could someone dedicate his life to such worthless crap? He stood up and stalked restlessly over to the window in his office.

God, he wanted his own life back.

No. He wanted any other life. He'd take his postman's life. He wanted his barber's life. Hell, he'd take that guy's life down there on LaSalle Street selling newspapers.

As long as Belle March believed he was a mailman or a barber or a newspaper vendor. As long as he could keep her safe.

As long as she didn't believe he was Sean Ryan.

He didn't turn around when he heard his office door open. "Jack?"

"I don't want to see anyone, Tom," he said woodenly.

"I suggest you don't turn around then."

He tensed and turned around slowly at the sound of Belle's voice. His eyes stayed glued on her face at the same time as he muttered irritably, "Tom?"

"Sorry, Jack. She can be pretty convincing," Tom murmured before he ducked out of the office.

"You shouldn't have come. I don't have anything to say to you," he said flatly once they were alone. But he couldn't stop his eyes from devouring her, making his words into the obvious lies they were.

She was wearing a dark gray pantsuit that was almost mannish in its elegant clean lines. But in typical Belle fashion the ivory blouse she wore was a confection of purely feminine froth. Her glory was gathered at the back of her head in a knot. Only a few escaped tendrils brushed her neck and cheek teasingly. His fingers itched with the need to release the knot and furrow in her rich curls. He didn't move an inch as she came toward him. But his nostrils flared in his otherwise impassive face when she got near enough that he could catch her scent.

"You don't have to say anything to me, Jack," Belle said in a low, mellifluous voice that made the hair on his arms stand on end. "I came to tell *you* something."

She came close and looked up at his face, her heart pounding very loud in her ears. His expression was stony but his blue eyes were lit with emotion as they watched her. Before Jack could stop her or she could secondguess herself, she raised her hand and touched his face. She smoothed her fingertips over his cheeks and jaw and forehead.

Her questing touch and the obvious depth of her emotion made his throat swell uncomfortably. His lungs struggled to inhale and his eyes burned when she pressed herself to him and put her arms around his neck. To be so suddenly enfolded in Belle's embrace, to be surrounded by her scent, to feel her body next to his, was such a blessing. He couldn't abide the idea of being tortured by it. Of their own accord his arms encircled her waist and he buried his head in her neck. Emotion shuddered through him.

She turned her face so that her mouth was close to his ear and spoke to him in a whisper.

"I don't know how it could be. I don't care. It's enough that you're in my arms. I won't speak of it ever again because now I understand that was what was worrying you. I'm sorry if I caused you worry. That's what I came to say."

He raised his head slowly and met her gaze.

"You're all right?" she mouthed in wonder as her fingertips skimmed his face.

He nodded, wondering mutely if his soul was showing in his eyes in that moment as much as Belle's was. She smiled tremulously at the same time as a tear trickled down her cheek. She stroked him with her fingers for an eternal moment.

"Now will you finally let me taste you, Jack Caldwell?"

Jack blinked in surprise at her question. But her fingers at his belt and the name she had used finally soaked into his awareness and he understood her. His throat constricted painfully. He watched in growing amazement and desire as Belle unclipped her hair and it fell in bountiful waves and curls around her shoulders. His fingers rose to caress her cheek softly.

"You have the face of an angel, Belle."

She smiled—the mysterious, elusive smile that had driven him crazy from the very beginning.

And then she sank to her knees in front of him.

Even though she made short work of shoving his pants and briefs down to his ankles by the time Belle grasped him by his root and delicately licked his head he was stiff and wanting. He clenched his eyes, another shudder of emotion coursing through him She eased him into her warm mouth and teased him with her quick tongue. His hands shook when he delved his fingers through her curls, eventually cupping the back of her head.

He glanced down at her and groaned at the sight of his cock slipping in and out of her full pink lips. Her mouth took him again and again, deeper, sinuously. *Oh God*, it was the sweetest torture. He was going to have to move soon…soon.

But he wished he could make this last forever.

"If you only knew, honey…" He paused as he watched her. The cheeks that hollowed out as she applied a steady suction were wet with tears. Jack palmed her head and thrust gently into her wet heat. She adjusted her angle and took him deeper.

"Ah, you *do* know. Don't you, beauty?"

For an answer she gave a low, steady purr of assent. The vibration that rose from her throat made Jack's head fall back. He groaned.

Love and desire unfurled inside her. She longed to enfold him in it, hold him securely inside her. Her need eclipsed her biological barriers, made her calm and sure. She closed her eyes and slid him into her throat. She breathed slowly through her nose and reached up to cradle his balls in her fingers. The look of tortured pleasure on his handsome face when her throat protested his presence, vibrating him, made her even bolder. She took another slow breath and swallowed him further. She pressed up gently with his balls and they brushed her chin.

"Christ, woman," Jack growled as he fisted her curls tightly and began to pump his hips. He panted raggedly as he watched himself slide out of Belle's lips only to be suctioned back into her enfolding depths again and again. He shouted when she wrapped her hand beneath her mouth, fisting and stroking him as well as sucking him.

"If you only knew how much I dreamed about doing this, honey. How much I wanted to fuck your sweet mouth," he murmured desperately. He felt his balls draw up even tighter. He thrust deeply. "How much I wanted to come down your throat, Belle. Just like…"

He withdrew and plunged between her tight lips again.

"Ahh, Ahh…Blessed Holy….Bloody…Fucking…Hell Lord Mother Jesus… *God*, that's so good!"

Jack blinked several times as his focus came back to reality a while later. He immediately glanced down to where Belle still knelt in front of him. His face tensed with concern when he saw how her shoulders were trembling and how wet her face was. He sank down on his knees next to her and cradled her head in his hands.

"Ah honey, don't cr—" His words stilled on his tongue when he realized that Belle wasn't crying but shaking with laughter. "What?" he asked in amazement when her golden eyes finally met his.

"I'd forgotten," Belle mouthed between spasms of laughter. "*Hell Lord Mother Jesus*? What does that exactly *mean*, Jack?" Belle snorted as the hysterical amusement that she'd tried to quell bubbled out of her throat again.

An uncertain grin tilted Jack's lips at her reaction but his eyes grew wary at the same time. He repeated her name soothingly as wiped her tears with his thumbs, but she just kept laughing.

"Belle, stop. Honey, it's okay. Everything is going to be all right," he assured her gently but firmly. He encircled her in his arms. He waited patiently—knowing it was bound to happen —until her wild laughter segued into profound, wrenching sobs. His hand moved rhythmically up and down her back as though he were massaging the difficult, clogging emotions out of her body. He spoke to her reassuringly in a quiet voice, even though he wasn't sure if she was even aware of him in the midst of her tumult.

But Belle heard him. His voice brought her back to herself —back to him. The painful spasms of emotion had begun to ease when Jack rose and readjusted his pants. He lifted her into his arms and brought her over to the leather couch. Belle tucked her head beneath his chin when he sat down with her in his lap. For several minutes neither spoke as Jack stroked her hair and pressed occasional kisses to her forehead. Eventually Belle's crying ceased with the exception of an infrequent hitch in her breath.

"I'll explain everything, Belle," he said starkly.

She glanced up to meet his gaze. "No. Not if it will worry you," she whispered hoarsely.

Anguish touched his features as he glanced around his office.

"Tom checks the house and this office for surveillance devices regularly, even though he insists it's not necessary. At one time I was completely convinced that someone had been listening in on my conversation with Jack Caldwell on the night before he died—the night I was supposed to die—even though Tom keeps insisting that Jack's accident was completely coincidental and unrelated. I'm beginning to think that he's right. But

I'll always have my doubts—my *fears* that he was wrong. So we'll speak of it today, Belle. But please. Never again. You have to accept me this way. It was bad enough what happened to Jack, Madeleine and Christopher. If something happened to you and all because I wasn't strong enough to leave you alone I would—"

Belle pressed two fingers to his lips. "Shhhh. I meant what I said before. I *do* accept you. I don't care what your name is or what you look like. It's enough that you're alive, that I know that it *is* you."

He hugged her to him. His eyes clenched shut tightly. "It was killing me. Do you know how much I wanted to strangle you for not playing along with my plans? Do you know how much I loved you for it? How much I still do?"

He pushed her back slightly so that he could look into her face.

"How?" he demanded in amazement. "How could you have known all along?"

Belle leaned in close to him. "I could say it was your eyes, or your body, or your scent," Belle whispered next to his ear, "but I think I recognized you on a more basic, instinctual level. My body knew you. But it was something even deeper that eventually made me reject what should have been obvious. I knew you because somewhere along the line, you became a part of me."

———

In the end, Jack decided that he didn't want to explain things to Belle there in his office. She called her practice and cancelled her appointments for the day. Tom drove them out to Jack's house. He winked at Belle as Jack led her by the hand toward the front door.

"Thanks, Tom," Belle said with heartfelt appreciation.

Tom shrugged. "Anything for love, right?"

Jack grunted. "Stop, or you'll have Belle thinking that all G-men are romantics."

"G-men? You mean Tom's a—"

"Hush, honey. I'll get to it soon enough."

————

Belle examined Jack carefully from where she sat on the edge of his bed as he changed from his suit into a pair of jeans and a short-sleeved ivory shirt. She wondered at how she didn't have the urge to call him Sean. The realization struck her that he would always be the man of her memories, the man she first fell in love with last year. But he was different now too, his spirit somehow altered, metamorphosed by his brush with death, by his grief, by his feelings of responsibility for his losses. In many ways he wasn't Sean Ryan *or* Jack Caldwell. He was at once familiar to her, but also different because of the changes that suffering had wrought.

Jack is as good a name for him as any.

She felt strangely comforted by the thought. Even though she didn't yet fully understand the story, she sensed that Jack Caldwell had somehow bequeathed Sean his identity. It was like a shield of protection, a magic spell all bound up in the power of a simple name.

And a face.

When he finished and walked over to where she sat on the bed, she couldn't stop herself from blurting out, "How did they do it?"

Jack sighed and sat down next to her. "The federal government can do a lot of things that the general public isn't aware of. But in this case it actually has become publicly known." When he noticed Belle's blank stare, he added, "Face transplants. That's how I got my best friend's face. That's how I got his life."

Even though Belle knew the truth must involve something along these lines, her stomach still clenched in dread. "They put his face onto yours?" she whispered shakily. "But then, he was…already dead?"

He nodded grimly. "His spinal cord was incompletely severed at the neck during the car accident. But he was alive when they brought him to the hospital. I'd only left his office at Ellsworth and Burke a few hours earlier when I got a call from his mother on my cell phone, telling me about Jack and Madeleine's accident. It was all so bizarre, Belle. If it hadn't been for their car accident, I would have been in a car that exploded later that night."

He saw her bewilderment and took a deep breath in readiness to explain.

"You know how I was going out to DC in preparation for Tariq Hasid's trial? I stopped in Boston because I wanted to go over some trial strategies with Jack. Everything I said about him as far as our relationship at the office was true. I just . . . you know, switched the names around. We liked to use each other as sounding boards."

He sighed deeply, his head tilting back.

"I respected Jack more than I can say. He went into private practice, but he could have gone far doing anything that he chose. He was the only person I've ever met who I can honestly say had what it took to be the President of the United States—a good one too."

"You miss him a lot, don't you?"

He nodded. "It's strange. I miss him, I have felt responsible for his death, but in many ways, I *am* him."

"What do you mean?"

He turned to her. "Jack was conscious intermittently when

they brought him to the hospital. He recognized me. He asked me if Madeleine was dead. He asked about Christopher. I respected him too much to lie to him."

"I had nothing to do with them asking him about the…" He grimaced. "Donation of his face. I was horrified when I found out that they'd asked him. See, by that time, the FBI had discovered the plot to kill me with that bomb in the car I would have driven to DC. If I hadn't have been in the hospital with Jack, I would have already been in that car and triggered the device. Hearing about Jack's accident had altered my agenda, and thrown a wrench in some really bad guy's plans. I was briefed about it by several agents from the FBI, the same ones who had been investigating some of the more viable death threats against me. Even before I went to Boston, they had been recommending that I go underground for a while. They insisted that the chances were too great that I was going to get hit. There were too many unknowns for them to cover all the bases."

"But you would never have backed down from doing your job, which was to prosecute Tariq Hasid," Belle said quietly.

His mouth pulled into a grim line. "Yeah. That's what I kept telling them. But a lot of things change when you see your best friend dying in front of your eyes, and you know that his wife and a good friend are on a slab in a morgue— maybe all because of you. Everything I told you about Madeleine was true, Belle. She was a lovely woman. And Christopher was my friend as well as being like part of Jack's family.

"There were several reasons why I eventually agreed to go underground. One of them was Jack himself. I'd made him aware of my situation, and then he heard more details from two of the agents in charge of the investigation. If I continued with the trial I had to seriously consider the idea that I should never see you again, Belle. Jack had just lost Madeleine, so he was in a prime position to make that *very* clear to me."

"But you said that Tom didn't believe that the accident was related to the terrorist plot against you."

He shrugged wearily. "He believes what he believes. I had my doubts, and continued to, although they've faded as time passed," he admitted. "Anyway, there was something else that decided me. Jack begged me to do it. To take his identity."

"He was worried about you, I'm sure," Belle said as she put her arm over his shoulders. She felt guilty about making him speak of this although she knew it was probably healthy for him to cathartically free himself from it. Still he looked exhausted from the weight of the memories.

"He was worried about me. But he was thinking about his parents too."

Belle's hand stilled on his back. "You mean they don't know? They still think that Jack Caldwell survived the accident?"

He lowered his forehead into his hand and closed his eyes, his pain and grief palpable. He nodded once. Belle didn't know how to respond to that. She felt empathy for the Caldwells of course, having also been kept in the dark about true events. But she immediately saw the difference between her own situation and Jack's parents. The person that she loved was still alive, while the Caldwells' son was dead.

"I know it seems strange and maybe wrong to you. But Jack and I had a long history together. We really were alike in many ways. See, one of the reasons that face transplants aren't done is that most people aren't too hip about the idea of donating their faces. But most importantly, the face isn't a vital organ. So all of the dangerous drugs that usually have to be taken when someone gets an organ transplant are seen as outweighing the risk of what is essentially a cosmetic surgery. Of course the government has various reasons for why they might consider face transplants desirable beyond aesthetic purposes, so they've sponsored a lot of research into it."

"You have to take all of those drugs?" Belle couldn't completely mask her anxiety at the thought.

"No. That's what I'm trying to tell you. Dr. Villarage has been doing government-sponsored research that involves the face recipient receiving special antibodies in advance of the procedure. The antibodies prevent rejection of the foreign tissue. It's pretty cutting-edge stuff. She's only done it on animals, and a handful of other human subjects."

"Oh my God. You could have died."

He nodded. "But I didn't. When Dr. Villarage ran a series of tests on Jack's and my tissues she found us to be amazingly compatible to begin with." When he met her eyes his gaze seemed to entreat her. "It really *was* like we were brothers, Belle. By some strange twist of nature or circumstances we really *did* share similar enough DNA to have been siblings. With the help of Dr. Villarage's antibody treatments, my body never even began to reject his tissue. In the end Dr. Villarage declared that Jack and I had been ideal subjects for the surgery.

"It's strange what it does to you psychologically, to look in the mirror and to see another man," he continued. "But in my case, at least it was the face of a man that I'd loved and respected. It's bizarre, but I feel like part of him is with me. For instance this scar—it's *his* scar. He received it from a shard of glass in the accident. But it eventually healed on *my* body."

Belle shook her head in rising awe as she experienced a degree of what he must have struggled with mentally and emotionally in forging his new identity.

"I don't know how Jack could have known but…"

"What?" Belle prompted when he stopped and became momentarily lost in thought.

"I think that he sensed that it could work, that the degree of loss and grief could be alleviated by the circumstances. Both for you and for his parents." He glanced over at Belle.

"Honey, I lied about never telling Jack about you. It was selfish of me, I know, but it was obvious by that time that you sensed me—Sean. I thought if I could diminish in some way what you had meant to me, then maybe you would accept me as Jack more easily. The point is that Jack knew that I had something to live for, *someone.* I think he felt the loss of Madeleine so acutely, that he wanted to give me a chance, even a small one."

"And he did," Belle breathed out with dawning wonder. Shivers ran through her. "Talk about a gift."

"You're telling me. But the one request that Jack insisted upon was that I not tell his parents and his sister Haley. The circumstances were so…fated. It couldn't have worked any other way, unless it was Jack and me. If there was one person on the face of the Earth who could step in and assume Jack's identity, it was me. I already loved his parents and his sister. I love my goddaughter, Erica—Haley's little girl. Even though I'll be the partial recipient of Jack's parents' wealth when they die, of course I'll leave it all to Erica. My parents had passed already, so we didn't have to be worried about dealing with their grief." He studied her intently.

"You think it was wrong of me, don't you? To have agreed to it?"

Belle's mouth fell open in surprise. Had her expressin been showing some indication of judgment? No, that wasn't it, she realized as she studied Jack's face. He was just asking for reassurance about something that he felt doubt about himself.

"I would never assume to pass judgment upon you after

everything you've been through. You had to make some terrible decisions with very little time to deliberate, I'm sure, given the necessity for creating some kind of viable cover-up story. *Of course* you made the right decision. I have no doubt of it."

He nodded slowly. "But in agreeing to Jack's request I felt like I was taking on an extra burden. I became obsessed with the idea of completely assuming his identity, because if the truth were revealed, I would suddenly put Jack's family at risk too. Which to be honest with you, isn't something that I think Jack had time to consider before he died."

She watched him with concern for the next few moments as he stared off into space, his mouth set in a grim line. His eyes abruptly swung over to meet hers.

"I considered never coming into contact with you again."

"You remember what I said that night we first were together. I don't want to be warned off. I want to be with you," she said with quiet steadfastness.

His mouth twisted with dissatisfaction. "I know. I know because I want to be with you too. I craved you each and every day that I was separated from you. But you haven't seen someone you loved lying in a hospital bed dying. He was so strong, so vibrant, and he was decimated into nothing but a mass of living tissue that he couldn't control. It was a cruel, awful death. *Not* what he deserved. If I ever found out for certain that I was responsible for someone else's life like I could have been in Jack, Madeleine and Christopher's case, I think I might lose it, Belle."

His blue eyes burned like crystalline shards when he met her gaze. "And if I thought I was responsible for something happening to you? There's no telling what I would do, honey. But it would probably involve some kind of vigilantism, something that I've fought against for my entire professional career," he finally muttered with stark desperation.

She felt strength and determination surge through her. "First of all, nothing is going to happen to me. Nothing except that I'm going to grow old and get gray hair and probably get really fat."

When she saw his mouth twitch ever so slightly at her words, she persisted. "And I realized something else today when I was talking to Clay." When she noticed his temporary confusion, she shook her head irritably. "Forget it. I'll tell you later. My point is that I realized that you're going to go crazy doing Jack Caldwell's work. Maybe you can't prosecute criminals as a U.S. Attorney like you used to, but there has to be some kind of work that you find more fulfilling. You knew Jack. Surely he had the potential to branch out into other lines of work that wouldn't be too far off his mark but which you might find more fulfilling."

He looked a little taken aback. "*That's* what you were thinking about?"

"Why wouldn't I? I want you to be happy."

He exhaled sharply and gave a bark of laughter. "You amaze me."

She smiled and stroked his hair. "It's not amazing. I just know you. You must have been going nuts doing that work these past few months."

"Yeah, I have been. Between doing meaningless corporate work and wondering whether or not Clay Rothschild was doing you, nutty is a pretty good way to describe me."

She nuzzled his ear. "I would never go to bed with Clay."

"Well you sure kept me on pins and needles. What do you think it was like for me, to see him kissing and pawing you after you went out with him? The only consolation I ever had was waiting for that stupid-ass expression he'd have on his face whenever you'd turn around and leave him standing there in front of your condominium with his dick in his hand and nowhere to put it. That almost made it worth it every time." His eyes turned hard with only a bare flicker of amusement. "I want to stress…*almost.*"

"You watched that?" Embarrassment made her cheeks hot.

He grunted and reclined on the bed. "Not every single time. I couldn't follow you everywhere, but enough times for me to have some serious doubts about whether or not you two were lovers. Tom was about to kill me for making him go over to your place all the time. He was the one who finally begged me just to try to make contact with you, so that he could lead a semblance of a normal life."

Belle chose the safer topic of Tom to pursue versus Clay Rothschild. "That story you told about Tom, that was—"

"A lie?" Jack asked abruptly. "Yes and no. What I told you about the kidnapping plot against Jack and how Christopher Aaron was hired, that was true. Jack's mom was always worried about him, but that incident really escalated her fear. Given my situation it worked out well that Jack's parents weren't surprised that I acquired another bodyguard after Christopher died. I couldn't tell you the truth, Belle. I couldn't tell you that Tom is a federal agent whose job is to protect me."

"I can't believe it," she murmured after a moment of deep thought.

Jack lifted his head from the bed. "Out of all the things that I've told you, you can't believe *that?*"

"It seems like you two really *have* been together for years."

He gave a small smile. "I guess the stressful circumstances created a close tie. Tom was there during all of my surgeries. He was involved in all of the decisions about making my assassination attempt appear successful." Jack rolled his eyes tiredly. "He's definitely seen me at my worst—both physically and mentally. And yet he still volunteered for what must be an incredibly boring assignment."

"And even though he believes that everything went smoothly, you still have your doubts?"

Jack stared sightlessly up at the ceiling. His eyes burned when he blinked. "I don't know. I doubt it more and more every day. I just don't want anyone that I love to be hurt because of their association with me. Is it too much to ask you? That you make the change permanent in your mind? The more you can accept me as Jack the less of a chance there will be for us to slip up, for my cover to be blown—for you to be put in harm's way. Jack gave this incredible gift to me and I've accepted it completely. Can you do the same?"

Belle stroked his hair. "*Yes*. I've already told you that I can. You feel the difference in you. But *I* feel it too. What I told you those other times is true. You're the same...but you're not."

He couldn't help but think of the way he'd treated her on that last night they were together. Belle had been right. He was harder than the man she had known.

"You must be disappointed in the change."

She blinked in surprise at his statement. Neither spoke for several seconds but Jack watched her with penetrating eyes as she considered how to respond. She suddenly laughed raggedly.

"This is so strange."

"Why, honey?"

"Because I feel like I'm betraying Sean by saying this, which is ridiculous because . . . well you *know* why it's ridiculous. But during those periods when I wasn't convinced that you were Sean—which, trust me, were a lot more frequent than you might think—I...I was falling in love with you. *Jack*."

A small grin tilted his mouth. "It may be ridiculous, but it doesn't sound unusual to me. There were times when I would have liked to kill Sean Ryan for standing in the way of our being together," he said with a low laugh. "This whole situation is beyond bizarre."

"There's one thing I don't get," Belle said after a moment. "Why did you tell me that story about the 'friend' who lost his wife? Did you know that I would assume you were speaking of yourself? Did you do it to convince me that you were Jack Caldwell?"

Jack shook his head and grinned up at the ceiling. "No, honey. I wasn't lying then. It was just like I told you. I really was talking about a friend."

"But Jack was already—"

"Not Jack. You."

He watched her as understanding began to dawn on her face.

"After that day in the park I kind of figured out what was happening. Somehow, some way, you were thinking of Sean when you looked at me. I thought that if you could hear your own advice, you might take it. My plan kind of backfired though, because instead you assumed I was talking about myself."

Belle laughed. "You shouldn't have relied on my clinical skills."

"Your sensitivity and your powers of observation do credit both to your person and your profession. I'm the one who underestimated you, honey. I'm still amazed—humbled, actually—that you somehow knew."

He closed his eyes, clearly exhausted. "You're tired," she said quietly as she smoothed her fingertip over his dark eyebrow. "Why don't you rest for a while?"

"There's more to tell."

"I think I have the essentials. Everything else will wait."

"Do you know what I really hate?" he asked after a moment.

"What?"

"Dennis McMann is a damned good prosecutor, but I could have nailed Tariq Hasid so much better."

She smiled wanly, completely unsurprised by his statement. "Hasid will never see the light of day again, and it's largely because of the case that you'd already built before your supposed assassination. Everybody says so."

He sighed. "I know. I wasn't referring to the *man*. I meant his image, the legacy that he's left. I could have nailed him better in the eyes of the world community."

Belle nodded. "Yeah, you could have. I have no doubt of it." She massaged his scalp. "Rest for a while."

"Will you stay with me?"

She nodded against his chest. "You're stuck with me for good, Jack."

SIXTEEN

WHEN HE WOKE UP, Belle was kissing his stomach with lingering, sensual caresses. Jack sighed. It felt sublime.

"Do you mind?" Belle asked as she glanced up and met the crescents of his partially opened blue eyes.

"I would mind it if you stopped," he answered in a sleep-roughened voice.

Belle kissed the furrow between his ribs, tasted him with her tongue, savoring the sensation of his thick smooth skin, inhaling his rich, masculine scent. "You never would let me have my way with you," she breathed out against him. She smiled and dipped her head again to experience the texture of his skin when it briefly roughed with goose bumps.

"And what would you call that in my office earlier? I was at your beck and call, your mercy and your every whim, Belle." His eyes glued on her with avid focus as she tongued his belly-button and returned his gaze. He couldn't figure out how she did it. When he'd first felt her tongue and glanced down at her, she'd looked curious and playful. But once the heat of his gaze soaked into her, she suddenly looked far from innocent and completely aware of what she was doing to him.

"You're a witch, Belle," he whispered as his hand came up to bury in her curls.

"A good one?" she asked huskily.

Jack inhaled deeply through his nose as he watched her trail her dark pink tongue along the strip of hair that swirled across his bellybutton and down into his jeans. Laughter rumbled in his chest.

"You can be a very bad one. But you're a very *good* bad witch." His laughter escalated and his eyes sparked with fire when she bit and flicked and released the first button on his jeans. "Whoa, little witch. Not twice in one day."

"Why not?" she asked irritably.

Jack continued to laugh. God, he loved her.

"Because I have some pride, honey. One-sided lovemaking is very nice once in a while and we both know what it meant to us before. But it's not what I want right now."

She responded by gliding her hand over the dense ridge in his jeans. "I think you'd probably find yourself settling for it, with a little encouragement." She smiled when she saw how he automatically shifted his hips up against her hand and how his eyelids narrowed as he watched her. "Besides, I think you deserve some payback."

He groaned as she mercilessly increased the pressure on him and reached for his fly. He couldn't bring himself to stop her with his hands. Only his mouth seemed to have a semblance of higher level—albeit rapidly dissipating—functioning.

"Belle, wait. How about a compromise?"

She paused. "What sort of a compromise?"

"I have a little fantasy. Will you humor me?"

Her glance was skeptical. Jack laughed. "You're killing me with that look. Have I been that bad with you?"

Belle raised one tawny brow. "You fucked my hair, Jack.

You stuck a candy stick in my ass. You tied me up and had your way with me. Your track record for making love to me hasn't led me to believe that you're very capable of compromise."

His light blue eyes darkened with arousal. "Well, if you think I'm going to apologize for any of that, you've got another think coming. If I recall correctly you were hardly complaining at the time either. Don't you even want to hear my fantasy?"

She glanced down at the considerable bulge in his jeans. "It won't hurt to listen. For a second," she added warningly.

His slanting grin and that flash of white teeth in his dark face made Belle go utterly still. *Damn him. He knows that smile makes me his slave.*

"Okay, here it is. We've talked openly in this room tonight. So I figure we've got nothing to lose. If there was damage to be done it's done already. I used to think about that night I was supposed to come back from DC incessantly. It made me bitter, more so than I care to admit, that I never had that night with you."

All teasing was forgotten when she heard the tone of his voice and sensed the profound shift in his mood.

"But you *did* have it." She reminded him of the night he took her virginity.

Jack shook his head slowly. "I was jealous and half-crazed that night. You have no idea how much I regret it, Belle. I thought of making love to you for the first time in a million different ways. But the only common theme in all of them was that we gave and took, that we shared ourselves with equal measure." He paused as he looked at her somberly. "So here's my fantasy—that we make love like we would have that night, that you call me by my name one last time. And then we'll leave that part of me in the past where it belongs. Can you do that, Belle?" he asked her quietly.

She blinked back the sudden swell of tears in her eyes. Without breaking his gaze she unbuttoned the remainder of his jeans. With his assistance she worked them and his briefs down over his long legs. Her eyes toured his muscular thighs, sprinkled with dark hair, and lingered on his cock. He thickened even more, as if the touch of her eyes was a caress from her fingers. She gave a small smile and drew his shirt up over his torso, taking her time to admire his lean muscular body, to skim her fingers lightly across his taut, smooth skin.

Jack helped her by sitting up and scooping the shirt over his head. He sighed in contentment and rising arousal as her fingers detailed his chest and shoulders. She watched him closely, loving how his eyes darkened when she circled one finger over a dark brown nipple and felt his flesh harden and pucker. She leaned down and licked him with her quick tongue.

"Belle."

His quietly spoken single word was a testament of love and desire.

He knew she wanted to love him slowly, recognized that she needed it. So he waited patiently despite a need that almost immediately sparked from a slow burn to a wildfire. And in truth he loved her gentle, sensitive touch, her flicking, teasing tongue. When her warm mouth began to inch down his abdomen and his cock jerked and strained in response, Jack put a hand on her shoulder.

"Let me undress you first. Stand up, honey," he muttered gruffly.

Belle stood in front of him as he sat on the edge of the bed. He pulled her between his knees and played with the frothy material of her blouse.

"This is pretty. I love the way you dress. You're so feminine." He palmed her breast. "So curvy." He pressed his face between her breasts and inhaled. "And you always smell so damn good. The first time I ever saw you, on that elevator, I was blown away."

"You were?" Belle asked softly as he released the knotted material at her collar. She watched his every movement as he took his time unbuttoning her blouse.

He nodded, all the while entranced with each new inch of apricot-hued skin that he exposed. "I didn't know it was possible for innocence and raw sexuality to be mixed so perfectly, until I saw you."

He flung back the edges of her blouse and palmed both of her breasts in two consecutive, rapid movements. Belle moaned softly at the sensation of him shaping and massaging her.

"You know how much I love your breasts. It was driving me crazy not to give them the attention they deserve. But I thought it would confirm your suspicions if I made love to you in the same ways as Sean." Jack peeled back her bra almost roughly, popping her large coral-colored nipples free from the cups.

She gasped and moaned when he immediately suckled first one nipple then the other. He did it deeply, greedily, with no preparation. Belle's knees almost gave way at the impact. Heat and wetness flooded her sex. Her eyes glazed with lust as she watched him. The image of him, his cheeks flexing as he sucked on her with such single-minded focus, was one of the most emotionally touching yet powerfully erotic things she'd ever seen.

"There were times when I thought you weren't that interested in them," she murmured as she continued to study him suckle her.

He didn't answer but continued to tenderly ravage her breasts with his mouth and hands. Only when they were flushed and her nipples were fully erect and distended did he finally move his dark head back to examine his handiwork.

"Belle, I love every part of you," he stated hoarsely. "But I could live off your breasts alone. Remember how I used to fuck them?"

"It was the first way you ever loved me, Sean."

His eyes rose to meet hers heatedly. They remained on her as he unbuttoned her pants hastily. In a matter of seconds she stood between his knees naked. He placed his hand over the smooth, pale, strangely erotic expanse of her belly. "You're going to carry my child here one day," he breathed out against her skin before he tongued her bellybutton. He burrowed two fingers into the juicy channel of her pussy.

"*Sean.*"

"Lie down on the bed and let me taste you. You're all honeyed up," he muttered almost incoherently as he pressed more kisses to her stomach. He felt suddenly desperate to be drenched in Belle's unique scent and taste.

"But you said equal," Belle managed between gasps as he continued to finger-fuck her.

"Fine," he muttered grimly as he grabbed her hips and backed up on the bed at the same time as he slid her body against his. "Then turn around and give me your pussy, honey. You can have your way with me if I can have my way with you."

She paused for a second but followed his instructions quickly enough when she realized what he meant. After thirty seconds of mutual stimulation Belle vibrated his cock with her uncontrollable, almost constant moaning. It was fantastically arousing to her to give pleasure at the same time as she took it. Sucking Sean had always gotten her hot, but to do it with his talented, hungry mouth on her made her burn exponentially brighter. Her pussy throbbed with almost unbearable pressure. The noises she made became muffled screams as she sucked his cock with rising desperation.

"Come off me," he demanded harshly. "It feels too good."

She slid him out of her mouth and waited with almost painful anticipation. He squeezed both of her ass cheeks and pressed her clit against his tongue. Hard. When she began to cry out and tremble with orgasm he applied suction. She screamed like a hot poker had been touched to her skin. His arm muscles flexed to hold her thrashing, undulating body steady against his mouth.

When she quieted he transferred his mouth to her entrance to drink the juices of his labor. He growled with arousal into her when Belle roused herself and sank his cock into her mouth deeply at the same time as she stroked him with her hand. Minutes passed in suspended gratification. But as time wore on Belle's moans vibrated him again, to the point that he knew he would lose control. She was incredibly talented in pleasuring him, but it was her increasingly wild sounds of aroused desperation resonating into his cock that would be his undoing.

He ordered her to release him while he made her climax again.

When the last of her orgasmic cries died down, Belle was left sagging against his bent knee, staring at his beautiful erect penis. She blinked several times to bring the awesome, up-close sight into focus. Mesmerized, she reached for him again but a teasing smack on her rear brought her attention around.

"Enough. I can't take any more."

Belle dismounted and lay down by his side. She took in his sweat-dampened forehead, the way his muscles were pulled rigid with desire. His lips were moist with her. She touched the tip of her tongue delicately to his mouth, curious. He remained motionless while her tongue slid over him with slow deliberation, tasting herself for the first time. His breath caught in his throat at the poignancy of her innocent yet flagrantly carnal actions.

His hand abruptly palmed the back of her head. He muttered starkly, "Surround yourself with it, honey."

His tongue plunged into her mouth, every bit as bold as it had been in her sex. He rubbed his tongue hotly against hers then sucked her into his mouth until Belle was tongue-fucking him, inundating herself with the exotic essence of both of them blended. She enjoyed it more than she could say, was vaguely surprised that the act of kissing could seem so illicit and deeply gratifying.

They broke away from each other eventually, both of them still hungry but breathless. Belle moaned when he came down on top of her, pressing her down into the soft mattress with his full weight. His cock glided along her belly.

She glanced up. His eyes were filled with so much emotion and desire they almost glowed. Belle felt locked in his powerful gaze as he placed both her hands above her head on the pillow. He massaged her clenching palms.

"Relax, beauty," he whispered soothingly. "Open your hands, relax your belly and thighs." He watched tensely as she complied, her eyes never leaving him. He knelt in front of her. "Now spread your legs."

Belle couldn't have ripped her eyes from his at that moment for all the riches in the world. Nothing compared to him. His muscles were tight and defined. The skin on his abdomen, shoulders and arms shone with light perspiration. His cock actually throbbed before her eyes with the intensity of his need. His eyes reminded her of a flame that was tightly controlled but held the potential to leap forward to scorch her at the slightest command.

He forced himself to breathe slowly through his nose. Belle lay spread before him, her sex fully exposed to his eyes, her golden hair tossed across the pillows, her lips parted, her hands curved loosely by her head into a pose of erotic supplication. He took his cock in his hand and leaned over her.

"I think that night I missed with you might have really been like this," he murmured huskily. "Are you ready?"

"Yes. I need you so much," she whispered.

For a moment he studied her silently. Then he bumped his cock up against her pussy, his fiery eyes never leaving her. And just when Belle thought he was going to make her suffer longer he bent one of her thighs back at the knee and surged forward with so much strength her eyes popped wide and she exhaled a shivering cry of shock.

"*Sean.*" She barely managed to say as he proceeded to take her with long, powerful strokes that rattled at the realms of her consciousness.

"Open your eyes, Belle." His voice was harsh. "Look at me."

She struggled to comply. She heard his demand, but her eyes focused clumsily. He always overpowered her when he first filled her, but tonight he overwhelmed her. The relief of orgasm tickled at her like an overpowering itch. She felt herself falling eagerly toward it when something interrupted her descent.

She blinked dazedly. "Sean would never spank me while he was taking my virginity, Jack," she said testily through panting breaths. Later, she wouldn't even recall that she'd said it.

He grinned. "He might have." He waited until she opened her golden eyes and focused on him. "And if he didn't, he would have wanted to. I want you to look at me while I take you. Give yourself to me."

Belle didn't have time to respond before he began to pound her again. His eyes were crescents of blue flame as he speared her soul as well as her body relentlessly again and again.

His strokes eventually became stabbing and erratic as orgasm loomed. "Belle, you're mine. No matter what, no matter who..." His face clenched tightly with cresting desire.

"Yes, *yes*. And you're mine—Oh, oh, Jack. *Jack*!" she cried out at the same time as she reached up and pulled his hips against her body with uncommon strength.

Orgasm slammed into them, the strength of it so powerful, that to Belle, it felt like a fusion of sorts.

After several minutes Jack realized that he'd collapsed on top of her and that she was bearing his full weight. He shifted off her.

She moaned in protest. "Don't go. You feel so good," she murmured.

"I'm not going anywhere. Just thought you'd appreciate breathing." He leaned down and kissed her lips softly. "I want to thank you for that."

"Thank you too. That was...indescribably good."

His smile flashed. "Not for *that*. But you're right. I meant thank you for calling me 'Jack'. At the end," he added when she looked at him blankly.

"I don't remember. I must have said it unconsciously."

He palmed her cheek. "I know. *That's* what I was thanking you for. It made me realize that I shouldn't feel guilty about asking you to marry me, asking you to take another man's name, because you really do accept me this way."

Her eyes appeared luminous. "You're name isn't what

matters, Jack. Neither is your face. *You're* what matters. And if that was a proposal, the answer is yes."

His smile widened slowly. He leaned down over her.

"Good," he said quietly. "Because if you're next to me, it's nobody's life but my own."

FLIRTING IN TRAFFIC

NOW AVAILABLE FROM BETH KERY

She went off like a red-hot firecracker on his foyer floor, then vanished. Esa never intended to participate in her best friend's unorthodox dating scheme-flirting with hunky construction workers in Chicago traffic. Her thoughts changed when she saw a long, lean slice of heaven strutting around the side of the highway. For him, she would be the carefree sex kitten her borrowed car with its suggestive license plates implied she was.

Though smarting from the wounds of a recent breakup, Finn can't resist the tempting redhead driving the come-and-get-me car, flashing him contemptuous looks with those brandy-colored eyes. The lure of taming the feisty little kitten is just too great to deny...

**Keep reading for an excerpt from
Beth Kery's *Flirting in Traffic*!**

ONE

ESA LAUGHED with a mixture of amusement and exasperation as her best friend poked at her shoulders and herded her out the door like she was a cow in the old Chicago stockyards.

"What's with you?" Esa asked as she closed the office door and locked it.

"I've got a date at six," Carla said, her face glowing with excitement and the new foundation product she'd bought on the internet last week while she was *supposed* to be filing Esa's Medicare claims. Esa sighed. That's what she got for hiring her down and out best friend to be her administrative assistant.

"You're nuts. We'll never make it downtown by six in Friday night construction traffic."

"We don't have to make it downtown." Carla said with a self-satisfied expression. "We just have to make it to the viaduct on 63rd and the Dan Ryan."

"You have a date with someone at 63rd Street and the Dan Ryan," Esa repeated dryly.

"Well, not exactly. It's not so much a date as it is a checking-out-the-goods session. Kitten's reporter called it a Scheduled Traffic Flirtation, I think."

Esa's steps slowed as they crossed the parking lot. She'd caught a nose-full of trouble on the cool autumn breeze. It was hard to say which gave off the more suspicious odor: the reference to her hugely successful, size four, mischievous little sister or the mention of Kitten's ridiculously popular magazine for single young Chicagoans, *Metro Sexy*.

"Scheduled Traffic Flirtation?" Esa asked warily.

Carla giggled as she grabbed Esa's arm and hurried her to the awaiting red convertible.

"You didn't read the article in *Metro Sexy*, did you? The one about singles flirting in Dan Ryan construction traffic? I'm the one who gave Kitten the idea. I've been waiting for the right moment to tell you. I'll explain everything once we get on the road. Give me the keys, I'm driving."

Esa caught a quick glimpse of vanity plates that read *SexKitten69* on the back of her sister's racy Ferrari convertible. You'd think she'd been driving naked to work for two days given all the lewd stares, shouted indecent proposals, suggestive cell-phone waving and creeps following them off the interstate. Esa had practically killed them during Smoky-and-the-Bandit style evasive maneuvers, trying to loose the horny jerks while Carla laughed hysterically in the seat next to her.

Kitten—*Rachel* that is. Esa refused to call her sister by that stupid childhood nickname—lived and worked downtown. Otherwise there was no way in hell her extremely pretty little sister would put up with the ridiculous behavior Esa had to endure driving that sports car on the interstate. But maybe Rachel just considered such idiocy part and parcel of her sexy image.

Suddenly her sister's insistence that she trade cars with her took on a sinister meaning. Rachel had claimed that she needed a more *staid* vehicle for her extended business trip to Indianapolis and had asked to borrow Esa's.

That was Esa all right, the staid, stodgy, boring older Ormond sister.

"How long have you been planning this?" Esa asked as she got into the passenger seat. She realized that she sounded bitter, but in truth she *was* a little hurt that Carla and Rachel had been plotting together without her knowledge. Sure, she was the gerontologist in the family and not the life of the party, sexy publisher but she was still a fun-loving city gal, wasn't she?

Or at least she used to be.

Carla, Rachel and her used to regularly stay out until three or four in the morning on the weekends, dining out at the trendiest restaurants, helping to plan Junior League charitable functions and then dressing to the nines for the lavish events, skipping out of work early on a Friday to catch a Cubs game, dancing and drinking at the clubs and creating all sorts of mischief in the romance arena.

The appeal of being a carefree Chicago socialite had dimmed quickly, however. Esa grew weary of the backbiting and vicious sniping between women. In addition, her parents —who used to wear patient, vaguely amused expressions when she and Rachel discussed Junior League events—could hardly be considered high-society headliner material. Esa and Rachel were not only newcomers to that scene, they were outsiders. It was a fact that became abundantly clear to Esa, if not her sister.

"We haven't planned it for long," Carla said with a wave of her hand before she pulled on her seatbelt. "A month or two. Long enough for me to have organized the Dan Ryan Construction Flirting chat loop online."

"The *what*?"

Carla's ecstatic expression faded quickly when she glanced down.

"Oh, shit."

"What?" Esa asked, more confused by the second.

"I forgot it was a stick shift."

Carla's blue eyes looked enormous when she met Esa's gaze. Her lush lower lip, shiny with freshly applied lipgloss, poked forward in a pout. Esa knew from years of experience that Carla's "helpless blonde" expression reeled the sharks in like filet mignon on the end of a hook. Fortunately for Esa she was both a straight female *and* a vegetarian.

"I can't drive a stick shift!"

"I know you can't. I was wondering what you thought you were doing," Esa replied with a smirk.

Carla's eyelids narrowed speculatively. The manic gleam returned. "You'll just have to drive." She plopped the keys into Esa's lap and clambered out of the driver's seat. "I told Vito I was a blonde bombshell. You're an auburn-haired girl-next-door. He'll never mistake you for me. What difference does it make who's driving?"

Vito? Esa mouthed in silent incredulity. Her knuckles turned white as she gripped the car keys. This just kept getting better and better, didn't it? She still hadn't moved when Carla flung open the passenger side door.

"Well?" she asked breathlessly. "Come on, Esa, you owe me after forcing me to go on that boring medical bookkeeping seminar last month."

"I sent you on that all expense paid seminar in Des Moines because I *thought* you might want to improve your job skills." Carla gave her a bland look.

"All right, I'll drive. Under one condition," Esa added when she saw Carla grin triumphantly. "Tell me everything about this stupid idea. I want to know precisely what kind of idiocy I'm going to have to bail you and Rachel out of."

"You won't be able to bail us out if you're in the clinker right there with us. Come on, Esa, picture it—a yummy, muscle-bound, bronzed construction worker-dude glazed from perspiration after some serious labor in bed." Carla's eyes sparkled merrily. "Don't *tell* me you're not thinking about how fun it would be."

Esa didn't put up too much of a fuss when Carla insisted she put down the top on the convertible once they'd reached 67th Street on the Ryan. The crisp fall air felt refreshing on her skin and temporarily made her forget that she was breathing the fumes of thousands of trucks and cars that communally moved like a gargantuan glass and metal slug on the pavement. Now that she understood that Carla's "date" wasn't actually mobile —some psycho stalker that could follow them into the city— but a stationary target, Esa felt a little better about her friend's crazy scheme.

"Since when have you been attracted to construction workers?" Esa asked as they inched forward in the clogged river of vehicles. The gargantuan project to widen I-94, other-wise known as the Dan Ryan, was already the stuff of urban legend even by Chicago standards, where everyone knew there were only two seasons: winter and road construction. The Dan Ryan project wasn't so much highway construction as it was road building on an epic scale like the Romans used to do. Commuting from Esa's downtown loft to her suburban office had become a downright nightmare.

Carla waited for the rattling L-train next to them to pass before she answered. "Are you blind, Esa? You must be the only straight woman in Chicago who isn't drooling over those hunks while you're driving to work in the morning. I mean there's got to be—what?—*thousands* of them parading around out there. The only thing better than tight butts in jeans are *flexing* tight butts in jeans," Carla checked her lipstick quickly in the mirror, "Strong thighs, bronzed biceps, broad shoulders—"

"Anything holding these guys' body parts together?" Esa wondered darkly. "It's a good thing I drive us to work or you'd be helping other horny woman in the city contribute to Chicago's traffic nightmare."

"Just stop it right now, Esa."

Carla's sharp rebuke nearly caused Esa to plow into the Ford Taurus in front of them.

"What's wrong with you?" she asked Carla in dawning amazement. Carla hardly ever got truly pissy, which is exactly what she appeared to be at the moment.

"I should be asking you the same thing," Carla said as she hurled her lipstick into her make-up bag. "Or better yet, I should be asking you who you are and what you did with my best friend, Esa Ormond. Clearly someone has stolen her and replaced her with some kind of alien robot whose idea of a good time is to write journal articles on the pros and cons of Viagra use and attend bingo night at the Shady Lawn Nursing Home."

"Carla, listen—"

"No, *you* listen. I tried not to complain too much when you started to refuse to go out with Kitten and me. I figured you'd just been burned a few too many times dating and were starting to focus more on yourself and your career."

"I did want to focus more on my career—"

"But *no*," Carla continued, oblivious to Esa's interruption or the loud beeping of the car horn behind them when Esa didn't immediately scoot forward ten feet in traffic. "Instead, you gave up everything. You've forsaken *any* type of the usual fun that a twenty-nine-year old single woman has. *Ever.* You won't so much as go out to have a drink with Kitten and I on a Friday night so we can laugh together or hang out with us to catch some rays on North Avenue Beach. Why don't you just go ahead and get your room reserved at Shady Lawn Nursing Home before your thirtieth birthday?"

Esa frowned. As if she really wanted to put her near-nude, mile-wide curves on display next to Carla and Rachel's svelte, gym-hewn bodies at the beach. But she'd be damned if she'd give Carla the satisfaction of saying that out loud.

"I'm Shady Lawn's physician, Carla. I can't help it if I have to spend so much time there."

"You have more fun socializing with those old bats than you do me."

The driver behind them gave up laying on the horn. He glared at Esa as he passed in the next lane. Esa was too busy staring at Carla in stunned disbelief to even notice. Finally, she clamped her mouth shut and shot forward a long stretch of road.

"Well that certainly came out of nowhere," Esa muttered after a moment.

Carla sighed. "Sorry. But I'd be lying if I said any of it wasn't true. You're no fun anymore, Esa."

"I'm *fun,*" Esa snarled.

"Sure, the residents of Shady Lawn think you're the life of the party," Carla muttered under her breath. She noticed Esa's glare. "Okay, if you're so fun, prove it. If Vito's all he's cracked up to be, I'm meeting him and a few other chatters from the online traffic group for a drink at *One Life*, that new club on Huron Street downtown. Go with me? Please? "

Esa hesitated, thinking about all the medical charts she

had stuffed into her briefcase. Carla's scolding warred with her practical nature. Even though she'd been acting so superior in regard to this whole flirting in traffic affair, Esa had to admit that it felt kind of good to have Carla beg her to take part in a loony scheme.

"I guess it'll be interesting if nothing else."

"Perfect." Carla clapped her hands happily before giving Esa a concerned look. "You're going to at least take off your glasses before going in to *One Life* though, aren't you?"

Before Esa could unclench her teeth Carla's blue eyes overtook half her face. "Look, we're almost to the 63rd Street viaduct."

"What's this Vito supposed to look like, anyway?" Esa asked, curious despite herself. Her gaze flickered over the road construction to the left of the car, a vast landscape of cranes, drills, broken-up concrete, exposed rebar and hard-working men. The project was so massive that a full crew would work until nightfall. At that point gigantic lights would be illuminated and abbreviated work would continue until well past midnight.

The sight of a man exiting the door of a construction trailer snagged her roving gaze. Her eyes widened. *Hey.* Maybe Carla was right about this sexy-construction-worker-thing. Talk about a long, lean slice of pure heaven. This guy was some serious eye candy. Esa focused on the subtle rolling motion of trim hips encased in low-riding, clinging jeans as he came down the stairs, work boots stomping.

Those long legs and that sexy saunter would have caught her eye anytime, anywhere. Surely a guy who moved like that just *had* to move well in bed. At five foot eight inches herself, Esa liked a tall man. She wanted to feel feminine in comparison to a date, not like Durgha, Queen of the Amazons. Maybe she was brainwashed by a sexist society, but was it too much to ask for a man whom she'd bet without a doubt could beat her in an arm wrestling match?

She found herself staring fixedly at the fullness behind the construction-guy's fly. She blinked dazedly. A warm, tingling sensation flickered in her lower belly and simmered down to her sex. The sensation took her by surprise it'd been so long since she'd experienced it.

She glanced forward just in time to stop them from plowing into a BMW.

The man drew her gaze again like a magnet, however. Her eyelids narrowed in fascination as her gaze traveled up a whipcord lean torso that slanted up tantalizingly to shoulders that weren't necessarily brawny, but extremely muscular and perfectly suited to his build. The dark blue t-shirt that he wore covered what Esa guessed were powerful biceps but left a pair of strong, tanned forearms exposed. He crossed those forearms below his chest in a casual gesture as he paused next to a pick-up truck. He started to talking to the driver.

Esa was so busy mentally slobbering that it took a few seconds to realize that Carla was talking.

"…I know what you're going to say. Guys can say they're Chris Hemsworth's twin online, and then you meet them and they're more like Quasimodo's ugly brother. But I don't know, Esa. I've got a feeling about this guy. He's six foot three, dark blonde hair, works out regularly at his club in addition to all that hard work that he does during the day, so you know his body's got to be rock-hard. He's thirty-one years old—"

A prickle of apprehension went through Esa when the man in the truck suddenly stopped talking to Mr. Adonis and looked point blank at Esa. Although his face remained mostly in shadow she saw his chin make a subtle pointing gesture. The man she'd been checking out so shamelessly turned around and pinpointed her with his gaze. Even at a distance of twenty feet, that stare lasered straight through her.

"We're here. This is it. Go slow Esa," Carla ordered in obvious excitement as they neared the 63rd Street viaduct. She sat forward in the passenger seat and examined the thirty or so men working in the vicinity.

"All right, all right," Esa muttered under her breath as she pressed on the break. She suddenly felt self-conscious and silly, like she was in the seventh grade and at the roller rink cruising past a cute boy standing at the rail. A hysterical laugh tickled her throat at the thought. She glanced over nervously at the two men, still feeling the one's stare like a tickle on her neck and shoulder. "I don't suppose Vito said he had blue eyes."

"Oh my God, Esa, that's *him,*" Carla said under hear breath when she finally zeroed in on the Adonis standing next to the truck. "Heaven help me I'm in love."

———

Esa experienced a flash of jealousy at Carla's proclamation. *She'd* seen him first, after all. Her ridiculous proprietary attitude only grew when Carla gave a high wattage smile and waved. She glanced over in time to see Vito's hand go up slowly in a return greeting. He said something quietly to the man in the truck. Esa saw a flash of white teeth when he grinned at something his friend said. Carla giggled in the seat next to her.

Cocky bastard, Esa decided irritably. She threw him a sour look before she glanced ahead.

"Carla, what the hell am I supposed to do now?" Esa hissed. "It's clearing ahead of me. I can't sit here and block traffic while you flirt."

Carla ransacked her bag, never taking her eyes off Vito.

She withdrew her cell phone and held it up significantly for him to see. "It's okay, Esa. You can drive. I've seen more than enough," Carla conceded breathlessly.

"What are you doing?" Esa asked as she stomped on the accelerator, leaving Vito in her proverbial dust. That smirk on his face really bugged Esa for some reason.

"I gave Vito my cell phone number online. He's going to text or call if he…you know…likes me."

"Why does *he* get to be the one to decide?" Esa asked irritably. "What a conceited bast—"

But her tirade was cut off when Carla's cell phone started beeping the tune to a popular rap song.

Esa stewed while Carla giggled and simpered, catching phrases like, "You must get so tired after working so hard in the sun for almost twelve hours…Oh you poor thing…Are you going to be at *One Life* then?...What?...I can't believe you lied about that. You are *so* bad…Seven thirty? Sure, we'll be there…" and then as Carla ducked her head and faced the passenger door window, "…Yeah, I really liked you too."

Esa rolled her eyes as she changed lanes. So touching, to be a witness to lust at first sight.

"How do you know he's not setting up dates with every woman on that stupid flirting chat loop, not to mention every single female advertising for a man in *Metro Sexy*?" Esa accused the second after Carla hung up.

"Don't be so boring. We're not planning on marriage and two point five children. It's just for fun."

"It's just for *sex*," Esa corrected.

Carla laughed. "And your point is? Sex *is* fun, Esa. It's not my fault you've forgotten that."

Esa stewed in the seconds that followed, unable to come up with a sufficiently acidic comeback. Besides…Carla was right. Wasn't she always encouraging her older adult patients to continue to express their sexuality in a safe manner? Sex was a crucial aspect of human behavior, after all.

Lately, however, Esa preached much better than she practiced. At what point had she become such a boring prude?

The question rankled.

She mentally schemed for a way of getting out of going to *One Life* with Carla but for some strange reason, Vito's grin kept popping behind her eyes like a cocky little dare.

She'd go all right...to protect Carla. Her friend was used to swimming with the sharks, but Esa's intuition hinted that this particular animal was downright dangerous.

———

Esa peered at her reflection in the mirror. For some asinine reason she'd actually listened to Carla and went to the lounge at *One Life* to remove her glasses. She really only wore them when she drove anyway, but all that talk about how boring she was certainly caused her to make a point of checking her appearance.

The sounds of a live reggae band filtered through the walls. Maybe it was the sensual beat of the music or maybe it was just all the reminders of how lame her life was that coaxed Esa to unfasten her blouse one button...then two. She gave her reflection a shaky grin after she caught a glimpse of the shadowed valley between her breasts. Not sexy Kitten Ormond, perhaps, but Esa still knew how to hold her own at a place like *One Life*.

The music immediately enveloped her once she left the lady's room. She went in search of Carla, whom she'd left sipping a sidecar and casting anxious glances toward the entrance. Her step faltered when she saw the back of a tall man wearing jeans leaning over and talking to her friend. She scowled when she noticed the burnished brownish-blonde hair and tight ass.

Well apparently Vito had arrived and was getting right down to the business of making time with Carla. Or *Jess* had, anyway. That was one of the many things that Carla had gushed on about after she'd hung up her cell phone earlier. *Vito* was really a *Jess*. Obviously Jess was a tad more concerned about meeting losers online than Carla, and was protecting his identity. Why the gorgeous Jess needed to use a chat group in a singles' magazine to land a date, Esa couldn't fathom.

Probably dumber than the concrete he poured on the job.

Her good friend's hoot of delighted laughter pierced through the music. Esa veered toward the bar, suddenly much in need of a stiff drink. Jess and Carla obviously weren't going to miss her.

After she'd finished half a martini, Esa felt light-headed. When was the last time she'd actually had one of these, anyway? Esa wondered as the band broke into *Red, Red, Wine*. Her body instinctively moved to the rhythm. She'd always loved the reggae classic.

Someone took her hand. Her mouth opened, the protest she'd been ready to utter melting like powdered sugar on her tongue when she looked up into the face of the man who held her fingers lightly.

Esa supposed the time period between when she stared into those arresting, amused blue eyes and when he spoke was only a few seconds, but her brain stretched it surrealistically long. Her heart skipped erratically beneath her peek-a-boo cleavage when Mr. Adonis smiled—not cocky like she'd imagined from a distance. No, instead that slow grin was the equivalent of potent foreplay. Ever so briefly, his gaze flashed down to her chest…as if he were a magician and knew precisely what effect he was having on her.

"Would you like to dance?"

Esa nodded, thoughts of loyalty to her friend evaporated to vapor by the sexiness of his smile. Carla? Carla *who*?

He tugged teasingly on her hand and she followed him out onto the small dance floor in a mesmerized state. When he turned and released her hand they immediately began to dance to the earthy rhythm without saying a word.

Hadn't she guessed as she watched him come out of the construction trailer that the man knew how to move? He *did* all right. Her gaze drifted over a handsome face and an angled jaw slightly whiskered with dark blond stubble before lowering over a blue and white button-down shirt that set off his golden-hued tan. His collar-length hair was a blend of light brown, blond and platinum hues that mingled together in a tousled, sexy mess. He must have showered after work because he'd changed clothing and Esa could smell his soap and the subtle, spicy scent of his aftershave. She looked down even further. The carnal rhythm of the music seemed to grant her permission.

Her hips moved with his in a tight, controlled roll to the sensual beat. A warm, tingly sensation of excitement swelled from her lower belly to her sex as her pelvis gyrated in perfect synchrony to his.

When Esa finally looked back up into his face again her breath caught in her throat.

He no longer seemed slightly amused. Instead his face had gone rigid. His eyes had taken on an almost dangerous glint. Esa wondered what it would be like to have him nail her with that stare while his cock pinned her down to the bed. A muscle leapt in his tanned, lean cheek, and Esa had the strangest feeling that he was reading her mind.

Considering the fullness behind his fly when she'd been shamelessly staring just now as they rocked their hips in unison, it wasn't too much of a stretch to suppose he was thinking *exactly* that.

He spread one hand on her hip in a possessive gesture, bringing her into contact with his body. She bit her lip to prevent a moan of excitement when her belly pressed against him. He was erect…deliciously full. Liquid heat flooded her. Her nipples tightened against her bra. She longed to press them against his chest to alleviate the ache and leaned forward to do so…

But the music ended.

"We gotta couple here who really knows how to *move* together," said a voice that was flavored with the accent of the islands. "If they smoked on that one, they're gonna burn a whole in the floor with this one…"

The sound of the lead singer's voice broke through Esa's bespelled state. She blinked, realizing she was pressed tightly against a very attractive, aroused male animal.

A sexy, aroused male who was also a complete stranger, not to mention her best friend's date.

"Excuse me," Esa mumbled.

She staggered into the women's room. The reflection that peered back at her from the mirror only vaguely resembled the one that had been there on her previous visit. Her cheeks and lips were flushed. Her russet colored eyes sparkled like she'd just swallowed a shot of potent liquor. Her wanton dancing had opened her neckline further and the ivory lace of her bra peaked out from the edge of the silk.

She looked thoroughly debauched.

Esa took a deep, unsteady inhale of air and turned on the cold water tap. God she'd *never* been flipped so effortlessly into the sexual 'drive' position in her life. Just the thought of the hot look in Vito's—no, *Jess's*—eyes when she'd gyrated against his crotch made heat flood her all over again.

She sighed dispiritedly and splashed some cool water onto her hot cheeks. Why did Carla end up with all the luck?

She exited the women's room a half a minute later and found herself sandwiched between a hard, yummy-smelling man and the wall.

"Don't you know it's rude to entice a man like that and then just disappear?" he asked in a low, slightly raspy voice that caused goosebumps to rise along the back of her neck.

"Sorry," Esa whispered as she looked up at him. His smile told her that he'd been teasing, however. Light angled across the upper portion of his otherwise shadowed face, making his eyes seem to glow with heat as he examined her intently. Maybe he hadn't been kidding afterall...

"I got sort of...hot dancing," Esa muttered, not even sure what she was saying.

His mouth tilted further with humor. Esa watched, mesmerized, as that sexy smile descended. He growled softly before he covered her mouth with his. He plucked with firm, persuasive lips once, then twice, seeming to assure himself that he had her agreement. It was Esa herself who opened and craned up for him however, requiring no coaxing.

His taste inundated her with a tidal wave of lust. His agile tongue stroked lazily, explored her thoroughly. Within ten seconds they were kissing with a wild, hot abandon. The amount of suction he applied was perfect, creating explosions of sensation in her body that were far, far from her mouth, making it imperative that she rub up against him.

He was warm and hard...everywhere. When she fully registered the impressive outline of what strained behind his fly she moaned in mixed arousal and misery and broke his kiss. She grasped for a measure of sanity but it was difficult to think with his long body pressed against her and his male scent filling her nose. Her hands rose of their own accord and explored his muscular back with hungry fingertips.

"You taste so *good*," he murmured, sounding genuinely amazed. He nuzzled her ear and then lightly bit her ear lobe, making Esa press her pelvis tighter to his, desperate to alleviate the ache that grew there with alarming speed. His hands cradled her waist and squeezed ever so slightly, as though he were taking her measure. When he gave a groan of satisfaction Esa was left with the definite impression that he liked the way she fit him.

She turned her head, blindly seeking out his mouth again. She moaned in excitement as she bathed once again in his intoxicating taste and their tongues dueled, teased and probed. *Sexual chemistry at its finest.*

"Let's get out of here," he mumbled against her hungry, nibbling lips a moment later. It gratified her to hear that he sounded as breathless as she was. "I don't live far away."

Esa's eyes widened in surprise at his bold proposal, not to mention the fact that she was actually considering it.

"Wh…what about Carla?" Esa asked, amazed at her sheer wantonness as she craned up to slide their mouths together and nip at his lower lip.

"What about me?"

She peered over Mr. Yummy's arm to see her friend standing in the corridor, her blue eyes wide with wonder. Esa straightened and pushed at her seducer's chest but he refused to move.

"Uh…I'm…you're…Jeez, Carla, I'm really sorry about this," Esa said breathlessly, the full impact of what she was doing hitting her like a ton of bricks had just landed on her chest.

"Why?" the man and Carla asked in unison.

"*Why?*"

"Yeah, *why*? It does my heart good to see you making out with a gorgeous hunk." Carla winked at the man pressing her to the wall. "You two were practically doing it standing up out there on the dance floor. From the looks of things you better go somewhere a little more private or risk being thrown in jail."

A low, sexy laugh rumbled in the man's chest.

"You're not mad that I stole Jess from you?" Esa asked Carla incredulously.

"*Jess*?" She pointed at Mr. Yummy. "*He's* not Jess. Jess's over there." She shifted her finger behind her to the table where she'd been sitting. "*He's* Jess's big brother, Finn." Carla's eyes twinkled with mirth. "Ain't I sweet? I brought a Madigan boy for you too."

Finn leaned down and brushed her cheek with his warm lips. He spoke so softly that Esa doubted Carla could hear him where she stood six feet away.

"'She had nothing to do with it. I was raring to come and meet you ever since I saw you in that red convertible and you threw me such a dirty look. Even your scowl turns me on. So what do you say, Kitten? My offer still stands. Course if your place is closer than mine, I'm all for that."

Esa's brain whipped and whirled like an out of control carnival ride. Why had he called her *Kitten*? Then Rachel's license plates flashed in her mind's eye. Oh…so he thought *she* owned that racy car. He thought *she* was the type to eye construction workers like they were walking slabs of luscious male flesh just waiting to be consumed by a carnivorous female.

He assumed *she* was the type to spend a night of lusty, raw sex with a complete stranger.

Excitement burned in her lower belly as she met his steady stare. Isn't this precisely the kind of thing she needed to break her out of her boring rut? Let him think she was a carefree, carnal sex kitten. Maybe she *was* the type to steam up the night with a complete stranger.

As long as the complete stranger was Finn Madigan, anyway.

———

Flirting in Traffic is available now for Amazon Kindle / Kindle Unlimited!

ABOUT THE AUTHOR

Beth Kery is the *New York Times, USA Today* and international bestselling author of over thirty novels, including the innovative serial novels, Because You Are Mine, When I'm With You, The Affair, and Make Me, all of which are also available now as complete novels. Beth holds a doctorate in the behavioral sciences and loves using her knowledge of human behavior, emotion and motivation to write characters with depth and complexity. Beth's book, Wicked Burn, was chosen as the best erotic novel of the year by the *All About Romance* reader poll and she has been nominated in several categories for reviewer's choice awards from RT Book Reviews magazine. Her novels have been translated into fourteen languages.

You can find out more about Beth's books at
www.bethkery.com , or by following her on
Twitter **@bethkery**, or her Facebook page,
www.Facebook.com/beth.kery.

ALSO BY BETH KERY

Single Titles

Wicked Burn

Daring Time

Sweet Restraint

Paradise Rules

Release

Explosive

The Affair

(also available in serial format)

Make Me

(also available in serial format)

Looking Inside

Behind the Curtain

Exorcising Sean's Ghost

Come to Me Freely

Flirting in Traffic

———

Glimmer/Glow Series

Glimmer

Glow

———

Because You Are Mine Series

Because You Are Mine

(also available in serial format)

When I'm With You

(also available in serial format)

Because We Belong

Since I Saw You

———

One Night of Passion Series

Addicted to you

(writing as Bethany Kane)

Bound to You *(novella)*

Captured by You *(novella)*

Exposed to You

Only for You

———

Home to Harbor Town Series

The Hometown Hero Returns

Liam's Perfect Woman

Claiming Colleen

One in a Billion

The Soldier's Baby Bargain

Made in the USA
Monee, IL
22 April 2020